Written in Stone

"*Written in Stone* is written with skill, as Adams continues to entertain her readers with a clever story and further develop Olivia, one of the most intriguing heroines of the genre and one created by a maturing and empathetic author."
—*Richmond Times-Dispatch*

"Well-paced mysteries, interesting back story, and good characters make this a must-read mystery."
—*The Mystery Reader*

The Last Word

"As in the two previous novels in the series, set in Oyster Bay on North Carolina's southeastern coast, Adams concocts a fine plot; this one finds its roots in World War II. But the real appeal is her sundry and congenial characters, beginning with Olivia herself. Adams's heroine has erected a steel curtain around her emotions, but *The Last Word* finds her emerging from her shell with confidence, a confidence matched by Adams in this unusual and appealing series."
—*Richmond Times-Dispatch*

"I could actually feel the wind on my face, taste the salt of the ocean on my lips, and hear the waves crash upon the beach. *The Last Word* made me laugh, made me think, made me smile, and made me cry. *The Last Word*—in one word—AMAZING!"
—*The Best Reviews*

"The plot is complex, the narrative drive is strong, and the book is populated with interesting and intelligent people . . . Oyster Bay is the kind of place I'd love to get lost for an afternoon or two."
—*The Season*

continued . . .

A Deadly Cliché

"A very well-written mystery with interesting and surprising characters and a great setting. Readers will feel as if they are in Oyster Bay."
—*The Mystery Reader*

"Adams spins a good yarn, but the main attraction of the series is Olivia and her pals, each a person the reader wants to meet again and again."
—*Richmond Times-Dispatch*

"This series is one I hope to follow for a long time, full of fast-paced mysteries, budding romances, and good friends. An excellent combination!"
—*The Romance Readers Connection*

A Killer Plot

"Ellery Adams's debut novel, *A Killer Plot*, is not only a great read, but a visceral experience. Olivia Limoges's investigation into a friend's murder will have you hearing the waves crash on the North Carolina shore. You might even feel the ocean winds stinging your cheeks. Visit Oyster Bay and you'll long to return again and again."
—Lorna Barrett, *New York Times* bestselling author of the Booktown Mysteries

"Adams's plot is indeed killer, her writing would make her the star of any support group, and her characters—especially Olivia and her standard poodle, Captain Haviland—are a diverse, intelligent bunch. *A Killer Plot* is a perfect excuse to go coastal."
—*Richmond-Times Dispatch*

Berkley Prime Crime titles by Ellery Adams

Charmed Pie Shoppe Mysteries

PIES AND PREJUDICE
PEACH PIES AND ALIBIS

Books by the Bay Mysteries

A KILLER PLOT
A DEADLY CLICHÉ
THE LAST WORD
WRITTEN IN STONE
POISONED PROSE

**A BOOKS
BY THE BAY
MYSTERY**

Poisoned Prose

ELLERY ADAMS

BERKLEY PRIME CRIME, NEW YORK

THE BERKLEY PUBLISHING GROUP
Published by the Penguin Group
Penguin Group (USA) LLC
375 Hudson Street, New York, New York 10014

USA • Canada • UK • Ireland • Australia • New Zealand • India • South Africa • China

penguin.com

A Penguin Random House Company

POISONED PROSE

A Berkley Book / published by arrangement with the author

For information, address: The Berkley Publishing Group,
a division of Penguin Group (USA) LLC,
375 Hudson Street, New York, New York 10014.

ISBN: 978-0-425-26295-5

PUBLISHING HISTORY
Berkley Prime Crime mass-market edition / October 2013

PRINTED IN THE UNITED STATES OF AMERICA

10 9 8 7 6 5 4 3 2 1

Cover art by Kimberly Schamber.
Cover design by Rita Frangie.
Interior text design by Tiffany Estreicher.

For Tim, because I am at home in your heart

Chapter 1

"Death by chocolate. That's what the coroner's report will read," Olivia Limoges said to the woman sitting next to her. She pushed away a plate still laden with a caramel brownie, a hazelnut petit four, and a square of peanut butter fudge. "I'll have to be rolled home in a wheelbarrow."

"That's why this place is called Decadence." Laurel Hobbs, local reporter and mother to twin boys, bit off the end of a strawberry dipped in white chocolate and moaned. "How can you resist the host of temptations being offered? Here we are, two of the lucky few invited to this exclusive event, and you're showing unnecessary restraint. Seriously, Olivia, try this one. Just take a bite."

Olivia glanced at the Amaretto cream puff and shook her head. "I think it was a mistake to drink both of those martinis during the cocktail hour. I could hardly refuse the chocolate martini I was given for the initial toast, and then Shelley pressed something called a Snickertini into my hand and stood there while I drank it. I didn't want to offend her on her big night, and Michel would poison me if I did anything to upset his beloved chocolatier, so down the hatch it went."

Laurel held up her hands. "No more talk of poisoning, strangling, or any other form of murder, please. I think we've had enough violence to last us several lifetimes. Besides, Michel would never turn on you. He's the head chef in the most celebrated restaurant on the North Carolina coast, and you own the place."

Gesturing around the desserterie, which was filled with Oyster Bay's most influential townsfolk along with a dozen journalists and television personalities from out of state, Olivia shrugged. "The Boot Top can't compete with an establishment serving every guest a dark chocolate shopping bag filled with white chocolate mousse. And did you see what Shelley used as a garnish? Sugared raspberries and a Decadence business card made of fondant. Incredible."

"No, you probably can't compete with that. I guess you should be happy that Shelley doesn't serve seafood or The Bayside Crab House would be in trouble too."

"Speaking of the Crab House, I should pick up some treats for my niece. I saw some starfish lollipops on the counter. Each one is made of raspberry-filled chocolate and costs more than an entire Happy Meal, but she's worth it."

Laurel grinned. "It's a good thing you're an heiress. You could buy every last piece of candy in here if you felt like it."

Olivia bristled. "Hey, I work as hard as the next person."

"You do. You spend all those hours between two restaurants and yet you stay so thin." Laurel shook her head in disbelief. "How can you be around such exquisite food all day and not weigh a million pounds? If I weren't your friend, I'd really hate you. I still haven't worked off the rest of my baby weight, and the twins are four! Oh well, now's not the time to count calories." She popped a truffle into her mouth.

"Look at Shelley. She's sweet, beautiful, and clearly enjoys sampling her own wares. A woman with Shirley Temple dimples and Marilyn Monroe curves. No wonder Michel fell for her. Ah, here he comes now."

Michel was glowing. Olivia barely recognized him out of his white chef's coat, but he cut a nice figure in his rented tux. "Can you get over my Shelley?" he asked, sitting next to Olivia and giving her a brotherly kiss on the cheek. "If I weren't madly in love with her, I'd be desperately jealous. She's got everyone under her spell. I told you she was an enchantress."

Olivia rolled her eyes. "Spare me, Michel. I've overindulged on tarts and cakes and bonbons, and I can't stand another ounce of sugary sweetness."

"Then you should try the chili pepper chocolate," Michel suggested. "Or the bacon flavored truffles." Olivia gave him a dark look, but he was too jovial to notice. He and Laurel began to compare notes on their favorite treats, going into endless detail about the perfect balance between sea salt and bittersweet chocolate.

"I'm going outside for some air." Olivia took her water glass and headed for the kitchen. Without asking permission, she breezed through the swing doors into the narrow space, surprised to find it empty of both cooks and waitstaff. Shelley had hired servers from a local catering company for her grand opening, and they were all busy in the main room, but where was the dishwasher? The assistant pastry chef? Or sous-chef?

The kitchen was a mess. The sink was full of stainless steel bowls coated in dried caramel, jam, buttercream, and chocolate in every shade of brown. The remnants of crushed nuts, chopped fruit, and mint sprigs were strewn across the cutting board, and every burner on the commercial stove was obscured by a dirty pot or sauté pan.

"Shelley's going to be up very late tonight," she said,

unable to stop herself from picking up a bag of flour that had toppled from the counter onto the floor. "She needs to hire some full-time help."

Like many of the stores lining the streets of downtown Oyster Bay, Decadence had a small concrete patio out back where the merchants and their employees would take smoke or lunch breaks. Shelley had placed a pair of Adirondack chairs, a picnic table, and a potted hibiscus on hers. The plant didn't look like it had long to live, but Olivia decided to prolong its existence by dumping the contents of her water glass into its bone-dry soil.

She went into the kitchen, refilled the glass, and repeated the process three times before the soil was moist to the touch.

"I think it's a hopeless cause," a voice said from the alley-way behind the shop, startling Olivia.

"Damn it, Flynn." She scowled at the handsome, middle-aged owner of Oyster Bay's only bookstore. "Is this how you spend your evenings? Creeping among the town's garbage bins?"

"Only when beautiful women are nearby," he replied nonchalantly and sat down at the picnic table. "Is this how you spend yours? Dressing to the nines and watering half-dead plants?"

Olivia studied the man who'd once been her lover. He was as carefree and confident as usual. His mouth was always on the verge of curving into a smile, and there was an ever-present gleam of mischief in his eyes. A textbook extrovert, Flynn loved to swap gossip with his customers and play with their children in the bookstore's puppet theater. He was lively and friendly and fun. Everyone liked him. He was everything Olivia was not, and that's what had initially drawn her to him. However, their strong physical attraction hadn't been enough to hold them together, and they'd both moved on to form more meaningful relationships with other partners.

"What are you thinking about right now?" Flynn asked. "You got this look on your face. Like you'd gone back in time and wanted to linger there a moment. Perhaps you were reminiscing about us?" He raised his brows and smiled a little. "We had some electric moments, didn't we?"

Trying not to let him see how accurate his guess was, Olivia joined him at the picnic table. "Where's Diane? It's a Saturday night in June. The stars are shining, the ocean breeze is blowing, and the town is stuffed to the gills with tourists. So why aren't you out wining and dining your girlfriend?"

"Because we had a big fight," he said without the slightest trace of emotion. "And because I wanted to talk to you."

"Oh?" Olivia's tone was guarded. "In the middle of Shelley's event? How did you know I'd be here?"

Flynn shrugged. "It was a sure bet that she'd invite you. Any small business owner with half a brain would. Do you know how many new customers I've gotten because you recommended my store?"

"I love Through the Wardrobe." Olivia was careful to praise the shop, not its proprietor. "I'd do anything to see it flourish. A town without a bookstore is an empty shell of a place."

Beaming, Flynn leaned toward her. "I'm so glad you said that. It makes it easier to ask you for a big favor."

Olivia gestured for him to continue.

"The *Gazette* and I are partnering to sponsor a story-teller's retreat next month for the Southern Storytellers Network. It's for people all over the region who make their living performing folktales. I'm going to schedule some children's programs at the shop, and the paper will arrange for adult performances at the library."

"This sounds wonderful, Flynn," she said sincerely. "But where do I come in?"

Olivia had to give her former lover credit. He didn't dance around the point or try to soften her up with compliments. He simply opened his hands so that his palms formed a bowl and said, "I need help funding the event. The expenses were supposed to be covered by the *Gazette*, a grant, and me. Unfortunately, the grant's fallen through. But we have to go on. Things have already been set in motion. Hotel rooms have been booked. Ads placed. Invitations sent and accepted. The bottom line is that we don't have enough money to pay for it all. We need a philanthropist, Olivia. The storytellers need you."

"Don't lay it on too thick," she warned. "How much are we talking about?"

Eyes flashing in premature triumph, Flynn reached into his shirt pocket and withdrew a slip of paper. "I've itemized all the costs. This way, you'll have proof that I haven't booked a Caribbean cruise at your expense."

Olivia didn't unfold the paper. She tucked it into her Chanel evening bag and promised to look it over in the morning. "I never make decisions when my belly is stuffed with chocolate."

Flynn laughed. "An excellent motto. After all, chocolate stimulates the mind's opioid production, creating feelings of pleasure that will eventually wear off. But if you'd like to prolong the sensation of euphoria, I'd be glad to assist with that." He stood and held out his hand for her. She took it, allowing him to pull her to her feet, and noted how he held still for a moment in order to study her pale, silvery blond hair, which was swept off her brow in a modernistic wave. He then lowered his eyes to her necklace of moonstones and black pearls. His gaze drifted down the curves of her body, taking in the form-fitting, vintage-style cocktail dress made of black lace with satin trim, and Olivia's long, tan legs.

"I'd try to kiss you, but your police chief boyfriend would probably hit me with his baton."

Olivia snatched her hand away. "I don't need him to defend my honor. I can clout you all by myself, thank you very much." She smiled to take the sting from the words and wished Flynn a pleasant evening.

When he was gone, she hesitated for a moment at the kitchen door and then decided not to return to the party. She walked down the alley and stepped onto the main sidewalk, heading for the public lot where her Range Rover was parked.

In order to reach her car, she had to pass by Fish Nets, the bar where her writer friend Millay worked. It was not an establishment Olivia regularly frequented as it reeked of tobacco, body odor, and stale beer. The music was too loud, the entertainment was limited to a stained pool table and decrepit dartboard, and the floor was covered in puddles of spilled liquor, discarded gum, and chewing tobacco spittle. And yet, Olivia had grown up among its clientele. Her father had been a fisherman, and most of the old-timers inside the bar had known her since she was a skinny, towheaded girl with the shy, sea-blue eyes.

Pausing at the door, she considered how ridiculous she'd look drinking whiskey with a group of work-worn men and women. She'd walk in wearing her cocktail dress and heels while Millay's patrons would be dressed in soiled and tattered jeans, frayed denim shorts or skirts, and T-shirts that had been washed so often that their logos were no longer decipherable. Their skin would be bronzed by the sun and weathered by wind and worry. Their hands were scarred and dirty and their language coarse, but they knew her. They knew her story. They knew her mother had died in a tragic accident, that her drunkard of a father had abandoned her when she was only ten, and that she'd come back to Oyster Bay after a long absence in order to reconnect with the past and strive for a new and better future.

They've accepted me from the first, she thought with a rush of gratitude and entered the bar. *These are my people.*

For a moment, her appearance stunned the crowd into silence, but it only lasted a heartbeat. Men and women warmly greeted her with catcalls and raucous shouts. Millay waved her over to the bar and polished a tumbler with a dish towel.

"Don't give me the stink eye. This one's clean," Millay said before pouring a finger's worth of her best whiskey into the glass. "It's the only thing in here that is, besides you. Aren't you supposed to be down the street with the rest of the snobs?"

"Why would I want to sip champagne and devour plates of sumptuous desserts with Oyster Bay's elite when I could be here, sitting on a wobbly stool and breathing in toxic air?" Olivia gestured at the taps. "Buy you a beer?"

Millay grinned. "Absolutely. I prefer the 'King of Beers.'"

She reached into the refrigerator behind her and pulled out a bottle of Budweiser. Popping the cap off with a neat flourish, she clinked the neck against Olivia's tumbler. "In the immortal words of Minna Antrim, 'To be loved is to be fortunate, but to be hated is to achieve distinction.'"

Olivia laughed. "Despite your best efforts, I believe you are genuinely adored."

"In this place, yeah. Beyond these walls, I'm that girl the old biddies point to and frown at in disapproval. I use too much makeup, my skirts are way too short, and I wear black boots all year long. I'm the scourge of the Junior Leaguers, and I take pride in knowing they're afraid to look me in the eye." She pretended to claw at the air with her left hand, causing the feathers hanging from her black hair to swing back and forth. Millay's ancestors, who were a blend of several races, had lent her an exotic beauty, but she preferred to draw attention to her artistic nature by piercing her eyebrows, wearing rows of hoops in her ears, and dyeing the tips of her jet-black hair neon pink, orange, or green. Lately, she'd taken to adding accessories to her textured bob. Tonight, she wore crimson feathers, but at the last meeting of the Bayside Book Writers, the twentysomething barkeep had celebrated the final round of edits on her young-adult fantasy novel by decorating her hair with glittery Hello Kitty clips.

"That's why you're such a talented writer," Olivia said. "You're fearless in life and on paper. You have the courage to be you, but you're also willing to be vulnerable. That's hard when you're used to wearing armor. Believe me, I know."

Millay shook her head in disgust. "What kind of crack was in that chocolate you ate? Don't go all fortune cookie philosopher on me, Olivia. Hurry up and finish that whiskey. You need to wash that sugar out of your system."

Smiling, Olivia complied. Millay immediately refilled her glass while a man sat down in the vacant stool to Olivia's right.

He lifted the faded John Deere cap from his head and said, "Evenin', ma'am."

"Good evening, Captain Fergusson." She gestured at her tumbler. "Would you join me?"

"Reckon I will. Thank you, kindly."

When Millay had poured two fingers of whiskey, he turned to Olivia and she raised her glass. "May the holes in your net be no bigger than the fish in it," she said, reciting one of the fishermen's traditional toasts.

He nodded and replied with one of his own. "May your troubles be as few as my granny's teeth."

Sipping their whiskey, they fell into easy conversation about the commercial fishing industry. Captain Fergusson supplied both of Olivia's restaurants with shrimp and had recently expanded his operation. He was now her primary source for blue crab and flounder as well, and she often met his trawlers at the dock when they returned with full cargo holds. Olivia would chat with the captain and his crew as she made selections for her restaurants. She liked Fergusson. More importantly, she trusted him.

Fergusson had been casting off while it was still dark to fish the waters around the North Carolina coast for the past forty years. And it showed. He was grizzled, his pewter-colored beard was wiry, and his eyes were beady and sunken from decades of gazing into the horizon. He was gruff, blunt, hard-working, and fair, and Olivia had grown quite fond of him.

As they spoke, other fishermen drifted over and inserted themselves into the conversation. Olivia bought clams, oysters, mussels, scallops, and a dozen different fish from many of them. Before long, she called for shots of whiskey for the entire motley crew. In between swallows, Olivia praised everyone she recognized for the quality of their seafood, and the men and their wives shared their predictions about the summer harvest. This naturally led to a discussion about the weather, and Olivia realized that to a bar filled with fishermen, construction workers, farmers, and yardmen, each day's forecast had a direct effect on their livelihood.

"You'd best get ready for a hot, dry summer," one of the women told Olivia.

Another woman, clad in a lace-trimmed tank top that was several sizes too small for her generous chest, pointed a cherry-red acrylic nail at a man chalking the end of his pool cue. "Boyd said his pigs have been lying in the mud for weeks." She cocked her head at Olivia. "Do you know about pigs?"

"Only that I like bacon." Olivia smiled. "But I didn't think it was unusual for them to roll around in the mud. I thought that's how they kept cool."

"Sure is," a second woman agreed. "But it ain't normal

for them to do it all the time. See, when they carry somethin'
around in their mouths—a stick or a bone or somethin'—
then you know it's gonna rain. When they just lie there in
the dirt for days on end, a dry season's comin'."

A man wearing a black NASCAR shirt elbowed his way
into the group. "The ants are all scattered too." He looked at
Olivia. "When they walk in a nice, neat line like little soldiers,
then we're gonna have a storm. I got a big nest right outside
my front door, and they haven't lined up in ages. It's no good."

"Woodpeckers aren't hammerin' neither," another man
added.

Someone else mentioned that the robins had left his yard
weeks ago and he was certain they'd gone west into the
mountains. "The animals know things we don't."

Everyone nodded in agreement, and then one of the
women turned to Captain Fergusson. "What's the sea been
tellin' you?"

"She keeps her secrets close, but the moon says plenty."
He put his whiskey down. Cupping his left hand, he raised it
in the air, palm up. "We got a crescent moon right now, and
she's lying on her back like she's waiting for her man to come
to bed. We won't see a drop of rain until she gets up again.
Mark my words."

The women tut-tutted and murmured about summers gone
by. Summers of unrelenting heat. Long days of dry wind and
parched ground. They talked of how the land had gone
thirsty even though the ocean was close enough to touch.
The salt had clung to people's skin, making them sticky,
short-tempered, and lethargic.

Olivia spotted a local farmer, Lou Huckabee, on the
fringes of the group. He'd been listening to the exchange
closely. "I'll still get you all your produce, Miss Olivia,"
he said above the music. "Don't you fret."

"I know you will, Lou. And every piece of fruit will taste

like it was plucked from the richest soil on earth, washed by the freshest rainwater, and delivered straight to my kitchens still tasting of summer sunshine. That's why I won't serve my customers anything else. You have a knack for growing things like no one I've ever met."

Lou dipped his head at the compliment, flushing from neck to forehead. "It's a callin', to be sure."

"To farmers," Olivia said and held up her glass.

"To farmers!" the men and women around her echoed.

Next, they toasted fishermen, fishermen's wives, an array of different types of laborers, Millay, Olivia's mother, and on and on until Olivia was dangerously close to being drunk. Despite the close air and the way the whiskey heated her body, she was too content to leave. And when Captain Fergusson began to tell a tale about a pod of dolphins changing into mermaids, she became as immediately enraptured as the rest of his inebriated audience.

While the old man spoke in a voice as weathered and worn as his face, Olivia thought about the note Flynn had given her. She glanced around at the people in the bar, reflecting on how each and every one of them had grown up listening to the stories of their parents and grandparents. Their elders passed down folklore on the weather, animal husbandry, treating ailments, courting, raising children, and more. And here they were now, sharing those same stories. Old, well-loved, and oft-repeated stories.

They are as much a part of us as our DNA, she thought. She knew that in the small, coastal town of Oyster Bay, the local legends centered on the sea. She'd heard them over and over since she was little, and she was curious to discover new tales, such as the kind Flynn's storytellers would share with them.

A burst of laughter erupted as Captain Fergusson reached the end of his story, and then the woman in the tank top took a long pull from her beer and said, "Them mermaids might not be real, but my daddy saw the flaming ghost ship last September. Said it came out of the fog like somethin' sneakin' through the gates of hell. He was supposed to bring his catch into Ocracoke that night so it'd be fresh for the mornin' market, but he sailed home with it instead."

No one laughed at her. Millay wiped off the bar and poured another round. "I've heard the name of that ship before. Would you tell me the whole story?"

The woman nodded solemnly, but there was a gleam of excitement in her eyes. Olivia saw it and smiled to herself. She'd seen the same spark in her mother's eyes every night at bedtime. Without fail, Olivia was sent to sleep with a spectrum of wonderful images and words floating through her mind. And though her childhood was long gone, a good story was no less magical to her now.

"A long time ago, a ship full of folks from England sailed to Ocracoke," the woman began.

Olivia turned away from the storyteller, so she wouldn't see her take out her phone. She quickly sent a text to Flynn, telling him she'd be glad to help defray the costs of the retreat, and then turned the phone off and put it back in her purse.

When the woman was done with her tale of murder, robbery, and revenge, the talk returned to the weather, as it so often did at Fish Nets.

"It's hard to prepare for a dry season," Lou Huckabee told one of the fishermen. "I can irrigate, but nothin's the same as real rain."

"That's true enough," the other man agreed. "Much easier to get ready for a storm. You know they're comin', and you know that, by and by, they'll pass on through."

Olivia sighed. "Still, we've had enough storms to last us a lifetime. I hope the big ones pass us over this year."

Captain Fergusson covered her hand with his, and Olivia sensed that he knew that she wasn't referring to hurricanes, but to the number of violent deaths that had occurred in Oyster Bay during recent years.

She squeezed his hand. "I could use a season of peace and quiet."

"It's all right, my girl," he said as tenderly as possible. "Life ain't always easy and it ain't always fair, but there's beauty in every day. You just gotta know where to look."

Olivia considered this. She looked around the room and decided that he was right. Tonight, the beauty had been in a rough place filled with rough people. It had been in their lore and their legends and the way in which their stories bound them all together, weaving a spell that could never be broken.

On impulse, Olivia told the captain about the storyteller's retreat. "They'll bring energy and tranquility and a little bit of magic to our town," she said, smiling widely.

For a long moment the old fisherman didn't respond. Then he rubbed his bristly beard and slurred into his cup, "Outsiders tend to bring us things that we don't want. Sure, stories can be like a fire on a cold night. But they can burn too. There ain't nothin' can cut deeper or sting with more poison than words can. You'd best keep that in mind, Miss Olivia. Words have power, and all things of power are dangerous."

And with that, he tossed back the last swallow of whiskey, slipped off his stool, and stumbled out into the night.

Chapter 2

Find out what your hero or heroine wants.

—RAY BRADBURY

The predictions of drought voiced by many of the locals at Fish Nets turned out to be true. Weeks passed with no rain, and Oyster Bay felt like it had been covered in a layer of salt-tinged dust. Plants withered and trees drooped. Even the grass in irrigated yards turned brown and brittle.

The beach was more crowded than ever. People yearned to submerge themselves in the cool water, to wash the heat and sweat from their bodies. They floated, weightless and happy, in the lulling arms of the tide. They didn't care if their noses and cheeks burned. They didn't care if they were late for work appointments or dinner reservations. They only wanted to be wet and buoyant for a little while.

Children splashed in the shallows and then lined up with their parents outside the Big Chill, where they pleaded for double scoops with rainbow sprinkles and extra cherries. They'd bounce with impatience on the sidewalk while their mothers and fathers complained about the wait and wondered if the thermometer would reach a hundred degrees by midafternoon. They'd gulp down low-fat yogurt smoothies and frown as dripping cones of rocky road ice cream soiled their kids' new souvenir T-shirts.

The locals tried to maintain an air of relaxed normalcy, but a drought put pressure on the businesses, and prices were already on the rise. Everywhere Olivia went, whether to the docks, her restaurants, or to Grumpy's Diner, the talk was all about rain. There wasn't a man, woman, or child in Oyster Bay who couldn't name the date of the last significant precipitation, and the television meteorologists offered no hope for any in the near future. Anxious exchanges between women at the grocery store were made in low whispers so the tourists wouldn't overhear, and fearful expressions were instantly transformed into polite smiles whenever a visitor drew close.

"When are we gonna get a storm?" a woman asked the cashier at the hardware store. She was in line in front of Olivia and had a plastic rain barrel in her cart.

The man glanced around to make sure no out-of-towners were present before replying. "Dunno. The wife says not 'til after the Cardboard Regatta anyhow," he said, mentioning the popular boat race that took place during the first weekend of July each year. "She's lived here all her life, and it's never once rained for that race. That's a good thing too, seein' as cardboard and strong rains don't mix."

The woman paid for her purchase and turned to Olivia. "You can smell a storm comin' before the rest of us, seein' as your place is out on the Point. Is anythin' brewin' out there? Anythin' at all?"

Olivia thought about her early morning walk. As was her custom, she and her poodle, Captain Haviland, had gone treasure hunting on the beach. They'd passed under the shadow of the lighthouse and meandered half a mile north before Olivia had unslung the metal detector from her shoulder and turned it on. The sand had refused to yield a single trinket, however, and the sun had risen so quickly and with such intensity that Olivia had turned for home without finding so much as a bottle cap.

"There's nothing on the horizon. Even the breeze felt dry," she told the woman. "There was no scent to it at all. It was like all traces of water have been burned away."

The woman nodded. "We've got to wait a spell, that's all. Most of us have been through this before. We didn't shrivel up and die then, and we won't now."

The conversation continued until Olivia was nearly late to her weekly meeting of the Bayside Book Writers. Fortunately, the group had chosen a supper of pizza and cold beer, so there wasn't much she needed to do to prepare the lighthouse keeper's cottage for their arrival.

Chief Rawlings volunteered to bring the beer, and Pizza Bay would deliver the pies, so all Olivia had to do was turn on lights and set out plates and napkins.

Millay was the first to arrive. She walked into the living room where the writers usually gathered, tossed her skull and crossbones messenger bag onto the sofa, and pulled a crumpled paper from the pocket of her sequined miniskirt. With a heavy sigh, she held it out to Olivia. "I got this in the mail the other day."

Olivia took a moment to study Millay's face, but her friend's expression was unreadable. Taking the letter, she smoothed it flat and read the single paragraph. After rereading it once more, she laid the letter reverently on the counter.

"You've been offered representation by a literary agent? This is amazing." Olivia shook her head in wonder. "When did you get this?"

Millay shrugged and averted her eyes. "Two days ago."

Surprised, Olivia said, "Have you researched the agency? Is it bona fide?"

"Yeah," Millay replied in a thin voice. "They represent lots of well-known YA authors and a bunch of other genres too. That's why I sent my query to them. I just never thought . . ."

"Millay, I know this is huge." Olivia saw the vulnerability in her friend's dark eyes. "Daunting even. But your book is ready. It's worthy of publication. You're worthy."

Millay looked unconvinced. "Maybe. Maybe not. I'll probably just get my hopes up, and then none of the publishing houses will buy it. It'll get passed around from editor to editor until it has nowhere left to go. Then what?"

Olivia laughed. "And I thought *I* was a pessimist. Come on, this is cause for celebration. Any one of us would kill for this letter. This offer. Let's break out the champagne."

"But this is going to change everything," Millay said, finally meeting Olivia's eyes. "Our whole dynamic was about the five of us finishing our novels. I didn't believe I'd get to this step so quickly." She sighed. "I don't want to be first."

"Who better to blaze into the unknown than you? Give yourself permission to be happy about what you've achieved." Olivia picked up the letter and thrust it at Millay. "Sign with this agency and start working on your next book. Take the leap."

Millay still hadn't reclaimed the letter.

Olivia wasn't one for pep talks, but she wasn't about to let Millay throw this opportunity away. "Approach this with the same fearlessness you use on drunk bikers or high school bullies or chauvinists or racists. Grab it by the—"

"Hello!" Laurel called out merrily upon entering the cottage. "I hope the pizza's here! I am *so* hungry."

She breezed into the kitchen, the folder containing Olivia's chapter tucked under her arm, and began chattering about her meager lunch. Suddenly, she stopped talking and shifted her gaze between Olivia and Millay. "There's a charged atmosphere in this room. Are you two arguing?" Without giving them a chance to respond, Laurel continued.

"When I was little, my parents made this ridiculous vow never to fight in front of me, but I could always tell when there was friction because I'd walk into a room and they'd be standing exactly like you are right now. Close, but not too close. And the air would be heavy with all the harsh words they'd just spoken. Certain words hang around long after they're uttered, you know. They have a way of clinging to things."

The comment was oddly reminiscent of the one Captain Fergusson had made to Olivia a few weeks ago in Fish Nets. "Go on," she said to Millay. "Tell her."

Millay rolled her eyes. "Fine." She waved the letter in front of Laurel. "It's no big deal, so don't scream or start getting all touchy-feely like you do, but I got an offer from a literary agency. They want to represent me."

Laurel said nothing. Her blue eyes glimmered, and her mouth hung open in astonishment.

"Here we go," Millay muttered unhappily, but Olivia could see a glint of pleasure in her face.

"Oh, Lord!" Laurel squealed. "I can't believe it!" She put both hands over her heart and drew in a deep breath. When she released it, a torrent of words came tumbling forth. "Actually, I *can* believe it! Your book is *so* good! I know it's going to sell like crazy, and we'll get to say that we knew you before you made it big. Oh, man! Does Harris know? Of course he does." She threw out her arms and advanced on Millay. "What are we doing to celebrate?"

Millay backed off a step and held out a warning finger. "No hugs, remember? And if you try to kiss me, I will go full-out ninja on you."

Laurel had to content herself with snatching up the letter and retreating to the sofa. Perching on the edge, she unfolded the missive and read it aloud.

The moment she started, Millay grunted in annoyance and gestured at the liquor bottles lined up behind Olivia.

"You need to start pouring something. Anything. But get me a drink, or things are going to turn violent."

Laughing, Olivia moved to fulfill Millay's request.

As she dropped ice cubes into a tumbler made of hand-blown glass, Rawlings and Harris came in together. They'd barely shut the front door before Laurel was sharing Millay's news. She jumped up and down with excitement, her blond ponytail swinging, the muscles in her toned legs tensing as she bounced on her tiptoes. To Olivia, she looked every bit the high school cheerleader she'd once been.

Millay had turned her back on the scene and was gulping her beverage without pausing for breath.

"Slow down," Olivia scolded. "You're not supposed to guzzle Chivas Regal. It's not a Slurpee."

"This is what I look like when I'm celebrating," Millay said, and wiped her mouth with the back of her hand. She had yet to greet Rawlings or Harris.

And then Olivia realized what was wrong. For some reason Millay hadn't told Harris about her good fortune, and here he was on the verge of finding out along with everyone else.

Olivia looked at him. Though he was smiling at Laurel and saying, "Yeah, I'm totally psyched for her," he was unable to conceal the hurt in his eyes. Olivia couldn't blame him. After all, he and Millay had been dating for months, possibly even a year. Olivia wasn't good at remembering such anniversaries, but she knew that if Rawlings had received that letter and hadn't told her first, privately, so they could revel in the news together, she would have felt slighted. The slight would then fester into anger. Over time, it would cause a small rift between them. She could almost imagine a crack forming in the hardwood flooring beneath her feet, a fissure meant to separate Harris and Millay.

Olivia wondered if Millay would try to repair the

damage, but there was an obstinate set to her jaw, and she refused to meet Harris's penetrating gaze.

"This is incredible," he said to Millay once Laurel had finally danced out of his way to share a gleeful embrace with Rawlings. The police chief had trouble returning the gesture as he was carrying two six-packs of summer ale in his right hand. After patting Laurel briefly on the shoulder, he edged around her so she could continue to bounce without causing damage to the bottles of beer.

Millay examined the chipped purple polish on her thumbnail. "Yeah," she said. "I thought everyone should find out together since we all started our books at the same time."

"Except me," Olivia reminded her. "And at this rate, I'll never finish mine. It's becoming dull. If I'm bored writing it, I can only imagine what a reader would feel reading it."

"Sometimes dull can be refreshing," muttered Harris, who cast a sidelong glance at Millay and then sank down into a leather club chair. He busied himself with removing his laptop from its case, placing his green ballpoint pen on the coffee table, and tidying the pages of Olivia's chapter into a perfectly aligned pile.

"Harris," Millay began, but was interrupted by the ringing of the doorbell.

"Pizza's here!" Laurel cried joyfully. "My treat!"

She returned a minute later and placed a trio of large pies onto the counter while Rawlings dug a bottle opener from his pocket. He popped off four caps, releasing a hiss of cool air and the scent of hops from each bottle, and asked Olivia to put two slices of ham and pineapple pizza on his plate.

She shook her head. "Does your clothing have to coordinate with your food?"

When he wasn't in uniform, Rawlings had a penchant for dressing in Hawaiian shirts, paint-splattered khaki shorts, and leather sandals. Olivia still hadn't become accustomed to what she dubbed his Jimmy Buffet duds and had bought him several polos and button-downs, but he refused to wear them. In fact, he retaliated by purchasing three more Hawaiian shirts brighter and more garish than their predecessors. Tonight's had a luau theme and was covered with leis, hibiscus blossoms, tiki masks, and cocktails garnished with paper umbrellas and pineapple wedges.

Rawlings patted his breast pocket. "This is my attempt to blend in with the tourists. It's part of a complicated sting operation that I'm not at liberty to discuss with civilians."

Olivia handed him his pizza and waved away the beer he proffered. "My chapter's on the chopping block, so I need something stronger than that."

"Come on, it wasn't bad. Your writing flows well, your dialogue is in keeping with the ancient Egyptian era, and I can visualize all of your characters. The problem is that I'm not really rooting for any of them." Millay took an enormous bite of pepperoni pizza and shrugged apologetically, whether for her table manners or her criticism Olivia wasn't sure.

Laurel spread a napkin over her lap and then immediately began to twist it between her fingers. She was always reluctant to criticize anyone's work. "I agree with Millay. Olivia, you continue to evoke the setting so vividly, but during the last few chapters I've felt like, well, there needs to be more going on with Kamila. She seems to be losing that fighting spirit she had in the beginning."

Olivia turned to Harris. "What do you think?"

"There's not enough drama," Harris said simply. "Or tension. You have a concubine who's in love with a pharaoh. Okay, cool. Your gal, Kamila, needs to get knocked up to secure her place in the palace. That's not happening, and so we worry about her fate. Great. Then, the God-King seems to be falling in love with her because she sings so beautifully, but he won't sleep with her. That's where you start to lose me. If this guy doesn't find her appealing, why should I?"

"Yeah, it's kind of like a bunch of vampires going ape for a girl because of how she smells," Millay added with disdain. "I want more of *you* in this woman, Olivia. Someone who doesn't take any crap. Someone who uses her brain to get ahead. I don't want Kamila to win this guy over with her body."

Olivia nodded. She knew her friends were right, but had no idea how to empower someone who was in essence a slave. She turned to Rawlings, letting him see the look of appeal in her eyes.

"What does Kamila really want?" he asked softly. "Security? A baby? To be loved by this man? If those are her goals, then I think you're writing historical romance and not historical fiction."

"No, I am not," Olivia objected. "I don't know anything about romance. I want my heroine to matter, for her to push the limits of a woman's place in society. I want female readers to view her as fierce and strong."

Millay gestured wildly with her beer bottle. "But she's neither of those things. She's spent sixteen chapters reacting to her fate, not creating it. You don't have a boring bone in your body, but Kamila is limp as a noodle. I'm sorry, Olivia, but I've kind of been hoping an asp would slither onto her sleeping mat and bite her in the ass."

After a moment's pause, Olivia burst out laughing. "At least that would breathe life into my deflated plot." Her smile vanished. "I don't know how I lost sight of what I wanted for Kamila. There's nothing at all heroic about her, and I'm not sure how to change that."

"I am," Laurel said. She helped herself to another slice of pizza, keeping them in suspense until she settled back on the sofa.

Millay gave Laurel a mock salute. "Our star reporter has all the answers. You've come a long way, baby."

Laurel cocked her head. "You're comparing me to the Virginia Slims slogan?"

"Totally. The other day I saw this sweet tote bag decorated with an iron-on of a woman smoking while her laundry was being blown off the line by the wind. She didn't give a damn. Just stood there, looking all gorgeous and cool and smoking. You're like that now. I can picture you letting the dirty clothes pile up to the ceiling while you sit at your computer hammering out award-winning articles."

Beaming, Laurel poked Millay in the shoulder. "You're the one who's signing with an agent, remember? You're the star." She turned back to Olivia. "Anyway, what I was going to suggest was that we all go to see Miss Violetta Devereaux at the library next Saturday. We can watch Harris race in the Cardboard Regatta, grab a bite at The Bayside Crab House, and then head over to the library. It'll be a memorable day."

"Who is Violetta Devereaux?" Rawlings asked.

"She's a storyteller. A whole bunch of them will be in town next week for their annual retreat," Laurel explained. "They're mostly spending time with each other, honing their craft and exchanging new versions of old tales and such, but the *Gazette* and Through the Wardrobe are sponsoring a few events for the public too."

Laurel didn't add Olivia's name to the list of patrons, and Olivia was relieved that Flynn had heeded her request to let her donation remain anonymous. She was about to ask Laurel for more details when Harris raised a finger.

"Will it be more like a ghost story or a one-woman play?" Harris said. "I'll go to anything as long as there are no puppets. I've got a thing about puppets."

Millay nodded in agreement.

"Listen," Laurel said. "Violetta is quite possibly the most famous storyteller of our time. Apparently, she tells such a compelling tale that you'll forget where you are when she starts speaking. She's inspired dozens of novelists, poets, and songwriters—not to mention other kinds of artists. People say it's impossible not to be forever changed after attending one of her performances."

Harris was clearly intrigued. "Whoa, that's serious."

"Hell, yeah," Millay agreed and sent a fleeting smile his way. "I bet this Violetta could teach us a thing or two about building drama. I'm in."

Laurel looked at Olivia. "What do you think?"

"It sounds like she's taken the key components of fiction and boiled them down until only the most essential elements are left. That's what I need to figure out. What is it that pulls the reader in and then refuses to let go? If Violetta can show me how to do that, then I'll listen to her all night long."

The day of the Cardboard Regatta began with a hazy sky and cloying humidity. Olivia skipped her walk altogether, hoping to grab breakfast at Grumpy's before the tourists filled every booth and counter seat.

Dixie Weaver, the diner's waitress and proprietor, was a dwarf. She zipped around the restaurant on a pair of roller skates with purple wheels. Her clothes came from the junior's department at Walmart, and she had a little girl's love of accessories and makeup. As a result, she usually wore too much of both, but no one dared comment on her fashion sense for fear of being barred from the diner, which would be a serious punishment as Grumpy made the best breakfasts in Oyster Bay. Dixie's coffee was also legendary. Rich and bold, it fortified both vacationers and locals for a long day.

Olivia sat at her favorite window booth dreaming of

Dixie's coffee. She craned her head in search of her friend while Haviland mirrored her movement. Olivia knew the poodle was also hoping Dixie would appear soon. After all, breakfast at Grumpy's meant eggs scrambled with ground beef, and Haviland loved to eat from a platter beneath the table.

Dixie skated out of the kitchen and spotted them instantly. She waved, and after handing a bottle of syrup to one of the customers at the counter, zipped to the front of the diner. "Do I have news for you!" She planted an affectionate kiss on Haviland's black nose, put a ceramic mug on the table, and filled it to the brim with her strong, dark brew.

"Coffee, divine coffee," Olivia murmured. She stirred in a dollop of cream and took a quick, gratifying sip.

Dixie slid into the booth next to Haviland and tugged her rainbow-striped kneesocks back into place. She wore a dozen multicolored bracelets on her left arm and a sparkly black wristband on the right. Her hair had been feathered and shellacked into place with half a can of Aqua Net in order to showcase her earrings. Made of turquoise and silver beads, they fell to the top of her shoulders and brushed against the straps of her American Idol tank top.

"I didn't know you were a fan of the show. I thought you were all about Andrew Lloyd Webber," Olivia said, waving her hand to indicate the diner's decorations. Every inch of available wall space paid homage to the composer.

"No reality show could hold a candle to Broadway," Dixie said. "But I love to listen to these kids singin' their hearts out. The whole thing's probably rigged, but I don't care. I sing along with every song. You should hear how my dogs start to howl!" She laughed and rubbed Haviland behind the ears. "I know you're waitin' on me, Captain, so I'll put your order in and then come back with my big news."

Olivia shook her head. "You're such a tease."

"Why do you think Grumpy and I are still married after all this time?" Dixie grinned saucily. "You wanna order or just let the chef fix you somethin' special?"

"I'll leave my meal in Grumpy's capable hands," Olivia said. "And I'd try to worm more info from you, since you're obviously bursting to tell me something juicy, but the woman at the *Cats* booth has her placemat raised in the air like it's a white flag."

Dixie scowled. "She'd better be surrenderin'. That harpy has run me ragged. She took one sip of water and then asked me for a refill. Demanded crisp bacon and then told me it was too crunchy to eat. Ordered white toast and then wanted to know why I didn't serve her wheat. Bet she'll leave me a crap tip too." She stood and gave her tank top an irritated tug. "She's lucky I'm not the type of waitress who spits in people's food."

She skated off, leaving Olivia to read the *Gazette*. Haviland looked out the window and seemed perfectly content to watch the passersby.

The paper was filled with short articles about the day's boat race and included numerous photographs of previous winners and their vessels. The regatta had increased in size each year, and because local merchants contributed to the cash prizes, the competition had grown fiercer than ever. So many entrants had tried to circumvent the construction rules that each craft had to be vetted by a special committee within twenty-four hours of the race.

This event was almost as well attended as the actual race and hundreds of bets were placed the moment the boats were unveiled. Of course, the authorities couldn't openly condone gambling, but Chief Rawlings and the rest of the force had chosen to pretend that they didn't know about the money exchanging hands on the docks, in the bars, and in the back room of the hardware store.

"Which horse are you gonna back?" Dixie said as she returned with Haviland's food and a frittata for Olivia. "Harris's? That boy sure knows how to build a boat. Oh, Grumpy wanted me to tell you that you've got cherry tomatoes, goat cheese, fresh basil, and corn mixed in with your eggs. Enjoy." She put Haviland's plate on the floor. After he jumped down to eat, she took his seat, folded her hands, and wriggled a little with excitement. "My cousin's here for the storyteller's retreat. I haven't seen him for ages. Probably because he's been in and out of jail since we were kids."

Because her mouth was full, Olivia registered her surprise by lifting her brows.

"What? Doesn't everyone have a few thugs hangin' on the family tree?" Dixie chuckled. "Lowell's pretty harmless as criminals go. He's just never been fond of payin' for things. He'd see somethin' he wanted, and if he couldn't afford it, he'd steal it. Most of the time he avoided gettin' caught, but the older he got, the more darin' he grew."

"So how is he involved in the retreat? Is he going to move through the audience picking pockets?"

Most people would have been offended by the question, but Dixie let out a roar of laughter. "Don't give him any notions, you hear?" She flipped the *Gazette* to the back page, pointing to the list of performer biographies. "See? Here he is. Lowell Reid. He's Miss Violetta's assistant. Takes care of her bookings, costumes, and props."

"That's a far cry from larceny," Olivia said. "You must be proud of him for straightening out."

"I am, but I'm a bit confused too. Last time I heard from his mama she told me that Lowell had been arrested. He was locked up somewhere in the western part of the state, and after he finally got out, this Violetta lady hired him. Lowell's mama said she was gonna be real famous soon because some college professor was writin' a book about her and the history of Appalachian folktales. Unfortunately for her, he died before he could finish his work. See."

Dixie pointed at a photograph of a middle-aged man seated in a cabin in the woods. Clutching a notebook and pen, he appeared to be deep in conversation with a very old woman. As Olivia studied the photograph, Grumpy stuck his head out of the kitchen and signaled for Dixie to pick up an order. She excused herself, leaving Olivia to wonder how the professor, whose name was Alfred Hicks, had died. The paper didn't mention the cause of death, but storytellers from the Appalachian region were quoted as saying they were shocked and saddened by his loss and were dedicating future performances to him.

As she ate, Olivia continued to read about the participants of both the children and adult programs. By the time she and Haviland had cleaned their plates, Dixie returned with the check.

"Professor Hicks was by no means old. And he must have been in decent shape to be hiking through the Appalachians," Olivia mused aloud. "It says here that he was in his late forties. Did Lowell mention how he died?"

Dixie nodded. Glancing around, she lowered her voice. "The officials said that his death was an accident. Word has it that he went out at night, lost his footin', and fell. Broke his neck. End of story. But when I talked to Lowell on the phone the other day, he said there was more to it than that. Somethin' he refuses to talk about. Somethin' that scared the tar out of him."

Intrigued, Olivia stared at her friend. "If Alfred Hicks didn't slip, then what happened to him?"

"I wouldn't say this with a straight face if it hadn't come straight from Lowell's lips, but he thinks the professor was killed." Dixie's face was pinched and humorless. "Murdered by the light of the moon."

"By whom?" Olivia asked.

Dixie leaned closer and whispered so softly that Olivia could barely hear her say, "By a ghost."

Chapter 3

The universe is made of stories, not atoms.

—MURIEL RUKEYSER

Olivia knew that Dixie was fully prepared to elaborate, but when Grumpy's face suddenly appeared around the side of the swinging door leading to the kitchen, it was clear that he wasn't pleased. Scowling, he beckoned for his wife to come into the kitchen.

"Lord, why do the orders have to stack up just when I've got somethin' interestin' to talk about!" she complained and skated away.

Olivia watched the woman in the *Cats* booth stuff the table's entire supply of sugar and sugar substitute packets into her voluminous purse before walking out of the diner. Dixie had been right in fearing the disgruntled customer wouldn't leave a tip, for when Olivia got up to investigate, she saw that the woman had done something far worse than stiff Dixie. She'd left a single quarter sitting in the middle of a puddle of syrup.

"What a piece of work," Olivia muttered and dropped a five-dollar bill next to the coin but clear of the syrup. If she left a larger tip, Dixie would surmise that the money hadn't come from the sugar thief, and she'd be offended.

Having restored balance on Dixie's behalf, Olivia signaled to Haviland that it was time to leave, and the pair headed down to the docks.

"It's already so crowded," she told her poodle, but he didn't seem to mind the mass of people. His warm brown eyes glinted in the sunlight, and his mouth hung open in a relaxed smile. Olivia grinned at him. "You're just hoping Diane and the gals who groom you will be here. You're shamelessly greedy. You just had breakfast and you're dreaming of treats."

At the sound of the word, Haviland barked and quickened his pace. Olivia let him walk in front of her. The big black dog cut a path through the throng of merchants and spectators, and Olivia followed in his wake, knowing full well that she'd have to rein him in before they got too close to the shrimp stall. Haviland adored shrimp, but he was restricted to one or two pieces and only if they had been deveined and steamed first. Left to his own devices, he'd gorge on shrimp until he got sick. And because none of the fishermen could resist slipping Haviland a snack, Olivia had to keep a close eye on him.

"Olivia! Hi!" Laurel called from behind a lemonade stand. "On your way to the waterfront?"

Whistling for Haviland to stop, Olivia veered away from the boardwalk to the tree-lined lane where vendors were hawking Cardboard Regatta T-shirts, model kits, and an array of carnival-type food.

"Dallas and Dermot volunteered to help our neighbor sell lemonade before the race," Laurel explained, smiling proudly at her sons. "The stand is raising money for charity and our neighbor, Bobby, is a Cub Scout. He'll earn a merit badge for volunteering and when the twins heard what he was doing, they begged to be allowed to assist him."

The boys exchanged proud glances and then one of them whispered to the other, "Mom's happy."

Because they were identical twins with no notable differences such as a birthmark or scar, Olivia could never tell Dallas or Dermot apart. When they were little, Laurel dressed Dallas in blue and Dermot in green, but now that the boys refused to be assigned certain colors, Olivia had no idea who was who.

"Go on." Laurel nudged the nearest boy. "Try your pitch on Ms. Limoges."

"Oh, you don't have to," Olivia said hastily. "I'm not thirsty at all, so let me just put some money in your jar or shoebox or whatever you have, and I'll be on my way."

Laurel shook her head and pointed at her sons. "Their preschool teacher said that they mumble too much. This will help them practice their public speaking."

Olivia handed one of the boys a twenty. "Okay. Tell me this. Will my donation help someone?"

"Kids with cancer," he said in a small, nervous voice, and fixed his gaze on Haviland.

"There you are. Succinct and to the point. Well done, sir." Olivia smiled at Laurel and then gestured toward the harbor, which was filled with cardboard boats performing test runs. "Are you going to miss the start of the race?"

At that moment a woman in a pink and green sundress and a little girl in a matching dress appeared next to Laurel. The woman dropped her designer handbag on the table and declared, "Your relief is here!"

While Laurel handed over the cash box and key, the little girl took the opportunity to stick her tongue out at Dallas and Dermot. It happened with lightning quickness, but Olivia saw the gesture and was annoyed by it because the girl was at least four years older than Laurel's twins.

"I'm sure your boys did the best they could, Laurel," the

mother said with false sweetness and peered into the cash box. "Oh my. There aren't many large bills at all. Well, never fear! My Ashley-Grace is going to sell more lemonade than any other child on record! She's a natural salesperson, and I've never met a soul who could say no to her. This exposure will be so good for her already flourishing pageant career."

The woman beamed at Ashley-Grace who turned to Olivia wearing an angelic smile. "Good morning, ma'am. You look lovely today. Have you sampled our unbelievably refreshing lemonade? Did you know that every glass—"

"Contains lemons," Olivia interrupted. "I'm severely allergic to lemons," she lied glibly. "And to most children."

Ashley-Grace's mother turned bright pink with indignation, but Olivia ignored her. "Don't be late, Laurel. Harris will look for us during the race. Good-bye, boys."

Dallas and Dermot were too busy giggling behind their hands to do anything but wave.

Reaching out to scratch Haviland's head, Olivia whispered, "Our work here is done."

Once again, the pair walked toward the sea of beach chairs and picnic blankets covering every inch of grass in the small park by the harbor. As soon as Olivia located the set of chairs Harris had set aside for the Bayside Book Writers, she took out a pair of binoculars and began to scan the boats lined up near the water's edge for her friend.

The captains in the junior race were steering their crafts to the starting buoys, and Olivia examined the vessels with amusement. For the most part, the boats created by the twelve- to eighteen-year-olds celebrated their hobbies and love of junk food. There were several skateboards, two boom boxes, a hot dog, a carton of French fries, three different candy bars, a cell phone, a horse, and a ballet slipper.

As with the adult race, two young men or women meeting certain weight requirements manned the boats in the juvenile division. They were each allowed a single oar. No working sails or motors were permitted.

Suddenly, a flesh-colored object obscured her view. Olivia lowered her binoculars to find Sawyer Rawlings standing in front of her. He was in uniform and cut a handsome figure, but Olivia also thought he looked hot and uncomfortable.

"Do you ever wish you had seasonal uniforms?" she teased. "Navy for winter, white for summer."

"Everyone would confuse me for the ice cream man," he said.

She arched her brows. "Ice cream men carry handcuffs and handguns?"

"Hey, we drive through the same neighborhoods. Besides, people would kill for something cold on a day like this."

"I can point you to the nearest lemonade stand," she said as he dabbed his forehead with a handkerchief. Olivia found the fact that he carried a handkerchief most endearing. Rawlings was an intriguing blend of old-fashioned southern gentleman and liberal modern man. His workdays were spent apprehending criminals, reviewing cases, and balancing budgets while his free time was devoted to painting, reading poetry, writing his novel, and hanging out with his sister and her family or with Olivia and Haviland.

Rawlings was about to speak when something caught his attention. Olivia turned to follow his gaze and saw that a teenage boy was poised at the top of a set of steps, ready to launch himself down. There was a sign reading "Skateboarding Prohibited" two feet from where he waited, the first two wheels of his board hovering in midair. The sidewalk at the bottom of the stairs wasn't clear of pedestrians, and someone was bound to get hurt if the kid took the plunge. Before Olivia could speak, Rawlings was in motion.

For a big man, the chief moved fast. He had the youth by

the elbow before he could leave the ground. Olivia couldn't hear what Rawlings said to him, but within seconds the boy was nodding deferentially. He then jogged down the stairs with his board tucked under his arm. Pausing at the bottom, he picked a wadded napkin off the ground, tossed it into the nearest trashcan, and turned to give Rawlings a brief wave.

Olivia smiled. Only Rawlings could command such respect using gentle tones and a paternal hand on the shoulder.

"He's a catch, all right," Laurel said, stealing up alongside of Olivia.

Irritated by the heat creeping up her neck and cheeks, Olivia asked, "Where'd your trolls go?"

"Steve's parents are taking them for rest of the weekend, and they are going to have their hands full. The boys are completely hopped up on lemonade." Laurel smiled and gazed out over the water. "The first race is going to start any minute now. Where's Millay?"

"I don't know, but she'd better get a move on." Olivia lifted her binoculars and scanned the boardwalk. "We've never had this many spectators before."

Haviland made a sniffing noise and Olivia glanced at him. "Do you want to find her, Captain?"

The poodle barked once and trotted off through the crowd. Olivia and Laurel sat in their canvas chairs and exchanged theories as to which boat would win the juvenile division.

"I'm rooting for the French fries," Laurel said. "You?"

"The hot dog. How could I pick anything else? The captain is dressed as a ketchup bottle, and the first mate is the mustard." Olivia shook her head. "Those guys must be boiling inside those costumes."

Laurel laughed. "That's why they're going to lose. How are they going to row in those getups?"

In the end, the ballet slipper won. Its long, delicate prow crossed the finish line seconds ahead of a giant banana. The triumphant shrieks of the female crew carried over the water. "Look! They're wearing tutus and tiaras!" Laurel exclaimed, peering at them through her own binoculars.

"They should've ditched the tutus and worn something unexpected. Camo maybe," Millay said, settling into the chair next to Olivia as if she'd been there all along. "Thanks for sending Haviland. I had no clue where to go. Harris e-mailed a picture of this spot at like seven this morning, but it looks totally different now. What gives with all these people, anyway? Is this what passes for culture in this town?"

Laurel handed her a Thermos. "Have some lemonade. You seem a little crabby."

Millay shrugged. "Harris and I got into it last night. I swear—all we do lately is fight. And then I had to go to work all pissed off while he went to sleep. The second I get off work he seems to want to talk about all kinds of heavy crap. I have to mute my phone just so I can get a few hours of shut-eye. The boy is either stupid or has a serious death wish."

"You'll figure it out," Laurel assured her, but Olivia wasn't as certain. Millay was showing all the signs of a woman who was ready for a change, and Olivia suspected Harris was one of the things she wanted a break from. It wouldn't be easy to do, especially since Millay and Harris would continue to see each other at the weekly meetings of the Bayside Book Writers. Still, Olivia knew Millay was capable of walling off her emotions. It was a skill the two women shared; one they'd both tried to stop using every time they got close to another person.

"I don't see Harris," Olivia said. "Millay, do you know what his boat looks like?"

"He told me it was a surprise," she said. "Something we'd all immediately recognize."

Laurel and Olivia swept their binoculars over the line of bobbing boats.

"They've gotten so elaborate." Laurel pointed at the center of the largest group. "There's a dragon with smoke coming out of its mouth. And a Viking longship. Look! The crewmen are wearing blond wigs and horned helmets." She continued to describe the vessels. A shark baring several rows of serrated teeth, a dolphin with a bubbling blowhole, a tugboat, a fire truck, a fighter jet, a pirate ship flying the Jolly Roger, a listing ferry, a yellow duck, a Loch Ness monster, and a spotted cow.

Olivia passed her binoculars to Millay. "You've got to see the church."

Millay located the boat with the steeple. The front half of the building was white and bore a sign saying "Sunday." Stained glass windows had been painted on the cardboard. The rear of the building was black and had a neon sign reading, "Saturday." In a painted window another sign read, "Bar Open." The captain was dressed as the devil and his crewmember was an angel.

"Awesome," Millay said with a grin. "Now that's original."

"But not nearly as cool as the boat coming out from behind that fishing trawler," Laurel said. "Hey! It's Harris!"

Olivia waited for Millay to hand over the binoculars, and when she met Olivia's gaze, her face was unreadable. Olivia peered out to the harbor and gasped. Harris had brought a scene from Millay's novel to life. Her heroine, Tessa, was a gryphon warrior and during the book's climax, she and her beast battled a fierce wyvern and its rider. Harris had carved the two beasts out of cardboard. Their necks were intertwined, and their green and golden eyes were glimmering with rage and bloodlust as they fought to the death. The gryphon's feathers had been painted a metallic gold while the wyvern's were black with a rainbow sheen. Their tails were entangled too—one ended in a tassel of fur while the other was a pointed spade. Glimmering claws skimmed the water, and two sets of wings—one a soft white and the other a deep indigo—reached high into the air.

"Who's rowing with him?" Laurel asked.

"Some guy from work," was Millay's flat reply.

Laurel turned to stare at her. "You can't still be mad at him. Not after seeing that boat. He made that for you."

Olivia guessed that Millay wasn't angry with Harris. She just wasn't in love with him anymore. That realization made her feel guilty. The guilt led to anger. And Millay had no idea what to do with that anger.

"Let him have his day," Olivia whispered to her.

Millay's dark eyes flew open wide, and then she nodded slowly. "I will."

The women watched in anxious silence as the boats lined up at the starter buoys. When the blast of an air horn signaled that the race had begun, Laurel leapt from her chair. Screaming and clapping wildly, she cheered for Harris without pause.

Millay remained seated until Harris's fantasy craft tacked around the final buoy. On the last stretch of open water, the contestants battled ferociously. Harris had broken away from the rest of the pack, but his lead was slim. The Viking longboat, the yellow duck, and the pirate ship were riding closely in his wake.

All the spectators were on their feet now, including Olivia and Millay.

"Come on, Harris," Millay muttered, gnawing at her thumbnail.

Harris pulled ahead by half a boat length and the crowd roared. He stopped rowing for a moment, waved, and yanked on a rope hanging from the wyvern's neck. A stream of green fire burst forth from its mouth, whipping the spectators into an even greater frenzy. However, during those few seconds in which he'd stopped rowing, the Vikings had caught him and now the two crafts were in a dead tie.

With only six lengths to go, Harris's boat caught fire.

It happened without warning. At first, there was a lick of green flame on top of the wyvern's head, and then a loud *whoosh* echoed across the water. Both the gryphon and wyvern were on fire, their heads and torsos engulfed in orange and yellow. All signs of the magical green fire were gone. Now, traditional flames blackened the intertwined creatures, melting them together as bits of charred cardboard dropped into the ocean.

"Get out!" a woman cried, but Harris wasn't abandoning his burning vessel. Even after the fire raced along the gunwales and his first mate dove overboard, Harris kept rowing.

Laurel reached for Millay's hand and clasped it tightly. "Why doesn't he jump? He's going to get burned!"

Olivia's heart was in her throat. What was Harris thinking? There was no longer any chance of victory, and without his crewmember, he couldn't even row straight. He was dashing from port to starboard, slapping his paddle into the water and giving it a furious push before switching sides. He had to stand to row in order to avoid the flames, and no matter how valiant his efforts were, they were utterly futile.

"He's sinking!" a man shouted, and Olivia saw that it was true. The heads of the warring beasts had collapsed, inviting a rush of salt water into the shallow hull.

Harris hurled his oar away and stood completely still as the Vikings flew toward the finish line.

"What the hell are you doing?" Millay murmured. Her dark eyes were fearful. "It's over. It's over, you idiot."

As if her voice had carried across the harbor, Harris turned to the shore. He folded himself over in a deep, courtly bow. And then, he put his palms together and dove into the water.

The Viking longship severed the golden ribbon tied between a pair of buoys, and the blasts of multiple air horns cut through the air. The crowd resumed its raucous cheering, but Olivia, Laurel, and Millay sat in anxious silence.

Horns continued to sound as the second and third place boats crossed the line.

"They're pulling him out." Laurel had her binoculars pressed to her eyes and was pointing to the spot where Harris's boat had been. It was completely gone from view. "Do you want to look?" she asked Millay.

"No," she said. "I'm out of here. He's going to be totally mortified by what happened, and my being around will just make it worse. See you tonight."

Laurel watched her go and then sighed. "That was such a romantic gesture. He almost won with a boat he built in his girlfriend's honor, and then it burned and sank. Poor Harris. I can't even imagine what he's feeling right now."

Olivia stared out at the water, "He probably believes that everything was riding on that race and he blew it. Actually, it was already too late, but he doesn't know that yet." Before Laurel could ask what she meant, Olivia folded up her chair and gestured toward the dock. "Come on, let's wrap our boy in a towel and take him home."

Supper at The Bayside Crab House was a subdued affair. Millay was a no-show. She texted Harris to make sure he wasn't hurt and then asked him to save her a seat at the storytelling event later that evening.

For his part, Harris was unusually sullen. Despite the fact that people kept stopping by their table to congratulate him on the most exciting and theatrical race in the history of the regatta, he was unable to recover his sense of humor. Strangers bought him drinks and asked to be photographed with him. A pretty young woman even begged him to sign her bare shoulder with a black marker, but he still remained moody and taciturn.

"Miss Violetta will help you forget about today," Laurel assured him after the woman had run off to show her friends Harris's signature. "That's what she does. Transports people with her stories."

Harris produced a small smile for Laurel's benefit. "I hope she's as good as you claim, because I'm really not in the mood for 'once upon a times' tonight."

Though she felt sorry for her friend, Olivia had been anticipating the storytelling event far more than any of the rest of the day's activities. She wanted to get to the library at least thirty minutes early in order to secure front row seats, but Rawlings, who'd just finished his shift at five, wanted to savor a platter of crab legs and a cold beer. Admonishing her to relax, he cracked his first crab claw with gusto.

Foiled, Olivia called the head librarian, an old friend of her mother's, and asked her to reserve five seats. Leona Fairchild had known Olivia since she was a baby and was more than happy to oblige, thus allowing Olivia to enjoy her meal of flounder in a lemon-garlic butter sauce with a side of steamed rice and green beans almondine.

When the four friends arrived at the library, Millay was waiting in the lobby. She slugged Harris on the arm and praised him for not going down without a fight. He was smiling and making jokes about his sunken boat by the time Leona escorted them into the conference room.

The room, an unremarkable space filled with rows of gray chairs and a stage area with a lectern and a retractable projector screen, had been transformed. The overhead lights had been dimmed, and Olivia thought the soft, white orbs looked like dozens of small, glowing moons. The stage was dark and empty, save for two wooden chairs. These had woven cane seats and Shaker-style backs and appeared handmade.

Olivia and her friends took their seats and spent the next ten minutes whispering to one another. For some reason, the presence of the vacant chairs had them speaking in low, hushed tones, though Olivia wasn't sure why.

Other attendees entered and sat down. They too were quiet and subdued.

"How can a pair of chairs create atmosphere?" Olivia asked Rawlings.

He thought for a moment. "There's an air of mystery in here. The dim lights, the old chairs, the anticipation. It makes me feel like a kid. Remember what it was like to sit in a movie theater in those long seconds before the projectionist began playing the film reel? Every part of me was tuned into that screen."

Olivia nodded. "Those chairs are our movie screen. And we have no idea what we've come to see." She noticed Dixie skating to an empty seat near the end of the row in the middle of the room and waved at her. Dixie tossed a phonebook on the chair, climbed onto it, and blew Olivia a kiss before curling her short legs inward to allow Grumpy to scoot past.

Grumpy's was the last available seat, and once he'd settled into it, the audience grew nearly silent. People looked at the stage, over their shoulders, and at one another. Their faces were filled with curiosity and nervous excitement.

These feelings heightened until, finally, a dwarf stepped onto the stage. He moved slowly, using both hands to drag a large trunk from one end to the other. When he reached his destination, he paused and fitted a key into the large silver padlock and unlocked the trunk. He lifted the lid, tossed the lock inside, and dusted off his hands.

"That must be Lowell, Dixie's cousin," Olivia whispered to Rawlings.

The dwarf was dressed in tan pants with patches on both knees, a charcoal-gray T-shirt, and a blazer of plum-colored corduroy. He wore a yellow bandana around his neck, and his hair was sandy brown and shaggy.

"Who cares about stories anymore?" he asked the audience, and perched on the edge of the low stage, as if this were the beginning of a casual conversation. When no one answered, he uttered an exasperated sigh and leaned back on his palms, swinging his legs a little and glancing up at the ceiling. He looked like a bored child.

"The story is everything," came a voice from the darkness. It was a woman's voice, deep and resonating. It echoed through the room, and Olivia felt it curl around her shoulders like a heavy shawl. "Stories last longer than deeds," the voice said. The woman wasn't speaking loudly, but her voice was almost a tangible entity, seeping over them like a powerful current.

The dwarf was clearly unimpressed by her reply. "We have books now," he argued. "We have television and movies. We have Twitter and Facebook and the wonders of the World Wide Web."

"And why do you think you turn to those things?" the voice asked softly, dangerously. "Every tweet, every post, every group of lines that you type is a story. Human beings connect with other human beings through stories. That's why you stare at the screen for so many hours. You are looking for other people's stories. And you want to share your own. You want your voice to be heard among all those other voices."

Shaking his head, the dwarf persisted. "Come on, stories are for kids. Look at us." He swept his arm out in front of him, incorporating the entire audience in his gesture. "We're adults. We've got no use for once upon a time."

There was a long pause. It was so long that Olivia grew uncomfortable. Why wasn't the woman answering? Harris had said nearly the same thing as the dwarf at dinner. So why didn't the woman hurry up and tell them what they'd all come to hear?

"Once upon a time, on a night so cold that the stars nearly froze in the wide, black sky, a man told a story to his son," the voice finally said, sounding a little less distant now. Less disembodied. The voice now spoke with a country accent. It was more familiar, more approachable. It was wise without being intimidating. "The son told the story to his son. Back when we huddled in caves and our bellies were never full and we were always cold. So cold. And the dark seemed to last for years. The son told the story to his son. History was born with that story. It told the secrets of survival. Spoke of a code of conduct. All that makes us human, all that separates us from animals came from that story. And we are still telling a version of it, thousands and thousands of years later."

The dwarf rubbed his chin, considering this answer. "Stories help us through the long, dark nights. Stories are the light of our souls moving out into the world." He stood up, walked to the trunk, and reached inside for an object. Taking out an oil lamp, he carried it to the front of the stage. Setting it down on the floor, he lit a match and put it to the wick. A blue flame instantly bloomed upward. The dwarf replaced the glass cover, blew out the match, and backed away.

"The story will outlast us all," the voice said. "But if we're lucky, we can become part of one."

A woman who looked to be in her early forties stepped from the blackness at the rear of the stage into the blue circle cast by the oil lamp. Her small frame was clad in a floor-length cotton dress. The fabric was a shade of deep purple dotted by tiny white flowers. She wore black gloves and boots, and waves of black hair tumbled over her shoulders with the exception of a lock of brilliant silver that framed her face. Her skin was ghostly pale in the ethereal light, and her large, round eyes shone like blue fire. Olivia thought she was one of the most beautiful women she'd ever seen.

"Once upon a time," she began, placing a gloved hand on the top rail of the closest chair. Staring out at the audience, Miss Violetta seemed to look every person in the eye. Olivia could feel the intensity of her gaze and was completely riveted by the woman's larger-than-life presence. As petite as she was, she seemed to loom above them, commanding every ounce of their attention. Olivia wondered if this was what it felt like to be hypnotized.

"Once upon a time," Violetta repeated, her accent thickening as her shadow stretched and lengthened. It rose up the back wall like a castle tower, and when she lifted her arms, the shadow turned into a tree. Tall and thin and a little frightening.

"Once upon a time, there was a girl who told a story that shouldn't have been told. Her daddy warned her not to tell it. He said she'd get herself killed if she didn't keep quiet. But she didn't listen. Soon enough, she'll be punished. She'll turn into a ghost. A haint." She raised a finger and pointed at someone in the crowd. Someone seated on the other side of the room from Olivia and the Bayside Book Writers.

"But not yet," Miss Violetta said in a voice as slick and smooth as a river rock. "Not just yet."

Chapter 4

We dance round in a ring and suppose,
But the Secret sits in the middle and knows.

—ROBERT FROST

Violetta didn't elaborate on that first story. Instead, she told a haint tale about a tiny mountain cabin that hadn't been occupied for many years. When it was finally sold to a young couple, the woman couldn't sleep at night because she was continuously woken up by the sounds of a baby's cry. Her husband didn't hear the cries, and eventually he began to think that he'd wed a crazy woman. Their marriage suffered. The woman slept less and less. She could hardly complete her chores. She burned the stew, wove crooked patterns on her loom, and failed to tend the vegetable garden. Weeks passed. The house grew dirty, the clothes were unwashed, and her loom sat silent in the corner of the cabin. One day, the husband came home from chopping trees in the forest to find that his wife had hung herself from the rafters.

"He took her down and held her close, remembering what she'd been like when he first courted her," Violetta whispered sorrowfully. "He buried her in the churchyard, and after the service was over he went on back home. The man reckoned his wife had truly lost her mind. He also felt sorry for himself because he was now all alone. But he wasn't." She paused to glance over her left shoulder. Peering into the blackness behind the stage, she took a step to the right. Her body went stiff. "That very night, he heard the baby crying. Heard his wife too, calling his name. Clear as a bell ringing over the hills it was. He wrapped a quilt 'round his shoulders and went outside. The moon was hanging low in the sky like a shiny silver coin, and there was his wife standing in the middle of the road. She was wearing her favorite dress and looked pretty as a new bride. She had a baby in her arms.

"The man rubbed his eyes, but she was there, just as real as you and me. She waved to him and then walked off into the woods. He followed her all the way to the river, but she vanished. He stopped chasing after her then 'cause everybody knows that a ghost can't cross a river. Even a frozen one. The man never saw his wife after that. Never heard that baby cry again neither. Years later he learned that the family who'd lived in his cabin caught the pox. It killed all of them. Folks said that the baby was the last one to die and he cried and cried all through the long night before he finally died."

Before Olivia could finish absorbing the tragic story, Violetta began another. This one was called Jack and the Giant. As with the traditional fairy tale, Jack was poor and hungry. He and his mother scratched out a feeble existence from the land. Violetta described Jack's constant obsession with food with the vividness of one who's known poverty and the hollow ache of an empty belly. In contrast, the giant was rich and feasted like a king. He ate mutton stew, roast pork, brown bread dipped in gravy, and dozens of berry cobblers at a time. He didn't live in a castle above the clouds, but in a cave deep in the hills. He smoked an enormous pipe and owned hundreds of hearty sheep and fat pigs. Jack, who played the banjo and was as foolish as he was brave, was a likable hero. Olivia laughed when he tricked the giant and sighed with relief when he was able to return to his simple cabin and present his mother with the giant's treasure.

He'll finally be able to eat, she thought happily. *He can stuff himself until he's good and full.*

But no sooner had Jack escaped the giant than he decided to take on the North Wind. Up until this point, Lowell's task had been limited to adding sound effects by using a rain stick, tambourine, banjo, and fiddle. He'd remained outside of the circle of blue light. But now, he unfolded a stepladder downstage left, donned a short wig of white curls, and climbed to the topmost rung. Perched atop the ladder, he played a set of high, chilly notes on his fiddle. He plucked the same strings over and over again until Violetta, speaking in Jack's voice, begged him to stop.

Having transformed into Jack, Violetta appeared to shrink to the size of a child. Hugging herself, she talked of how cold the mountain winters were. How there was a hole in the chinking between the logs next to Jack's bed. The wind whistled in through this hole, making Jack shiver. Snow snuck in too, covering Jack's quilts with a dusting of white. Onstage, Jack shuddered and rubbed his arms, and Olivia suddenly felt cold. Because most public places used too much air-conditioning for her taste, she always carried a cardigan in her bag. She hurriedly slipped it on and folded her arms over her chest. The air felt damp. It passed beneath her clothes and chilled her skin. The sensation increased as Lowell continued to play his shrill song and Jack, through chattering teeth, pleaded with him to stop blowing.

After that story, Violetta told a pair of folktales about how the turtle cracked his shell and why the wolf howls at the moon. She finished the show with another ghost story about a hermit who hid his treasure in the heart of a hollowed-out trunk and became so afraid that it would be found that he began to dress up in bearskins and scare off anyone who came near his cabin. Over time, he began to lose his mind. People said his eyes glittered like diamonds and he attached bear claws to his gloves. When he died one winter alone on the mountain, his ghost remained, walking on all fours like a bear. The legend was that anyone who came too near the treasure would hear the man's growl and be forever cursed with bad luck, sickness, or death.

Her strange tale left the audience reeling in horrified delight. Violetta delivered the last sentence and then simply strode from the stage and into the darkness beyond.

"There'll be a reception in the lobby when the lights come back up," Lowell announced when she was gone. "We hope you've enjoyed our Appalachian tales."

The crowd applauded timidly at first, still too stupefied by Violetta's final story to make much noise. Olivia shook herself from the storyteller's trance and clapped louder. Soon enough, the room swelled with appreciative noises, including whistles and cries of "wonderful!" and "amazing!"

"I couldn't agree more," Olivia said to Rawlings. "I could have stayed here all night listening to her. It was like being under a spell. An extraordinary spell."

"She certainly drew me in," Rawlings agreed. "I forgot where I was. *When* I was."

Millay pointed at the oil lantern. "What was with all the blue light? That woman's eyes were crazy blue, and the skin around her eyes seemed kind of blue too. She must have gotten hold of Dixie's makeup kit. It was kind of creepy. She looked like an alien."

"All the better to hypnotize you with, my dear," Harris said, doing his best imitation of an old crone. "By the time we see her out in the lobby, she'll probably blend right in with the crowd."

"She won't be there," Laurel said. "She only appears in

public when she's telling stories. And she always performs in partial darkness like she did tonight."

Olivia studied her friend. "Have you been researching her for an article?"

Laurel nodded. "At first, I was just going to highlight a few of this weekend's key performers, but Violetta stands above the rest. She's as strange and mysterious and beautiful as a fairy tale queen. That's partially why she's become so well known among the country's storytellers, though as you saw, she possesses plenty of talent too. She rarely gives interviews. The last one was over a decade ago."

Suddenly, the overhead lights were turned to their brightest setting, and Olivia blinked her eyes in discomfort. The abrupt flood of light broke Violetta's spell. People ceased whispering, and the nervous energy they'd held on to all evening burst forth in rapid, animated speech. Gathering their belongings, they filed out of the room. Laurel lingered behind, and because she was seated at the end of the row, none of the Bayside Book Writers could move.

"Why are we waiting?" Harris asked. "They'll eat all the good stuff if we don't get out there."

"The reception is being sponsored by the *Gazette*," Laurel said. "Trust me, there isn't anything too impressive. And we're waiting because I want to introduce myself to Dixie's cousin. Dixie promised to put a bug in Lowell's ear about getting me an interview with Violetta."

They heard a rustling behind the stage, and Lowell came out. Without looking at them, he extinguished the oil lamp's flame, folded the stepladder, and gently laid it down on the stage floor.

Laurel made her way toward him. "The show was wonderful."

Lowell turned. "Thanks," he said and continued to collect his instruments.

"We're friends of Dixie's. She told us you were first cousins. I can see the resemblance. You have the same color eyes." Laurel's words poured forth like a rushing river. "Listen, I know you're still working, but I wanted to find out if Miss Violetta had any free time tomorrow. I'm a reporter with the *Gazette*, and I'd love to talk with her."

"She's not gonna see you," he replied as he packed his fiddle into a case. "It don't matter who you know or what you're willing to pay. She wouldn't sit down with God Himself even if He asked her real nice, so you don't stand a chance."

Clearly taken aback, Laurel looked at the floor. Her cheeks were flushed.

Olivia wanted to learn more about the intriguing storyteller too, and so she decided to help Laurel obtain an interview. "I sense that Miss Violetta values her privacy," she said to Lowell. "Would she agree to a phone conversation?"

Lowell shook his head. "She doesn't do phones. That's why I'm in charge of her bookings and travel arrangements."

This gave Olivia pause. Was it possible that Violetta faced strangers only when in her entertainer persona? Did she suffer from a complex social phobia perhaps? "Would it help if Laurel sat in a different room?" she asked on a whim. "They could speak through a crack in the door."

"Sorry, lady, but it's not gonna happen. My boss—"

"I'll see you." Violetta's voice swept over them like a wind. It was cool and strong and musical. "But not here. I need a dark, quiet place, and I gotta be able to smoke."

Olivia thought quickly. "I have a small cottage on the beach. You'd have to drive there, but it's private and you can sit on the back porch. The moon is weak tonight so there's very little light . . ."

Violetta didn't answer. Millay and Harris exchanged looks as the silence stretched on and on. Lowell had stopped what he was doing and was staring at Olivia in surprise.

"I'll come," Violetta finally said. "But I don't want an audience. Just you, gal."

"Laurel's the reporter. I'm just her friend." Olivia wondered if she should have let Laurel do the talking.

This was followed by another long silence.

"Lowell and I will follow you to this cottage by the sea," Violetta commanded softly. "Give me ten minutes. I need to collect myself first."

Olivia looked at Lowell and nodded. Laurel clasped her hands over her heart and scooted into the aisle, gesturing for the rest of the group to pass.

"Do not start jumping up and down," Olivia warned in a low whisper.

Grinning, Rawlings promised to meet her at her house after the reception. He then congratulated Lowell on a great show and strode from the room.

"Well, since we're not invited to your private party, I'm going to toss back a few glasses of free booze and then head into work." Millay saluted Olivia and sauntered off.

Harris hesitated for a moment and then followed her.

Onstage, Lowell closed the lid of the trunk and began to slide it across the floor toward the ramp in the back.

Laurel turned to Olivia, her eyes shimmering with excitement. "You have no idea what a big deal this is! Thank you! Thank you! I have to call Steve and tell him I might be home late and then jot down some key questions. Oh, Lord, I cannot believe it. See you at the cottage?" Without waiting for Olivia to respond, she dashed up the center aisle and disappeared through the doorway.

Lowell had gone outside through the fire exit close to the stage, leaving Olivia alone. She walked to the back of the room and dimmed the lights again. She wanted five minutes to think about how Violetta's brand of storytelling magic could breathe life into her dying manuscript. Taking a seat in the middle of the room, Olivia could still sense Violetta's presence. It lingered like the fresh, metallic scent following a summer rainstorm.

Suddenly, she felt chilled again. Rubbing her arms, which had erupted in gooseflesh beneath her cotton sweater, she turned to her right and saw a figure sitting across the aisle.

"There's always one person who doesn't leave," Violetta said. "Somebody like you who wants to soak up the power of the stories for just a little bit longer."

Violetta didn't sound the same as she had onstage. Her speech was no longer clear and crisp. It was now the mumbled cadence of her native mountain drawl. It wasn't seductive or hypnotizing, but Olivia still hung on to every word.

"I was hoping to learn your secret," she confessed. "I'm writing a novel, and my characters have gone flat. You're able to inject unique and magnetic personalities into dozens of different voices. We can't see these characters, and yet they're there, as real as the people sitting next to us in the audience."

Dipping her chin to acknowledge the compliment, Violetta focused her electric blue gaze on Olivia. "What's your story about, then?"

Olivia told her as succinctly as possible. She knew that Laurel was probably on her way to the lighthouse keeper's cottage and didn't want to keep her waiting. As she talked without pause, she studied the lovely, enigmatic storyteller. Violetta still wore her old-fashioned mountain dress, boots, and gloves. Her face was remarkably unlined for someone in her early forties. It had such a chalky hue that Olivia assumed she must have been wearing stage makeup.

"That ain't your story," Violetta instantly proclaimed when Olivia was done. "Some tramp livin' in Egypt a billion years ago? You can't give her a voice 'cause you don't know her. You want her to live and laugh and sing and weep? Then give her *your* story. Fill her with your joy and loneliness and all the love you've found and lost and found again. If you don't, she'll always be a paper doll. You want a marionette. You want somebody that can dance at the end of your string." She mimicked the motion with her small hands. "You're in control, but she's connected to you. See?"

"Is that why your stories feel so real? Because you've been cold and hungry? Because you figured out how to survive using your wits and courage?"

A humorless laugh bubbled from between Violetta's lips. "That makes me sound like some storybook hero. Things were the same for all of us mountainfolk. Ain't nobody drivin' Mercedes where I come from. Bein' rich meant that your ribs weren't stickin' through your skin. Everybody struggled."

Olivia didn't want to steal Laurel's thunder, but she couldn't help but ask, "How did you discover your gift?"

Violetta shrugged. "My daddy and granddaddy told their tales to me. Most nights, it was how we passed the time. I didn't think I could ever tell 'em like they could. In the beginning, I was scared that I was no good, but I got over that. Soon as I saw that lots of folks wanted to hear our stories, I tried real hard to tell them like no one else could. I'd rather sing for my supper than spend my days scratchin' in the ground and sewin' quilts."

"Did you ever marry?"

"Nope. You?"

Olivia smiled. "Never even came close." She didn't want to talk about her relationships, past or present, so she waved her arm around the room. "Why are you more comfortable in the shadows?"

Violetta's eyes flashed, and Olivia wondered if she'd crossed a line. She was about to apologize when the other woman touched her cheek with her fingertip. "I have things to hide. More than most folks."

When it became clear that she would say no more and moved to rise, Olivia said, "Trust me, I have my share too. Old family secrets. Things I can't talk about even with those who know me best. Those who love me for who they think I am."

Violetta waited a few heartbeats before speaking again. "I'm the last true Devereaux. When I die, the whereabouts of a certain treasure will die with me. That's a relief to me and a source of mighty vexation to others." She grinned, her thick makeup nearly cracking with the strain. "Fools. The place has been tucked away inside my stories for years. But what isn't meant to be found shouldn't be found. Some secrets are a curse."

Olivia thought of the discovery she'd recently made in which she'd learned that the man she believed to be her dad was the twin brother of her biological father. Her real father, a successful television exec named Charles Wade, had had an affair with Olivia's mother, Camille. When Camille realized that Charles wouldn't leave his wife, she cut all ties with him and married his brother so that her child wouldn't be born a bastard. Olivia ended up being raised by one parent who doted upon her and another who saw the brother he'd come to hate every time he looked at her.

Camille had locked Olivia's birth certificate in a safety deposit box, no doubt waiting for the right time to tell her daughter about her true parentage, but she died in the midst of a hurricane when Olivia was seven. Thirty-odd years later, Olivia had met her true father and disliked him on sight. He treated Oyster Bay and its people with disdain, and that was something Olivia just wouldn't stand for. She felt no connection to Charles Wade.

Her lack of interest in the man who'd sired her was the polar opposite to what she was experiencing now: a strong feeling of connection with the woman across the aisle. Olivia wanted to know Violetta's secrets. No longer out of curiosity, but because she had a strange desire to befriend her.

"When you first came onstage tonight, you said that you'd be a ghost before long. What did you mean?"

Violetta folded her hands in her lap. "Jesus knew Judas would betray him from the very beginnin'. I was born knowin' I'd be kissed like that one day. My Gethsemane is this town." She fixed her blue gaze on Olivia. "But it's a good place. I like how the water stretches on and on until you can't tell the difference between earth and sky. Last night I saw a million stars. They were floatin' on the water like diamonds. Bits of fiery ice."

Olivia smiled. "You should climb to the top of the lighthouse tonight. The view will take your breath away."

"Maybe I will, but for now, you'd best go on." Violetta abruptly rose to her feet. "I'll see you in the parkin' lot directly." She paused. "Remember. If you're brave enough to put your real story down on paper, then it will speak to folks. It'll be a gift to them. But pourin' out your heart is only part of it. After you're done with that bit, you've gotta spin the most complicated yarns you can. The best stories are equal part truth, equal part lie."

"I'll keep that in mind," Olivia promised. "Thank you for talking with me."

With a nod, Violetta walked off toward the stage, and Olivia picked up her handbag and headed out of the room. As soon as she entered the hallway, she heard the din coming from the reception up ahead. The lobby had a high glass ceiling and a marble floor, so sounds echoed around the space as if they were reverberating inside a large cave.

Edging her way through the crowd, Olivia noticed several flamboyant outfits. One woman was wearing a turquoise caftan dress and a necklace of orange beads while another was dressed like a Romani gypsy complete with hoop ear-rings, peasant blouse, and head scarf.

"They must be the other storytellers," Olivia murmured to herself, stepping to the side as a man gesticulated with a serpentine-shaped walking stick.

Leona Fairchild was standing near the buffet table. She held a plastic champagne flute in one hand and gave Olivia a thumbs-up with the other. Olivia smiled at the head librar-ian, equally pleased by the event's success, and continued winding her way past Oyster Bay's art patrons, the library staff, and the mayor.

Dixie and Grumpy were positioned near the rolling cart of used books for sale just inside the front doors. Dixie's plastic flute was empty, and she was reaching for her husband's when Olivia approached. "That was somethin', wasn't it?" Dixie said.

"Indeed it was. And I can see how invaluable Lowell is to Violetta. He keeps everything moving along so that the stories can flow into each other without interruption."

Beaming with pride, Dixie elbowed Grumpy in the ribs. "I told you he'd straighten out." She turned back to Olivia. "Grumpy doesn't trust Lowell as far as he can throw him. He doesn't like it that I'm lettin' him stay at our place."

"We don't have any room," Grumpy said, his voice a low growl.

"Two of the kids could sleep in a tent in the yard. They love bein' in the open air."

Grumpy frowned. "Yeah, because then they can sneak out with their friends and get into all sorts of trouble. And we'd never know they were gone unless one of their brothers or sisters decided to rat on them."

Olivia knew that the Weaver children were a handful. Each of their four or five kids—Olivia was constantly forget-ting how many they had—seemed to be more mischievous than the next.

"It seems to me that Violetta needs Lowell around for more than just performances," she said, hoping to distract the married couple before their argument could escalate. "He handles her bookings too." Olivia pointed at Dixie's roller skates. "Since I haven't seen him in a pair of those, does Violetta do all the driving or does Lowell have a modified car?"

"He was one of the first dwarves I knew with a pedal extender," Dixie boasted. "Put it on his car himself when he was only seventeen. He was always good with tools."

"Yeah, especially with lock picks and bolt cutters," Grumpy muttered, and Dixie gave him a slug to the stomach.

Olivia pointed at Dixie's glass. "I think you need a refill. See you two later."

Dixie raised her brows. "Where are you goin'? The chief's still here, so are you runnin' home to warm up the bed for him?"

"I'm on a mission," Olivia replied. "One you'll read about in the *Gazette*, I hope."

Leaving Dixie to mull over her enigmatic statement, Olivia stepped into the humid night.

The chill she'd felt inside the library instantly became a memory, and she shucked off her sweater. By the time she reached her Range Rover, she was already thirsty. Tossing her sweater on the passenger seat, she leaned against her car and drank from the tepid bottle of water she kept in the center console. As she rehydrated, she gazed at the dull-gray sky.

"Everything looks washed out," she murmured to herself. The moon was as colorless as sand, and even the stars seemed to have lost their luster, turning as dry and gritty as the rest of the North Carolina coast.

Olivia decided to ask Violetta if she knew any stories about drought once Laurel was done with her interview. She sipped her water and reflected on how she could apply Violetta's advice to her novel. After ten minutes passed, and then another five, she grew restless.

"Where are they?" she demanded of the silent parking lot.

The lights from the library shone in the darkness, and swarms of gnats and moths gathered around the streetlamps lining the sidewalks. Olivia's gaze followed one of the lit paths that curved behind the library. Wondering if Violetta was waiting for her by the staff entrance, she tossed her empty water bottle onto the passenger seat and headed for the back of the building.

However, she saw no sign of Lowell or Violetta, and when she tried the door that led into the conference room, it was locked. She found that strange. After all, she'd seen Lowell exit through it twenty minutes ago.

Olivia was rapidly becoming irritated. Laurel would undoubtedly have reached the lighthouse keeper's cottage by now and would be pacing the floorboards in anticipation. The thought increased Olivia's indignation.

"Hello!" She pounded on the door. "Lowell? Violetta?"

She put her ear against the warm metal and listened for the slightest sound, but she heard nothing.

"Damn it all," she muttered and strode around to the front entrance again. Shoulders squared, she pushed through the boisterous crowd. She was just about to break free from the press when a hand closed around her arm.

"I thought you'd gone," Rawlings said.

She shook her head. "I'm supposed to have left, yes. Violetta told me to wait in the parking lot, but she's never come out."

Rawlings shrugged. "She's an artiste. It's in her DNA to be theatrically late."

"I don't do late," Olivia replied with a scowl and

continued down the hall. She hadn't made it very far when Lowell came racing toward her. He was moving as fast as he could on his short legs, his body wobbling from side to side in his haste. His face was ashen, and his brown eyes were dark with fear.

Seeing Olivia, he stretched his arms out as if preparing for an embrace. And the second he reached her, he clamped his hands around her wrists. His entire body was trembling violently.

"What's wrong?" Olivia said, looking him over for any sign of injury.

Lowell's only reply was to utter a string of expletives. He couldn't seem to stop. They shot out of his mouth like gunfire.

"Lowell!" she shouted. "Lowell! Is it Violetta?"

He stopping cursing and nodded wildly. Without another word, Olivia dashed down the hall and into the conference room.

The space felt empty, but Olivia cast a quick glance down each row as she rushed toward the small room behind the stage. Violetta was in a chair, her head tilted backward at an awkward angle, her hair tumbling down her shoulders in black waves, her eyes open wide. She stared at the ceiling, unblinking, and her tongue protruded from between slack lips. Her face and neck were blue. Olivia had the absurd thought that the shade was beautiful. It reminded her of the ocean beneath a summer sky.

Violetta Devereaux, the famed Appalachian storyteller, was dead.

As the truth of this washed over Olivia, she retreated two steps, covering her mouth in horror.

This fascinating and enigmatic woman who'd breathed life into so many tales, who'd amazed audiences all over the country with her incredible voice, had been forever silenced.

"You've been murdered," Olivia whispered, forcing herself to look at Violetta's tortured expression, blue skin, and swollen tongue once more. "Strangled." And then she remembered that Rawlings was in the building.

Rawlings. She seized on the name. *Rawlings.*

She ran to him. She ran in search of comfort and safety, and to tell him that something evil had stolen into the library. At that very moment, a killer was exiting the building or hiding in the stacks or casually sipping champagne in the lobby.

Olivia burned with anger as she rushed down the hallway. This place was sacred. Her mother had worked in this library. She'd been absolutely content here. She'd smiled brightly when she assisted patrons and hummed softly while shelving materials. This building was a sanctuary to so many, and a killer had dared to taint it with violence. Olivia wanted someone to answer for that.

And so she ran.

Chapter 5

I would rather that my spark should burn out in a brilliant blaze than it should be stifled by dry-rot. I would rather be a superb meteor, every atom of me in magnificent glow, than a sleepy and permanent planet.

—JACK LONDON

Rawlings saw Olivia coming. He also saw something in her expression that conveyed her urgency. Tossing his plate on the closest table, he moved to meet her.

When they were near enough to touch, he bowed his head close to her lips so that whatever she had to say would be heard by him alone.

Olivia grabbed his left arm with both hands. "Violetta's dead. Someone's killed her."

She could feel his body stiffen beneath her fingers. "Show me."

As they hurried down the hallway, Olivia had the sense that she was in an underground tunnel. The fluorescent ceiling lights cast a sickly yellow glow on the gray carpet, and the door to the conference room seemed to recede as they walked toward it. Olivia felt like she was in a Lewis Carroll story.

"Steady," Rawlings said. He took her elbow, and before she knew it, they'd passed the rows of chairs and were confronted by Violetta's blue face. Olivia couldn't help but stare at the sight as if she hadn't seen it just a few moments ago. She expected the color to have drained away somewhat by now, leaving a doughy white in its stead, but the summer-sky hue remained. Even in death, Violetta Devereaux possessed an otherworldly beauty.

"Did you touch anything?" Rawlings asked, reaching for his phone.

"No."

Rawlings gave a series of terse instructions to the officer on the other end of the line and then stood in silence for a long time.

Finally, he looked at Olivia. "Can your librarian friend stay calm in a crisis?"

"She's a rock."

"Good. Have her lock all the doors. No one gets in or out without my say-so. If she asks why, tell her we have an emergency on our hands, but don't go into any detail."

"Understood." Olivia hustled back to the lobby in search of Leona Fairchild.

As Olivia hunted for the librarian, she also kept an eye out for Lowell. Rawlings would need to speak with him sooner rather than later. Pivoting this way and that, she stood on her tiptoes and studied the sea of faces in the lobby, but she didn't see Lowell or Ms. Fairchild anywhere. What she did notice was that a group of people were saying their good-byes and heading for the front door. Olivia felt a stirring of panic.

She pushed ahead of them, ignoring their indignant looks.

"What in the world—?" Dixie began when Olivia rushed over and clamped her hand on Grumpy's wrist, exactly as Lowell had grasped her wrists ten minutes earlier.

"I need you to block this exit," she told Grumpy. "No one

can leave. I don't care what you tell people, but no one gets out of this building. Chief's orders. Something horrible has happened. More cops are on the way, and they'll take over when they get here. Until then, you must guard this door."

Dixie fired off a series of questions, her voice becoming more shrill and more demanding with each one, but Olivia didn't even look at her friend. Confident that Grumpy would take charge, she went off to resume her search for Lowell and Leona.

She found the librarian coming out of the staff kitchen. A woman wearing a white chef's coat embroidered with the words "Roll With It Catering" followed her. The caterer carried a tray of finger sandwiches while Leona had a pitcher of soda in one hand and ice water in the other.

"Excuse me," Olivia said, blocking the librarian's path. "I need to speak with you immediately." She took the pitchers from Leona and entered the kitchen.

"What's going on?" The librarian drew her brows together. She was displeased by Olivia's abruptness but too concerned to object.

Olivia placed the pitchers on the counter, splattering droplets of brown cola over the surface. She hadn't meant to make a mess, but her hands were shaking too violently to avoid it. "Violetta Devereaux is dead. Please don't ask me for details. All I can say is that we have a . . . situation. Rawlings would like you to lock all the doors right away. We need to keep everyone inside the building until his team arrives."

Leona went pale. She drew in a deep breath and steadied herself on a chair back. Olivia watched the older woman push down her emotions, nodding to show Olivia that she understood and was prepared to follow the chief's orders. She pulled a set of keys from her pants pocket and gripped them hard in her right hand. "What should I tell people?"

"That you're merely following instructions given by the

police, who will brief them as soon as possible. Don't say anything else."

By the time Olivia returned to the conference room, Rawlings had finished his preliminary examination of the scene. He met Olivia halfway up the center aisle. "Where's her assistant?"

"Lowell may have left already," Olivia said. "I didn't see him anywhere."

"My officers are two minutes out. Can you stand guard over her? Make sure no one comes close?" Rawlings gestured to where Violetta sat lifeless in a chair, her unseeing eyes fixed on the ceiling tiles. Olivia followed her dead gaze, wishing that the storyteller could have died looking at something beautiful, something full of color.

Olivia's throat tightened. She glanced at Rawlings and nodded.

Once again, she was alone in the conference room, but this time, she no longer sensed Violetta's presence. She was gone. The echoes of her last words were gone. There was only an oppressive silence. Olivia stood in the middle of it, feeling the weight of too many unanswered questions.

The police separated people alphabetically, took their statements, and eventually had to release them. As soon as she finished giving her statement, Olivia sent Laurel a text saying that the interview with Violetta was canceled and that she was sorry not to have let her know sooner. She told Laurel to go home and that she'd call her first thing in the morning. Olivia then retreated to the staff kitchen to escape the sight of the coroner's men rolling their gurney down the hallway. She didn't want to witness Violetta's departure from the building. She didn't want to think of the captivating storyteller being zipped into a body bag, like a butterfly being tucked back into its cocoon.

"Laurel will be furious with me when she finds out what happened," Olivia told Leona with a weary sigh. She longed to climb into bed, Haviland curled up at her feet, and burrow under the covers until the sun painted her room a warm bronze. "She'll have plenty of time to file a piece on Violetta's death tomorrow. Someone might as well rest tonight."

The librarian took off her reading glasses and wiped the lenses with a tissue. "I'd like to think that Violetta will have a little peace too—just a few hours before every part of her life is scrutinized under a magnifying glass—but I'm sure there's already a post on Facebook. There's no privacy in this modern world. Not even for the dead."

"At least they're beyond caring," Olivia said, but she was troubled by Leona's remark. She knew what a murder investigation would entail. She was all too aware of how the secrets, memories, and relationships that formed Violetta's history would be brought to light for dozens of strangers to analyze. Nothing was off-limits. Nothing was sacred. Everything would be typed into black-and-white reports and scoured by police officers, and later by journalists and inquisitive members of the public.

Leona looked tired. Her face was drawn and her movements were slow and clumsy. It was unsettling for Olivia to watch her go through the simple steps required to brew a pot of coffee. Leona was brisk and efficient, but that was before someone had died in her beloved library, before she had puzzled out that the death was a suspicious one.

"Why?" she said to Olivia as she filled the coffeepot with water. "Why would anyone harm a storyteller? Why here? She was from the other end of the state. Why now? In *my* library?"

Olivia gave a weary shrug of her shoulders. "I have no idea. Maybe there was animosity between her and another performer."

Leona turned, paper filter in hand, and frowned. "Oh, please. Does that sound like a reasonable motive to you? Where is Violetta's assistant?"

"I think he bolted after telling me about her," Olivia admitted. "Not through the front door though. Grumpy and Dixie didn't see him. And he obviously didn't use the conference room exit."

"That leaves only the exit near the book drop." Leona's frown deepened. "But we keep that locked, so he either slipped past Dixie or he's still in the building."

"Hiding in an air duct?" Olivia shook her head. "No, he's gone. You should have seen his face. He was terrified."

Leona put the filter in the basket and began to scoop grounds into it. "He could have been putting on a performance."

Olivia hadn't considered that. Lowell had seemed genuinely stricken. She could still feel his grip on her wrists, how his thick fingers had trembled. His hands were exceptionally strong. They'd left bruises on her skin. Bruises that were already darkening from a yellow blue to a plum purple. Olivia recalled how Lowell had dragged the laden steamer trunk across the stage. He was certainly powerful enough to have strangled his boss, but why would he?

The treasure, she thought suddenly. Violetta had mentioned that people had been trying to locate the treasure for her entire life—that she'd hidden the clues to its whereabouts in her stories. Thus far, no one had been able to solve her puzzle. Had Lowell begun working for Violetta in hopes of finding the treasure? Had he grown tired of listening to her tell the same tales over and over without his ever getting closer to the prize?

"What are you thinking about?" Leona asked above the gurgle of the coffeemaker.

"That you're right. I don't know Lowell from Adam. He could have been playing me." She closed her eyes and rubbed her temples. A headache had bloomed there an hour ago and showed no signs of ebbing. "I've learned by now that no one is as they appear."

Leona put a hand on her back and rubbed it gently. "Some of us are, hon."

Olivia opened her eyes and smiled up at the woman she'd known all her life. "Is that coffee any good?"

"No," Leona replied. "Would you like a cup anyway?"

"Yes. It'll give me something to do for the next five minutes."

She was about to take her first sip when Rawlings entered the kitchen. He didn't look tired at all. He seemed taller and more broad-shouldered than when he'd simply been another guest attending Violetta's performance. Now he was the picture of authority, despite the fact that he wasn't in uniform and had left his sidearm at home. Olivia stared at him, slightly awestruck by the ease with which he was able to morph into his chief of police persona, shucking his civilian demeanor like a reptile shedding its skin.

"Dixie's asking for you," he said. "Everyone's free to leave, and I think she'd like to see you before she and Grumpy head home."

Olivia bid Leona goodnight. As soon as she and Rawlings were out in the hall, she said, "Did you find Lowell?"

He shook his head. "I sent an officer to the B&B and one to the Weaver residence. No sign of him at either location."

"It doesn't look good for him," Olivia said.

"No. Running never looks good," Rawlings agreed.

When they reached the lobby, Dixie was sitting on a wooden bench, idly spinning the wheels of her left roller

skate around and around with the flat of her hand. She
jumped up when she saw Olivia and the chief.

Olivia paused and touched Rawlings on the arm. "Call
me when you can."

"I will." He brushed a strand of hair from her cheek. "Are
you all right?"

"Sure," she lied, gave him a little smile and walked away.

Dixie waited for Rawlings to leave before speaking.
"Lord have mercy, 'Livia! Folks are whisperin' that Violetta
was killed and that Lowell might have had somethin' to do
with it." Her ale-brown eyes grew moist. "He's done bad
things, but he wouldn't go and kill anybody!"

"Have you seen him?" Olivia asked.

Dixie looked hurt. "No. Not since the show. I was sure
he'd find me straight off, actin' all high and mighty because
he's workin' with the famous Miss Violetta, but he never
made it to the lobby. Next thing I know, Violetta's dead and
he's gone."

Grumpy slung an arm around his wife and propelled her
through the doorway. "Come on, babe. He's sure to call you.
He doesn't know anybody else in this town, and he's probably real shaken."

"You go get the car, shug." Dixie scooted out from beneath
his arm. "I wanna talk to Olivia for a sec."

Grumpy bent down, kissed Dixie on the crown of her
head, and walked into the parking lot. The shadows had
deepened around the cars, and a scattering of wispy clouds
covered the moon. The night felt old, and Olivia was eager
to get home.

"What don't you want to say in front of Grumpy?" she
asked Dixie.

"That Lowell could be hidin' in the woods near my
place," she said. "He's got a record, 'Livia. He's goin' to
expect folks to point a finger at him."

Olivia studied her friend. "And if he is there when you get home? What will you do?"

Dixie's jaw tightened in anger. "What would you do if it was your brother?"

That gave Olivia pause. Would she deceive Rawlings to protect Hudson? How far would she go to shelter someone she loved, even if it meant breaking the law? "I don't know," she admitted.

"That's the difference between us, then," Dixie said. When Grumpy pulled up with the car, she climbed in without saying goodnight. The door slammed and the engine growled. A pair of red taillights glared at Olivia through the darkness.

The next morning Olivia was jolted awake by the persistent ringing of the phone and, assuming the caller was Rawlings, she answered. Laurel was on the other end of the line, and she didn't sound happy.

"You sent me home!" Laurel cried indignantly. "I'm a reporter! A reporter who's been scooped thanks to you."

Olivia lay back on the pillows. Her body felt stiff and sore, as if she'd run for miles without stopping. Her mouth was dry and gritty. She drank some water from the glass on the nightstand while Laurel ranted.

"Are you even listening?" her friend demanded.

"I'm sorry that I told you to go home," Olivia said, her words hoarse, her voice ragged. She took another swallow of water. "But the cops wouldn't have let you back into the library anyway. You'd have waited outside until all hours of the morning to get a few aggrandized statements from members of the audience. No one could have told you anything of import."

"But I still could have broken the story," Laurel protested, but with less heat. "Anyway, it's done now. You sound terrible, by the way."

"I've felt better. Perhaps if I'd had more sleep . . ." She let the accusation hang in the air.

Laurel sighed. "Guess we're even now. Listen, I have a bunch of background material on Violetta—stuff I'd compiled for her article. Do you think the chief could use it?"

"Absolutely. And if you don't mind, I'd like to read it too." Olivia closed her eyes for a moment, blocking out the sunlight and Haviland's plaintive look. The poodle was hungry, and it was well past breakfast time. "I saw her last night, Laurel. And frankly, I'm relieved you weren't there. All of that incredible energy, that powerful force that she was able to exude . . . it just vanished."

"She told us she'd become a ghost," Laurel whispered. "How did she know?"

Olivia thought back on the beginning of the performance. And then her eyes flew open and she sat up in bed. "Here's another question. Who was she pointing at in the audience right after she raised the subject of the ghost?"

Laurel gasped. "Do you think she saw her killer? That she knew she was almost out of time?"

"Maybe. We should let the chief know who was seated there."

Laurel didn't reply. As the silence grew, Olivia could practically feel her friend's reluctance to speak. "What is it, Laurel?"

"Don't you remember who came in late and took the last seats on the end of that row? The exact place Violetta pointed to?"

Dread washed over Olivia. Its coldness was incongruent with the bright white sheets and the warm sunshine streaming through the windows. "Damn it all. It was Grumpy and Dixie."

"Are you going to tell Rawlings?"

The question echoed the one Dixie had asked her the night before, and Olivia felt the sudden burden of it. "I have to," she said miserably.

An hour later, she opened the door to the deck and stepped into the heat. The stark light had bleached the colors from the sand and sea oats. Except for the glassy ocean, the whole world had been rendered a dull beige. Cradling a mug of coffee, Olivia watched Haviland race down the path over the dunes, heading for the water's edge. She tried calling Rawlings again, but he didn't answer.

She showered, slipped into a gauzy sundress, and drove into town. The church bells were pealing, and people dressed in their Sunday best hurried from sanctuary to car, reluctant to be away from the luxury of air-conditioning for more than a moment. The noon sun perched high in a hazy blue sky, and the heat shimmered off the sidewalks in ripples.

The moment Olivia entered The Bayside Crab House, Haviland turned left for the kitchen. "No, you don't," she scolded. "We have paperwork to do."

Haviland gave a sniff of disapproval but trotted into the manager's office. Olivia liked to do her bookkeeping on Sundays when her sister-in-law, Kim, was home with her two kids. Kim handled the restaurant's day-to-day operations, but Olivia made the major decisions. Settling into the desk chair, she placed orders, reviewed the budget, and e-mailed a Raleigh advertising firm about the restaurant's fall campaign.

She'd just sent the e-mail when her half brother, Hudson, knocked on the office door. "Hungry?"

She smiled at the man she hadn't known for very long. Hudson was gruff and taciturn like their father, but he had a softer heart than Willie Wade and adored his wife and children. He also wasn't as enamored of whiskey as Willie had been. Hudson rarely drank, and when he did, a cold beer satisfied him. Her brother was a hard worker and an excellent cook, and over the past year, Olivia had grown quite fond of him.

He's not your brother, a voice whispered.

Olivia studied Hudson's tall frame and dark eyes. They were Willie's eyes, but they weren't hard or angry. They were much kinder. Willie Wade was not known for his kindness.

He is *my brother. No one knows that Charles Wade is my father. The facts don't matter. What matters is that I need Hudson and his family, and they need me.*

"I had a late breakfast," she said, still smiling. "How about a salad?"

"You got it." Haviland nudged Hudson with his paw and whined once. The big man studied the poodle. "I might have something for you too."

He returned shortly with a grilled chicken Caesar salad for Olivia and a small bowl of ground beef mixed with peas for Haviland. "What do you think of the specials for next week?" he asked after serving Olivia her meal.

"I think the mahimahi and cilantro fish tacos will be a huge hit," she said. "And the blackened grouper is always a top seller, but my favorite is the firecracker shrimp with a side of wasabi slaw."

Hudson was clearly pleased. "It's got quite a bite."

They finished reviewing the menu and Hudson left to go back to the kitchen while Olivia ate and continued to work. As she completed her last task, images of Violetta invaded her thoughts. Turning to the computer, she typed Violetta's name into Google's search box.

"Who were you?" she asked. Over a dozen results appeared on the screen.

Most of these focused on Violetta's performances, but

Olivia finally found a site on the arts of Appalachia that had a link to the storyteller's biography. Violetta Devereaux was born in 1958 in Whaley, North Carolina, to Josiah and Ira Devereaux. The fourth of five children, Violetta had three older sisters, Hattie, Mabel, and Flora, and a younger brother, Elijah.

Violetta's father worked their mountain farm while her mother tended their two-room cabin and made rugs on her loom. She sold these, along with quilts and blankets, or traded them for goods. The children worked from the time they could walk. In addition to their regular chores, they were also tasked with gathering plants to sell to a wholesale drug company. "We collected Galax and goldenseal, witch hazel and snake root and more. We got paid the most for ginseng," Violetta was quoted as saying. The direct quote gave Olivia pause, and she scrolled to the end of the piece to see who'd penned the biography.

"Alfred Hicks," she spoke the name aloud for no reason in particular, but when she did, it sounded familiar. "How do I know you?"

Unable to recall the context, she resumed her reading. The Devereaux children didn't have much in the way of formal schooling, and the family possessed very few books. Their chief entertainment came in the form of Bible readings and tale telling when the family gathered around the potbellied stove each night. Josiah was an avid storyteller, and Violetta soon learned to mimic his methods. As she grew into a young woman, Violetta began performing for neighbors and local church groups. People found her so captivating that she considered entering the regional competition. However, she couldn't afford to travel. The family struggled financially. During a particularly lean winter, Violetta's brother, Elijah, fell ill. The severely undernourished child died on Violetta's eighteenth birthday. Wracked by grief, she made two vows. The first was to leave home and never return. The second was to never marry or bear children.

In the spring following Elijah's death, Violetta packed up her few belongings and moved to the outskirts of Blowing Rock where she began her storyteller career in earnest. To supplement her income, she took in washing and continued to sell plants to local drug companies. Violetta survived, but she remained poor and relatively unknown until, during her late thirties, she competed in a major storyteller's competition and was awarded a handsome grant. Violetta toured the state and later, the nation, performing for children and adults alike. She never reunited with her family following Elijah's death. Those close to the Devereauxes claim that the character of Jack in Violetta's stories was modeled after her late brother, but Violetta never confirmed this theory. When questioned about her reclusive nature and refusal to commit any of her stories to paper, Violetta responded by saying, "Some of my tales are about life and laughter, but others are dangerous. Cursed. Strung together, some of the lines and phrases can form a noose, strong enough to hang a man with."

The article finished with a glowing review of Violetta's performance at the National Storytelling Festival in Tennessee.

Olivia let the information sink in for a moment. She then opened a new window and typed Alfred Hicks's name into the search box. She gasped when the first result announced that Hicks, a professor at Western Carolina University, had died last winter.

"'Suffered fatal injuries resulting from a fall,'" Olivia murmured. Her words dropped like anchors into the empty air. "Lowell told Dixie the professor's death was no accident. He claimed that it had been the work of a ghost."

She stared at the screen again, trying to locate where

Hicks had died. "A trail on Beech Mountain," she said and opened yet another window. This time she used Google Maps to zoom in on Beech Mountain and its environs. Scanning the small towns close by, she saw that Violetta's hometown of Whaley was practically at the mountain's base.

"So what?" she asked the screen. "Is the connection important?"

Olivia was just about to conduct a search on Violetta's estranged family when her cell phone rang. Recognizing the number, she answered at once.

"'Livia? Lowell's here. At the house." Dixie's whisper was low and anxious. "I'm not gonna call the cops. I'm callin' you."

"Has he said anything?"

Dixie snorted. "Yeah. He said he wanted a beer. And then he said that he wanted another one. And another one after that. He's as rattled as a loose shutter in a hurricane."

Olivia tried to control her impatience. "Has he said anything of significance?"

"He told us about Violetta. About findin' her. And about runnin' away."

"Why did he take off?"

Dixie hesitated. "He said he needs a place to hide. That if he doesn't, he'll be next."

"He knows the killer's identity?" Olivia couldn't conceal her eagerness.

Another long pause. "He says it's the ghost. The one from the mountains that pushed the professor off the trail," Dixie said. "I have no idea what to make of it. You'd best come over. He might talk to you. But just you."

Olivia didn't reply immediately. Dixie was asking her to have a friendly chat with the suspect in a murder investigation. She also wanted her to keep Lowell's whereabouts from Rawlings. Olivia hated to deceive him, but she saw no other choice. Someone needed to hear Lowell's story, especially if he was prepared to go underground like a crab scuttling into a burrow. "I'll be there in fifteen minutes," she said.

"For what it's worth, I don't think he did it."

Olivia heard the doubt in her friend's voice. "Are you sure?"

"No." She hung up.

Reaching down to wake her sleeping poodle, Olivia held her hand on Haviland's soft head. "It's time for you to morph into guard-dog mode, Captain."

Haviland sprang to his feet, instantly alert. Olivia felt a powerful rush of affection for him. She leaned over and kissed his black nose, breathing in the scent of his fur. He smelled of salt water and sunshine.

She then led her dog outside into the heat. And quite possibly into peril.

Chapter 6

Do not stand at my grave and weep,
I am not there; I do not sleep.
I am a thousand winds that blow,
I am the diamond glints on snow.

—MARY FRYE

The Weaver's double-wide was at the end of a gravel road lined with loblolly pines and wax myrtle. Their yard was a southern redneck cliché. Scattered in between copses of weeds was a rusty sedan on cinder blocks, a kennel with a chain-link fence, stacks of tires, a flipped wheelbarrow, and an assortment of mismatched lawn chairs in various degrees of disrepair.

Dixie occupied one of three molded-plastic chairs positioned beneath a green awning that was attached to the roof of the mobile home. She raised her hand in greeting as Olivia pulled her Range Rover to a stop next to Grumpy's Harley.

Olivia let Haviland out and he raced to Dixie. He licked her once and then sniffed her all over, as if he could smell her anxiety. She whispered briefly to him, and then stood up and walked to her outdoor refrigerator.

"Beer?" she asked Olivia, fishing out a can of Pabst Blue Ribbon.

"No, thanks. I'd love a glass of tap water though."

Dixie turned to the trailer and hollered, "Come on out here, Lowell! And bring a glass of water with you! The McDonald's cups are clean!"

"McDonald's?" Olivia raised a brow and took the chair next to Dixie's.

"They're old as the hills, but we love 'em. They've got pictures of the Hamburglar. My kids were wild about him when they were little."

Olivia shook her head. "I have no idea what you're talking about."

"You have lived a very sheltered life, my friend." The door to the double-wide creaked open, and Lowell poked his head out. After peering nervously around the yard, he joined Dixie and Olivia under the awning. He presented Olivia with her water without meeting her inquisitive gaze. She thanked him and examined the glass she'd been given.

"See?" Dixie pointed at a dwarflike figure dressed in a black-and-white prisoner's uniform and a black cape and hat. "That pint-sized bandit ran around stealin' hamburgers. He was Lowell's hero when we were kids. I used to have a whole set of these, but my boys have broken half of 'em."

Considering Lowell had served more than one jail sentence for robbery, Olivia found it strange to be drinking from a glass decorated with a cartoonish thief.

As if reading her mind, Lowell gave her a wry smile. "Not only am I better looking than that guy, but I went after much cooler stuff. A patty of defrosted meat stuck between a pair of stale buns? He should have been emptying cash registers."

Olivia noted that while Lowell's accent was much like Dixie's languid drawl, he didn't cut the *g*'s off the end of his words like she did. He had her ale-brown eyes too, but his hair was darker and his forehead larger. There was a hardness to his jaw too. Dixie could be stubborn, but she was never hard. Her eyes always sparkled with humor, and she was usually on the brink of laughter. Not now. Lowell's presence had her looking tense and haggard.

"I'm sorry about Violetta," Olivia told Lowell gently. She knew she had to tread carefully or Lowell would clam up, so she decided that courtesy was her safest move. "And I'm sorry that you had to be the one to find her."

Lowell, who'd been sitting on the edge of his chair, relaxed slightly. "I still can't believe it. I can't believe that was Violetta. She was . . . did you go back there?"

"Yes." Olivia glanced from him to Dixie. "It was awful. I was shocked to say the least."

Lowell seized on the word, as Olivia expected he would. She knew she needed to gain his trust if she wanted to learn anything of significance. "Shocked. Yeah, I was shocked too. That's not even good enough to describe how I felt." He passed a hand over his face. "The way her eyes were open, staring at nothing. And her mouth . . . I could tell she'd suffered. She wasn't Violetta anymore. She was something out of a nightmare."

The comment surprised Olivia. Lowell had served jail time. He'd seen and done things most people hadn't, and yet, the sight of his dead boss had caused him to come undone.

It could all be an act, she reminded herself. "Is that why you took off?"

He nodded, his gaze sliding from her face to the woods.

"Your reaction is completely understandable," Olivia said. "So why not come forward? Is there more to the story?"

When Lowell refused to answer, Dixie frowned at him. "Tell her what you told me. She's not gonna laugh. She's not like that."

Lowell's eyes narrowed, and he stared at Olivia. "Do you believe in ghosts?" His question sounded like a challenge.

She was feeling less and less sympathetic toward him by the moment. "No. I believe memories, regrets, or mistakes haunt people. But I don't subscribe to the idea that restless spirits wander the earth. When you're dead, you're dead."

"I thought that once too," Lowell said. "But not anymore."

Olivia threw out her hands in exasperation. "Are you going to talk to me or not? I have better things to do than sit here and try to pull words out of your mouth."

Lowell screwed his mouth into an ugly sneer, and Dixie put a hand over his. "If you don't get this out, it'll eat you up inside. And while that's happenin' the cops are gonna find you, and when they do, you'll need this lady to put in a good word for you."

"I don't need her help. I didn't hurt Violetta. All I want to do is get out of town."

Now Olivia did sense fear in the small man. "Does this have to do with Professor Hicks? Were you working for Violetta when he died?"

Lowell was silent for so long that Olivia didn't think he would answer. All the anger and defensiveness had drained from his face. His eyes had gone glassy, as if he were hundreds of miles away, and the memory he became lost in was clearly an unpleasant one. "He wanted to write all of her stories down, but she didn't care for that. She told him he could put the Jack tales on paper because they didn't belong to her. They belonged to everyone."

"While the other stories, like the haint tales, didn't?" Olivia guessed.

"That's right. Some of them were passed down from her daddy and granddaddy, and she made up a bunch too. The one about the ghost in the forest, the one where folks are looking for silver dollars, the one about the man going crazy and acting like a bear, and some others are hers. You can tell because she talks about places where she grew up. Land-marks and stuff."

Olivia nodded to show that she was listening.

"Hicks was real persistent. He was like a pit bull hanging on another dog's throat. Just wouldn't let go. He followed Violetta. Wrote her letters. Left gifts at her doorstep. But she only let him in after he promised to dedicate his book to Elijah. That's her brother who died when she was still living at home."

Now that Lowell had begun to talk, the words came pour-ing out. Olivia suspected he'd been waiting to speak to someone about the professor for a long time. "I assume that she gave him permission to print her stories in the end," Olivia said.

"Most of them," Lowell said. "But I saw him during her shows. He attended them so he could write down the ones she didn't want him to print. Even from the stage I could see him scribbling away."

"Why? He couldn't have published them without her permission."

Lowell shrugged. "I asked him that same question, but he wouldn't give me a straight answer. I didn't want him pulling one over on Miss Violetta. She was good to me. A real classy lady."

He sounded sincere, but Olivia decided it was time to push him. "What about the treasure Violetta alluded to? Did she mention it in all of her performances?"

Staring her right in the eye, Lowell shook his head. "Only when she felt the past calling to her. It's just a made-up story anyhow. There's no treasure."

Olivia studied Lowell and came to the conclusion that he was an accomplished liar. She said nothing, letting the silence grow uncomfortable.

Dixie was the first to react. Downing the rest of her beer, she nudged Lowell with the empty can. "Tell her how the professor died."

Lowell shot her a reproachful look and then pushed himself out of the chair. "I need a drink."

To avoid watching his ungainly passage to the refrigerator, Olivia focused her attention on Haviland, who was stretched out behind her in a soft patch of grass. Their conversation and the buzz of insects had lulled him to sleep. His paws twitched as his dream self chased phantom prey.

The pop and hiss of a pull-tab puncturing aluminum caused Olivia to glance up. Lowell drank several swallows of beer and then burped loudly. "We were all up on Beech Mountain that night," he began, his gaze fixed on the trees again. "Hicks wanted to follow the track of one of Violetta's haint tales. It was about two young girls who were being shadowed by a ghost. They crossed a log bridge over the river to get away, because the mountain people believe ghosts can't move over water. This haint was protecting the silver coins he'd hidden inside the heart of a hollowed-out trunk."

"Was Hicks after the coins?" Olivia asked. "Are they the treasure?"

"There's no damn treasure!" Lowell yelled, lurching to his feet.

Haviland jerked awake with a growl and bared his teeth at the small man.

Olivia put a hand on her dog's head. "It's all right, boy."

Lowell slowly resumed his seat, his expression guarded.

"Let me ask a different question, then," Olivia said. "Why did Hicks go at night? And why were you with him?"

There was a long pause. "The haint tale took place just after twilight. In the dead of winter. Hicks said he wasn't just gathering Violetta's stories. He wanted to write a book about mountain people too. Claimed he had to live some of her tales if he was going to get the words right."

Olivia made an encouraging noise.

"So there we were. The professor, a local man Hicks hired as a guide, and me. I'd lived up in the mountains for a few months, but I didn't know my way around the place where Violetta grew up. She wouldn't go near it herself. There was still a little daylight when we left the cabin Hicks was renting, but it got dark real quick. I went out of curiosity and because I didn't really trust the guy, but if I knew how things would end, I never would have gone." He slapped his thighs. "I don't exactly have legs for hiking. Always thought Dixie's way of getting around was the smartest. Stay on flat ground and roll on four wheels."

Dixie nudged him with her bare foot. "Then what in hell's name were you doin' in those hills? You like fast cars and loud bikes. Hot meals and warm beds. Soft women and all-night bars. Why'd you take that job?"

"Not many folks were looking to hire an ex-con. The money was fair and Violetta was a good boss. She didn't treat me like a freak. She knew what it felt like to be different. As it turned out, I liked being onstage." A smile played around the corners of his mouth. "People stared at me because I wanted them to. They weren't the kind of stares we're used to, Dix. I wanted them to look at me."

Dixie flashed him a grin. "I get that. Why do you think I wear rainbow kneesocks and tutus? I want folks to know that I'm more than a dwarf. I'm a diva on wheels."

He smiled back at her, and Olivia could see that the two cousins genuinely cared for each other. There was tenderness in Lowell's eyes when he looked at Dixie that made Olivia want to know him better.

"It must have been so cold that night," she said softly, hoping to return to the scene of Hicks's death.

Lowell took the bait. "My breath froze as soon as it left my mouth. After an hour or two, I couldn't feel my fingers or toes or certain other parts of my body. Important parts."

That earned another smile from Dixie, but Olivia wasn't interested in levity. "Go on," she said.

"The sky was coal black, but there was a full moon. We had just enough light to see by. When we finally got close to the place where Hicks thought the hollowed-out trunk was, it started to snow. Not the pretty Christmas kind of flakes, but the wet, get-under-your-collar stuff." He gestured at the dry yard with his beer can. "Hard to imagine how cold it was in this kind of heat. How wet and icy cold. I kept saying that I was turning back, but I didn't. I was worried about bears. Coyotes too."

"I thought bears hibernate in the winter," Dixie teased. "You think they'd wake up just to snack on your scrawny hide?"

Lowell didn't laugh. "They don't go into a deep sleep like bears in the North, and I didn't want to take any chances."

Olivia tried to picture the scene. An isolated mountain covered with dark trees, long shadows, and snow. Three shivering men following the landmarks described in Violetta's story, climbing up and up as the night wore on.

"When we couldn't tell the difference between a log and a stone, the guide called it quits. Hicks refused to leave, so we started going down without him. He was yelling something to us from a crag when . . ." He paused to finish his drink. "When he was pushed."

He twisted the beer can in his hands until a silver gash appeared in its side. "I know it sounds crazy, but when I looked up, I saw something move toward Hicks. It was more like the outline of a person than a real person. A shape with huge black eyes. It put its hands out, and next thing I knew, Hicks was falling."

Dixie shuddered. Olivia waited for Lowell to continue, but his eyes had gone glassy again.

"Did the guide see the shape too?" she asked.

"No. He was focused on the trail." Lowell fingered the jagged edge of his can and then dropped it on the ground. "I didn't think it was real. With the snow and the moonlight, I thought my eyes had played tricks on me. But I saw it. And I saw him fall. I see it over and over every night. I can't sleep for seeing it."

Olivia believed Lowell's account of Hicks's death. He'd witnessed something that hadn't made sense to him. It had frightened him to the core.

"Did you tell the police about the figure?"

Lowell snorted. "Come on, lady. They'd have thought I'd been into the white lightning."

Dixie and Olivia exchanged befuddled glances.

"Mule kick?" Lowell said. "Hillbilly pop, wild cat, blue John, bush liquor—"

"Moonshine?" Olivia interrupted. "And had you?"

"Not until later, after the men went out to collect Hicks's body. They called the cops, but it took them ages to come, and I was pretty far gone by the time they showed up." He laced his hands together and stared at his palms. "Our footprints were gone by then, too. It was like we'd never been there at all."

Olivia considered the implications of the snowfall. "So if the shape had been a real person, his tracks would have been covered as well."

"It wasn't flesh and blood, I tell you." Lowell's voice was a low and angry rumble. "You could see the tree branches right through it."

"No wonder you can't sleep," Dixie whispered. "But that thing belongs to the mountains. You told me that it looked like someone strangled Violetta. It takes a strong person to do that, Lowell. Not a ghost."

"Then where'd he come from? Her killer?" Lowell challenged. "I was only outside loading the car for a few minutes, and when I went in to get the last of our stuff, that's when I saw her."

"Did you hear voices?" Olivia asked. "Any signs of an argument or a physical struggle?"

Lowell shook his head. "I closed the door behind me each time. Violetta didn't care for surprise visitors, and it was my job to make sure no one got near her."

His failure to protect Violetta hung in the air. Olivia wanted to be convinced by the shame she saw in his eyes, but she wasn't willing to trust him completely. He'd have to tell her the truth about the treasure first.

"She pointed at someone in the audience at the beginning of her performance," Olivia said, unable to look at Dixie. "Did you recognize anyone in the crowd?"

"Most of the other well-known North Carolina storytellers were there. They always came to watch her, to see what made her the best. Other than them, I only knew Dixie and Grumpy."

Olivia allowed herself to relax. "But Violetta didn't know the Weavers, so she could have been gesturing at a fellow storyteller or another resident of Oyster Bay."

At that moment, Grumpy opened the door to the double-wide and jogged down the warped wooden steps. He was shirtless and barefoot, and carried a bulging garbage bag in each hand.

"Olivia." He dipped his chin in greeting and then disappeared around the back of his house. Haviland rose, stretched, and followed Grumpy, undoubtedly hoping he'd be offered something to eat.

Lowell watched the poodle until he was gone from view and then turned to Olivia. "Violetta never met Dixie, but she knows Grumpy. At least she used to."

Olivia was stunned into silence.

"It's no big thing," Dixie was quick to add. "His family lived in the next town from hers. They went to the same church growin' up. But he joined the army at nineteen and didn't go back to visit much. She might have known him when he was a boy, but that's all."

"Why didn't you tell me this before?" Olivia asked.

"I didn't know," Dixie mumbled. "Not 'til we got to the show. Grumpy said somethin' about how long it had been since he'd seen Violetta. You know I get jealous right quick, so he didn't say anything about it until we pulled into the library lot. That's why we were late. I was askin' him all about her, but he didn't have much to say, and we had a bit of a fight."

Olivia nodded. "Okay, but the chief needs to know these details. And Lowell? For what it's worth, I don't think you're responsible for Violetta's death."

"I told you—" Dixie began.

"But I know you're not telling me the whole story either. If someone's after you, there has to be a reason why." She spoke as gently as she could, leaning toward Lowell in a conspiratorial manner. "What would motivate someone to track you down? Revenge? Blackmail? Do you possess valuable information?" Lowell's face immediately closed off, and Olivia raised her hands in surrender. "You don't have to confide in me. Just trust me when I say that Chief Rawlings is a good man. He won't string you up because you ran. He will listen without passing judgment."

Lowell laughed derisively. "I'm not going to tell some cop that I'm being hunted. Or what I saw the night Hicks died. I'm not talking to anyone. I'm done talking." He turned to Dixie, his fists clenched in anger. "I could have been miles away by now."

While he'd been speaking, Grumpy had reemerged from around the corner of the house and come up behind their group of chairs. He towered over Lowell, his long shadow falling across the dwarf's face. "You owe Violetta," he said simply. "She took a chance on you. Now you've got to repay her by doing what you can to help find her killer. You know who her friends are. Who her enemies are. No one else here does. Call the chief. And if you don't, I will."

Lowell shot Dixie a dirty look, and Grumpy stepped in front of his wife. "Don't go making this about Dixie. You owe Violetta, Lowell. Now do what needs to be done."

Olivia had never heard Grumpy string that many sentences together at once. He stood, his muscular arms crossed over his chest, his bare skin glistening with sweat, and glowered at Lowell. To Olivia, he looked like a tattooed Goliath.

"When they toss me back in the slammer, it's on you," Lowell snapped, slid off his chair, and waddled away.

Without another word, Grumpy walked off in the opposite direction, leaving Olivia and Dixie alone.

"I don't think I made things any easier," Olivia said by way of apology. "And to be honest, I'm concerned about what happened to Hicks. If he was murdered because of some connection he had to Violetta Devereaux, then Lowell's fears might be justified. Though she was not strangled by a ghost."

Dixie looked miserable. "I can't have ghosts or killers 'round my kids. Much as I'd like to smother them half the time, I don't want them in danger because Lowell's here."

Olivia took her car keys out of her purse and shook them. In response, Haviland appeared from the far corner of the yard, a tennis ball clamped between his teeth. He dropped it at Olivia's feet, panting and smiling. She tossed it for him and he raced off, a blur of black against the brown and yellow grass. "I'll drive Lowell to the station. In the meantime, put your dogs on long leads and make sure your guns are loaded."

Dixie managed a tight smile. "What good's a rifle against a ghost?"

Rawlings called Olivia at five that afternoon and asked to meet her at The Boot Top's bar. She was already at the restaurant, and having been subjected to one of Michel's monologues on his girlfriend's attributes, she was primed for a cocktail.

Gabe, The Boot Top's bartender, served Olivia her drink a few moments before the chief sank into the leather club chair next to hers. Rawlings scooped up a handful of mixed nuts, chewed feverishly, and swallowed. "Sorry, but I'm starving. Had to skip lunch today." He filled his palm with more nuts.

"Let me get you something." Olivia signaled a passing waiter and placed an order. By the time she returned her attention to Rawlings, he'd emptied the bowl of cocktail nuts. "How are you?" she asked.

He smiled at her. "Now I know that you love me. You asked about me before the case."

"Aren't the two intertwined?"

He sighed. "I suppose they are. And I'm frustrated because this is a frustrating case. We have a hundred suspects and no obvious motive. The ME is supposed to report to me within the hour. He told me the cause of death was asphyxiation, but he wouldn't elaborate. Said there was an abnormality he had to research before sharing his findings."

Gabe approached their table carrying a glass of ice water in one hand and a platter of assorted cheese, olives, and sliced meat in his other. "I'll be right back with some fresh bread." Gabe smiled at the chief. "Would you like something else to drink?"

"No, thanks. I'm still on the clock." Rawlings watched

the bartender walk away. "That kid gets better looking every day."

"He says it's the surfing, but I think it's because he's young, sun-kissed, and content. Contentment is very attractive. It's why every bar stool will be occupied tonight."

The chief popped a wedge of Brie into his mouth and chewed thoughtfully. "He's sincere too. People respond to that. I've spent too many hours today with individuals who pretend for a living—who wear costumes and makeup, and can trick us into believing they feel something they don't."

"Are you referring to the storytellers?"

"It was exhausting to gather their statements." Rawlings took a long drink of water. "They couldn't give a straight answer. Every phrase was embellished. Every reply a soliloquy."

Olivia helped herself to a square of Havarti with dill. "Were you able to track down all the attendees?"

Rawlings nodded. "For the most part. We drafted a seating chart while we were still in the library. Mrs. Fairchild showed us where she sat the VIPs, including you, my dear, and the rest of the guests helped identify their neighbors. We have a few more preliminary interviews to conduct, but they'll be done by the end of the night."

Gabe returned with warm bread and two servings of bacon-wrapped shrimp stuffed with basil and garlic.

"And what about Lowell?" Olivia speared a shrimp with her fork. "Were you satisfied with his story?"

The chief shook his head. "Not by a long shot. He could be playing me. While he told a convincing tale about being frightened, it's not enough to distract me from what I consider to be very suspicious behavior. The bottom line is that he fled from a crime scene. For the moment, I've decided not to bring him up on charges for that, but only because he came to the station voluntarily. Though Lowell told me that you had a hand in getting him there. Well done."

Olivia waved off the compliment. "Lowell genuinely believes that Alfred Hicks was murdered. I don't know exactly what he saw, but it scared him, and he doesn't seem the type to spook easily. I also think there's more to this treasure business than a professor's desire to publish Violetta's stories."

"I agree. I've requested a copy of the sheriff's file on Hicks. And Laurel tells me she's gathered a stack of background material on Violetta. I was hoping you and I could go through those papers after supper."

Olivia couldn't hide her pleasure in being asked to assist with the investigation. "How will I be compensated for my time?"

"I'll pay my debts with physical labor." He grinned.

The couple fell silent. They sipped their drinks, sampled the food, and watched the restaurant's patrons. Olivia savored these quiet moments with Rawlings. He was the only person in the world with whom she could sit in comfortable silence for long periods of time.

A woman at the bar threw her head back and laughed loudly at something her male companion said. He whispered something into her ear, and she laughed again. Then he got up and headed to the restroom. Once he was out of sight, the smile slid from the woman's face, and she glanced at her watch and frowned.

Olivia's eyes met the chief's, and she guessed that the woman's performance had him thinking about the case again. "Why would anyone want to hurt a storyteller? The competition for performing tall tales can't be that intense. People can win grants and stipends, but is that motivation enough for murder?"

"A grant changed Violetta's life," Rawlings pointed out.

Then he gave a little jump and pulled his phone from his pocket. Glancing at the screen, he said, "It's the ME. Be right back."

He strode from the bar area and hustled outside. Gabe suddenly appeared at the table. "Another round?"

"I'd better not," Olivia said. "I have a feeling I need to stay sharp tonight."

When Rawlings returned, he wore a befuddled expression. "The ME believes the killer slipped a plastic bag over Violetta's head and then wrapped a piece of fabric around the bag and pulled tight. After she asphyxiated, the killer removed the bag and took it with him. The line on her neck isn't very deep, so the ME doesn't think she was strangled with a sharp object. That rules out any kind of thin wire or rope, but it still leaves us with too many possibilities."

Olivia thought back on the scene. "There was no sign of a struggle. If someone tried to kill me that way, I would have clawed at the plastic bag and kicked out with my legs. I don't remember seeing scratches on Violetta's neck."

"No. She was still wearing her gloves and her hands were bound to the chair. There are faint lines on her wrists. Here's the strange thing," he began, and then paused and turned over his palms, gazing at them intently. "The ME said that it wasn't just her face that had that bluish tint. Her hands and chest and legs were the same color. She was blue everywhere."

Now Olivia was confused too. "What does that mean? Was it makeup? Body paint?"

Rawlings shook his head. "No. Her *skin* was blue. The ME thinks it's a blood disorder, but he needs to run more tests."

Olivia didn't know what to make of this strange information. She mulled it over and then drew in a quick breath. "That's what Lowell meant when he said Violetta knew what it felt like to be different. That was their bond. That's why they understood each other so well."

"The dwarf and the woman with the blue skin," Rawlings said softly. "Two misfits."

By this time, the bar had filled up with people. The Boot Top's patrons sipped drinks, talked, and laughed. Olivia observed the attractive vacationers and handful of locals. She saw their stylish clothes and relaxed postures, their perfect white teeth and toned bodies, and she realized that not one of them had an ounce of Violetta's charisma. Hers had been a presence too powerful to ignore. She could eclipse every woman in the room by uttering a single word.

"Have you ever heard of a blue star?" Olivia asked Rawlings. He shook his head. "A blue star is extremely large and very, very bright," she said. "It burns quickly, and when it dies, it doesn't shrink like other stars. It explodes, forming a supernova. The light it gives off is spectacular. And beautiful."

Rawlings reached across the table and took Olivia's hand. "We'll give her justice. It's the only thing we can offer her now."

Olivia squeezed his fingers hard. "Then let's get to work. I want to know her whole story. I want Laurel to be able to tell it when we're done. That way, Violetta can shine again. If only for a little while."

Chapter 7

Injuries may be forgiven, but not forgotten.

—AESOP

Olivia and Rawlings settled on opposite ends of the living room couch. Paperwork was strewn across the surface of the coffee table along with a bottle of sparkling wine and a glass of chocolate milk.

After waiting patiently to be let out, Haviland pushed the door to the deck open using his nose and front paw, and then looked back over his shoulder at Olivia.

"Go ahead," she told him, momentarily glancing from the papers in her hands. Haviland wormed his head through the crack he'd made, widened it with his shoulders, and disappeared outside. Still holding on to the paper, Olivia got up, shut the door, and poured herself some wine before returning to her seat.

"Do you want me to tell you when I've come across something interesting?" she asked Rawlings.

He removed his reading glasses, rubbed his eyes, and shook his head. "No. Just make a note of it and we'll talk later."

She watched him circle a phrase in Hicks's case file. A frown had appeared on his face, and a trio of deep lines were etched across his forehead.

He's spotted an inconsistency, she thought, having seen the expression before. Rawlings had discovered a detail that probably seemed insignificant to the sheriff's department. But for some reason, Oyster Bay's police chief thought it demanded closer scrutiny. He tapped his pen against his lips and stared off into the middle distance, and Olivia sensed he was on a snow-covered mountain on a cold January night, peering about in the moonlight in search of answers.

She returned her attention to the documents Laurel had brought to the station. The majority were press releases and reviews of Violetta's performances, and though Olivia skimmed them, they were all similar. The reporters who'd attended one of Violetta's shows were amazed by her ability to transport the listener to another place and time. But Olivia had experienced that for herself. She wanted to know what Violetta was like offstage.

"No wonder Laurel was so eager to obtain an interview," she muttered under her breath.

Rawlings looked up from his file. "Not finding what you're looking for?"

"No. I want to know why Violetta left home so soon after Elijah's death. Was the grief too much? Was she haunted by his memory? I also want to know if she insisted on performing at night in order to hide her blue skin. And most of all, I want to know about the treasure she alluded to. It's got to be the reason she was killed."

"You're making assumptions. Try to pick a question you can actually answer," Rawlings suggested. "Take the treasure, for example. Lowell claims that Professor Hicks was following Violetta's haint tale—that he was searching for the hollowed-out tree trunk where silver coins were hidden.

Hicks believed he was close to finding the spot. He was so convinced that he was willing to stay on Beech Mountain alone on a cold and snowy night after Lowell and the guide, a local man named Dewey Whitt, had called it quits." He tapped his chin with the pen. "Let's say that Hicks actually did find the right tree trunk and someone wasn't happy about that. So that someone pushed Hicks off the cliff to protect the secret location."

Olivia tried to envision the scene. "Or to keep the coins for himself."

"Are silver coins that valuable? Are they worth the price of murder? Now that's a question you might be able to answer," Rawlings said and turned back to his reading.

Reenergized, Olivia grabbed her laptop from her desk. She noticed Haviland at the deck door and slid it open. A waft of ocean-scented air snuck inside, and Olivia heard the faint *whoosh* of a wave curling onshore. She didn't dare linger there, or the rhythm of the water would pull her out of her work and coax her to come closer in the manner of the moon manipulating the tide. Inhaling a deep breath of salt and sea, Olivia closed the door.

She launched an Internet search on the values of silver coins but was given too many results, so she narrowed the field by looking for rare silver dollars. After writing down some notes on the mint years and current market values, she paused to take another sip of wine.

"Find anything?"

Olivia shrugged. "The coins are worth as little as fifty bucks to as much as fifteen thousand for an uncirculated silver dollar from 1801. It's pretty unlikely that the Devereaux family had one of those unless a distant relative worked at the mint."

"We'll have to look into the closest branches on her family tree—get a picture of her parents and sisters—but I don't have the time or the men to spare investigating beyond that. There were more than the Denver and Philadelphia mints at one point, weren't there?"

Olivia turned back to the computer for an answer. "Washington, DC, Carson City, San Francisco, West Point. And we have no idea where Violetta's grandparents or great-grandparents were from. I'm sure Harris could be persuaded to trace her lineage. If the coins are the motive, then the Devereauxes must have owned a handful of Liberty Busts or Morgan Silver Dollars minted in a particular year. Those coins are worth over two grand apiece." She shook her head in disbelief. "If they truly owned something this valuable, why wouldn't they spend it?"

Rawlings grew thoughtful. "I have no idea. Forty or fifty thousand dollars is a huge sum of money to people living in poverty. But a tenured professor? Would he venture up a mountain at night for that kind of money? Based on a tall tale?"

"I don't know," Olivia admitted. "I still don't believe that Hicks waited for darkness because he wanted to relive Violetta's story. For some reason, he needed secrecy. I'd bet my house that he offered Lowell and this Dewey Whitt fellow money or a share of the spoils if they agreed to accompany him." Warming to her subject, Olivia touched Rawlings on the knee. "Think about it. Lowell had a criminal record. He was a professional thief, but he was no outdoorsman. He and Hicks needed a local. What do you have on Whitt?"

"As of this point, very little." The chief put the file down and took off his reading glasses again. He curled his fingers around Olivia's hand. "It's getting late. I can't focus anymore."

"I'm going to make two calls before we turn in," Olivia said. "I'll have Harris search the genealogy sites and I thought I'd ask Grumpy to talk to his parents about Violetta's family. You and your team can cover the facts and statistics while—"

"His people will provide the gossip." He smiled. "It's a good idea. There are always little seeds of truth in the stories people tell about each other. I need to know Violetta's story. She's a complete stranger to me at this point, but somewhere between the hard, raw data and the memories of those who knew her lies the truth."

Olivia considered this statement as she walked to the kitchen. She'd burned the copy of her birth certificate that her mother had hidden in a safety deposit box, but that action couldn't permanently erase the record of her parentage. Those facts, unrelenting and irrevocable, were available through the state's vital records database. And though Olivia planned to conceal the truth in order to protect her relationship with Hudson and his wife and children, it existed all the same. It was out there, waiting to be found should anyone care to look for it.

With a sigh, Olivia dialed Dixie's number, her hand tracing the wrinkled edge of a painting her niece had made for her in May. It showed a park bench positioned in the center of a garden filled with dozens of flowers. Caitlyn had painted herself flying a kite in the background, a smiling Haviland at her side, while Olivia read a book on the bench. The kite strings wound across the upper half of the painting, loop-de-looping through fluffy white clouds and golden sunrays. Butterflies hovered over the flower petals, and one had landed on the pages of Olivia's open book. Caitlyn had written, "The Perfect Day" in her little girl block lettering along the top edge.

"You all right?" Dixie said when she answered the phone. "It's late for you to be callin'."

"I'm sorry to bother you, but the chief needs some help with Violetta's case."

Normally, Dixie would jump at the chance to be in the middle of a police investigation, but this one was too close to home. After a pregnant pause, she said, "What can I do?"

"Actually, it's Grumpy we need, but I have a feeling you'll have a better chance of convincing him to get involved than I will."

Dixie snorted. "I wouldn't be too sure of that. He's real unhappy about Lowell stayin' here."

Olivia could understand Grumpy's reservations. Like her, he probably sensed that Lowell knew more than he'd admit to about Hicks's death and Violetta's treasure. His very presence could put the entire Weaver clan at risk. "I can book him a hotel—"

"He's my cousin," Dixie interrupted. "We take care of our own in my family. And I need this to be ironed out real fast, so tell me what you want Grumpy to do."

Olivia did. She then called Harris, who was delighted to assist with the case.

"Immediate family only?" he asked when she explained what she needed. "Or are you going to give me a challenge?"

"We're looking for skeletons in closets," Olivia said. "If some dark secret was passed down through the generations, we need to know what it is. If there's nothing sinister, then maybe you'll find some clue about the silver coins. Violetta was either killed because someone wanted to silence her or—"

"Because she wouldn't speak," Harris finished for her. "Millay's kind of turned me into a night owl, so I'll get started tonight. I should have something for you by tomorrow afternoon, but some of the genealogical sites will take longer. Maybe two or three days for copies of certain documents."

Olivia shook her head, even though she knew Harris couldn't see her. "The killer's probably still in Oyster Bay, so do whatever you can but do it quickly." She softened her tone. "Are you doing okay otherwise?"

Harris sighed. "I'm losing her, Olivia. And please don't try to pretend that I'm not. I knew from the beginning that Millay wasn't into long-term anything. Her job and the Bayside Book Writers are the only commitments she'll make." He chuckled humorlessly. "And come on. Look at me. How could I expect to hold her interest? I haven't traveled cross-country on a motorcycle. I haven't jumped from a plane or been arrested. My life is boring. I'm totally predictable. The two things she can't stand."

Because she didn't know what else to say, she asked as kindly as she could, "What will you do?"

"I can't stop where this is headed," Harris answered miserably. "I am who I am."

"I'm sorry, Harris." Olivia wished she could offer him better comfort, but she knew there was nothing she could do except listen. "I know it hurts."

Harris barked out a dry laugh. "Yeah, just a bit. But thanks for not telling me to fight for her. That's what everyone else says. They don't realize that she's already gone. She just hasn't said the words yet."

Olivia could feel Harris's pain coursing through the speaker and was suddenly very much aware of her own contentment. Rawlings was in the next room. Haviland was there too, curled up on the rug near the fireplace. She had friends and family. People to call her own. The sea stretched out beyond her back door, full of whispers and promises. "You're not going to leave the Bayside Book Writers, are you?" she asked Harris.

He hesitated. "My company's opening an office in Houston, and my boss approached me about getting the new software department off the ground. The money's really good, and the people they're bringing on board to design the games are the best and brightest. They're going to change gaming forever."

"You sound excited about the offer," Olivia said, though she didn't want Harris to accept it. She wanted their group to remain intact. The Bayside Book Writers meant more to her than receiving critique or inspiration for her novel. Other than Dixie, its members were her closest friends. She could be herself around them. They accepted her, flaws and all. Loved her even. After so many years without friends, she hated to lose one of them.

But she also understood that Harris needed to get away if he ever hoped to recover from his impending heartbreak and that he needed someone he respected to encourage him to leave. "Maybe it's time for you to have an adventure, Harris. Texas is full of possibilities. Rodeos. Rib-eating contests. You could come back wearing a ten-gallon hat and boots with spurs."

Harris laughed, and for a few seconds the hurt loosened its hold on him and he sounded as carefree as the boy he'd once been. The Peter Pan look-alike. Back before he'd fallen for Millay. Before he'd been shot trying to protect her.

That's why she's having trouble saying the words, Olivia thought. Harris was a hero. The whole town knew what he'd done for her, and the whole town would judge Millay harshly if she dumped him.

"She's going to make me do it," Harris whispered glumly, as if he knew what Olivia had been thinking.

Olivia had to agree. "You took a bullet for her. She'd be despised by everyone if she left you."

"That's why I'm going to take this job in Texas. She needs me gone. So I'll go because that's how much I love her." Harris's voice was hoarse and world-weary. "Being with her was worth this agony. Every second she was near me I felt completely alive. She was like a drug. Maybe after six months in my self-imposed Texas rehab, I can come back and be the cool ex-boyfriend."

"Or the one who got away," Olivia said.

Harris gave a rueful snort. "That's the master plan. But don't tell anyone. I'd rather not look like a total jackass if it doesn't play out."

After promising to keep his confidence, Olivia hung up. When she returned to the living room, it was empty. Rawlings and Haviland had gone to bed. Olivia turned the lights off and climbed the stairs to the master bedroom. Rawlings was already stretched out with a pillow tucked under one arm, and Haviland had his head in his paws on the floor by her side of the bed.

Olivia got under the covers and moved closer to Rawlings. He slid both hands under her nightgown, his palms sliding up her thighs, over the hill of her backside, and he traced the slope of her spine. His lips brushed against her neck and then searched for her mouth. She met his kiss hungrily. Her conversation with Harris had created a need in her—a need to feel that what she had with Rawlings was safe. She plunged her fingers into his hair, demanding that his kiss be deeper, that his body respond to her desire faster.

They made love feverishly and then lay back breathing hard. Haviland had relocated to the closet and only reemerged after Olivia and Rawlings began to whisper about the case.

When they were too tired to speak rationally, Rawlings said, "It may not seem like it right now, but it helps me to talk things over with you. You and I are good together in so many ways, Olivia. We should do something about that."

Olivia felt a stirring of alarm. "What do you mean?"

Rawlings sat up on one elbow and looked down at her. His face was in shadow, but every contour and line was familiar to her. She could feel him frown as he searched for the right words. "This business of me keeping a change of clothes and toothbrush here. It's not enough. I want more than a drawer."

Relieved, Olivia smiled. "You can have the whole dresser. I'll empty it tomorrow."

"I'm not talking about a piece of furniture. I'm talking about us merging our lives."

"What, like living together?" Olivia asked.

"For starters," Rawlings said.

Despite the fact that she was too exhausted to consider such a major decision, Olivia envisioned the chief's poetry books on her nightstand, his shampoo in the shower, his family photos on the bureau. Instinctively, she drew away from him. "Why can't we just stay as we are? We're happy."

Rawlings flopped onto his back again. "We are. But I want to take the next step. I want to come home at the end of the day and see you. Or be waiting for you when you're done at the restaurant. I don't want us to have to plan to get together. I want us to just be together. Permanently."

Turning her face toward the window, Olivia stared at the pale moon. "Let's talk about this another time. I'm so tired that my head feels foggy."

Rawlings put a hand on her shoulder and traced small circles on her skin. "Just think about it, okay?"

She didn't answer, and within a few minutes, his breathing slowed and his shoulders rose and fell in a steady rhythm. Olivia was too unsettled to follow suit, and after tossing and turning for almost an hour, she went downstairs and reclined on the sofa. Haviland followed her, looking confused, but after she stroked his head, he stretched out on the rug and closed his eyes.

Olivia's gaze drifted over her tidy bookshelves, taking in Egyptian sculptures, miniature paintings from Russia, Greek amphorae, carved jade from China, Lalique crystal, and other souvenirs from her extensive travels. She'd never shared her space with another human being, and though she loved Rawlings, she didn't know if she wanted his things in her house. She didn't know if she wanted him here all the time either.

I'm too used to being alone, she thought as the French carriage clock on the mantel chimed out the hour. Olivia listened to its airy bells, recalling the little shop in Paris where she'd bought the clock from a stooped gentleman with half-moon glasses and a merry laugh.

This was her home, where she was surrounded by memories and keepsakes from her past. Everything had its place in her haven. Her sanctuary. Could she throw open her doors and invite Rawlings to share it? To alter it?

"Not yet," she whispered in the dark. Pulling the cashmere lap blanket she'd bought in Nepal over her shoulders, she closed her eyes and dreamt of snow-covered mountains.

The next morning, Olivia was at her usual window booth at Grumpy's Diner when Laurel found her.

"Rough night?" Laurel asked playfully as she sat down across the table.

Olivia didn't smile back. She raised her coffee mug and said, "This is my second cup. By the time I'm done with my third, I might be able to have a civil conversation. Until then . . ."

"Got it." Laurel turned to greet Haviland, who was much more enthusiastic in his hello, and then waved at Dixie.

Dixie collected menus from the family at the *Tell Me on a Sunday* booth and then skated over to Laurel's side. She peered at Olivia's cup but didn't top it off. "I know better than to mess with her brew," Dixie explained to Laurel. "Especially when she hasn't had her beauty sleep. How about you? Want somethin' to eat?"

Laurel said, "I had breakfast hours ago, but I'd love a muffin and some hot tea, please."

Dixie nodded and turned to Olivia. "Grumpy said to come on back once the caffeine's done its thing. His folks get up as early as we do, so Grumpy's already chatted with them." She jerked her thumb in the direction of the kitchen. "He was on the phone for twenty whole minutes. I don't think they've talked that long since his granny passed on and they wanted to know if Grumpy wanted any of her things."

Olivia put her coffee cup down. "I'm ready if he is."

"No, you are not." Dixie scowled. "You sit and sip and visit with Laurel. Grumpy has to get these brunch orders cooked before he starts chewin' cud. A distracted cook is a bad cook."

"That's true," Laurel agreed. "I can't even have the radio on when I'm fixing supper. Steve has to keep the boys out of the kitchen or I'll burn everything."

Dixie nodded. "There's a fine line between crisp and charred, and Grumpy knows not to cross it, but if his mind wanders . . . well, let's just say I've made him redo plenty of orders since we opened this joint. Usually happens when he's worried about one of the kids. Today, he's wound tighter than a fishing reel. I'll let you know when it's safe to come back." Dixie gave them a little curtsy and skated off.

Olivia took another swallow of coffee, reveling in the feel of the hot liquid sliding down her throat. "Rawlings told me to thank you for the files on Violetta. I read through most of them last night, but I don't think I learned anything of value. Harris is searching through genealogical records, and I'm hoping that Grumpy's parents can tell us more about her childhood. They live a town away from where Violetta grew up."

Laurel's blue eyes went wide. "What a small world. Did Grumpy know her?"

"When they were kids, but he hadn't seen her for decades."

"I wrote a short piece for the *Gazette* this morning, and it read like most of the articles I gave the chief. Violetta's professional life completely overshadowed her private one. I interviewed a bunch of the other storytellers, but none of them seemed to really know her intimately. The only interesting thing I learned from them was that she was a genuine recluse. Painfully withdrawn. She always dressed in long skirts and long-sleeved blouses, and she either went straight back to her hotel or drove home directly after a performance."

Olivia frowned. "Then why come to this storyteller's retreat at all? She didn't need to hone her craft, and the money she earned from Saturday's show could hardly have been worth a trip across the state. We need to ask Flynn how he contacted her. Did he speak with Lowell? Convince him to travel to Oyster Bay?"

"I don't know, but I wrote down the names of at least two storytellers who were seriously jealous of her," Laurel said. "Both of them believe Violetta used her fear of people to manipulate judges into awarding her grants and monetary prizes. One of them, an Amabel Hammond, accused Violetta of faking the whole condition in order to win competitions. This woman also knew Professor Hicks. They went to grad school together, and she now teaches at Appalachian State, which isn't too far from where Hicks taught at Western Carolina University."

Olivia knew that Sawyer Rawlings didn't believe in coincidences, especially when it came to murder investigations, and made a mental note to share this detail with him. "And the other storyteller?"

Laurel pulled a small notebook from her purse. "Greg Rapson. He grew furious when he talked about how Violetta had been dubbed 'A Living Legend' and the 'Virtuoso of the Spoken Word.' He said she was overrated."

"Furious? That's a pretty strong emotion."

"I know. But he called Violetta really nasty names. Late-night cable terms, if you know what I mean. I was especially shocked because he teaches college kids. What kind of example is he setting for them?" She scratched behind Haviland's ears, and he licked her hand in gratitude.

Olivia nodded. "Okay, so he's crass, but is he a murderer? Does he or Amabel have what it takes to win competitions?"

"Apparently they do. They've both placed second behind Violetta a number of times." Laurel jabbed her finger into the soft notebook paper. "The strange thing is that they acted pretty neutral about her at the beginning of our conversation. But after they'd had a few beers, they began to show their true colors. It was Millay's idea to seek them out when they were drinking, so I tracked them down at that bar within walking distance of their B&B. I felt kind of slimy because I didn't tell them I was a reporter, but I thought the chief should know what they said."

Dixie reappeared with a cup of tea and a softball-sized banana-nut muffin. After serving Laurel, she pulled a jar of honey out of her apron pocket and handed it to her. "This is the good stuff. I only give it to folks I like. Liquid gold, Grumpy calls it." She eyed Olivia's empty coffee mug. "All right then, you can come on back."

Grumpy was frying three eggs and half a rasher of bacon when Olivia entered the kitchen. She sat on a stool and watched him work without speaking. The bacon grease sizzled and spat, and Grumpy's spatula clanked against the griddle, flashing silver like a startled trout. He plated the food and slid a pile of crisp hash browns next to the bacon. "Order up," he said to Dixie. "Anything else?"

"A short stack of blueberry pancakes. Sausage on the side." She picked up the platter and skated out of the kitchen.

Grumpy had the pancake batter all ready to go. He gave it a quick mix with a whisk and then poured three identical circles of batter onto the griddle. While air bubbles formed in the cooking pancakes, Grumpy strode into the walk-in and reemerged with a bowl of fresh blueberries. "My folks remembered Violetta's family well enough," he began. He put two sausage links on the griddle. "Decent, hardworking people. Kept to themselves, but that describes most folks on the mountain. Anyhow, my ma and pa only saw Josiah during wintertime. He didn't go to church, and Ira handled all the town business. Word was that he had some kind of disease that forced him to stay covered up all the time."

He was blue, Olivia thought, her pulse quickening. Was that the family's secret? Was their blood disorder a treasure or a curse? And did it factor into Violetta's murder? Or Hicks's?

Grumpy dropped blueberries onto the cooking pancakes. They sank into the dough, and he waited a moment before flipping them with practiced flicks of the wrist. He then gave each sausage a quarter turn. "Ma also told me something sad. And I want you to know that she's not one to stretch the truth," he added.

Olivia could imagine Grumpy's parents as plain, no-nonsense people who knew how to do hundreds of things most of contemporary society couldn't do. His mother probably canned her own fruits and vegetables, dried her own herbs, and sewed most of their clothes and bedding while his father built their house from the ground up, raised livestock, grew most of their food, and could repair cars, appliances, and farm equipment.

"Go on," she said.

"A few days after Elijah died, Ira Devereaux broke down in the general store. My ma was there and took her home and gave her coffee with whiskey. Ira told her that Elijah could have been saved had Josiah been willing to send for the doctor and get him the medicine. Ma said that folks rarely sent for a doctor. They cost too much, and times had been especially tough for the Devereauxes. Still, Ira told my ma that Josiah was really rich. Kept some secret stash buried in the heart of some trunk. Ira didn't know where it was, or she'd have dug it up herself. But he wouldn't fetch it. Said it was cursed and he wouldn't touch it even to help his own son."

Olivia was hanging on his every word. "And because Elijah didn't get the help he needed, he died?"

"That's what Ira believed, and when Violetta found out about all this, she went half-crazy. Said she'd never look on her pa's face for the rest of her days. Her ma's neither. Folks say her hollers echoed up and down the mountain. And then she left home for good."

He slid the pancakes into the middle of a white plate and lined the sausages up on the side. "She never went back. Even when her folks died."

"And her sisters? Did your mother know what happened to them?"

Grumpy nodded. "They got married and moved west. Utah and Oregon, I think. Except the sister closest to Violetta in age. She became a college teacher. Said she was going to have a better life than her folks did. I knew her as Mabel, but my ma said she changed her name. I can't remember what she said. Anna. Annabelle. Something highbrow sounding."

"Amabel?"

"That's it." Grumpy rang a bell, signaling that an order was ready for pick up. "How'd you know?"

Olivia pointed to where Laurel sat. "Laurel interviewed her last night. Amabel's here. In Oyster Bay. I find it very strange that she hasn't admitted to being related to Violetta. Even worse that she doesn't seem upset by the fact that her sister's been murdered."

Grumpy wiped his hand on his apron. "Sounds like she's got something to hide."

"Yes, it does." Olivia didn't think Amabel was the only one. "People have come to our town with their stories. But it seems they've brought their secrets along too."

Chapter 8

If you're a pretender, come sit by my fire, for
we have some flax-golden tales to spin.

—SHEL SILVERSTEIN

When Olivia told Laurel that Amabel Hammond was Violetta's sister, Laurel nearly spat out a mouthful of tea.

"What kind of journalist am I? How did I miss that?" she cried and pushed away the remains of her muffin.

"Amabel isn't her legal name. It's Mabel. I assume she got married," Olivia said. "Look, what's important is that you learned there's no love lost between Amabel and her sister. I think you should tell the chief everything you, Amabel, and Greg talked about last night."

Laurel put some bills on the table. "I'll call him on the way to Through the Wardrobe. Pay up. You should come too."

"Why?"

"Amabel and Greg Rapson are doing a joint program for the kids there in fifteen minutes. Steve's bringing the boys so we can blend in while spying on the storytellers."

Olivia added more cash to Laurel's pile. "I hope they're not putting on a puppet show," she joked.

Laurel scooted out of the booth, Haviland close on her heels. "What do you and Millay have against puppets?"

At the mention of Millay's name, Olivia decided it would be a good idea to have her join their investigative party. After years tending bar, she was adept at reading people.

"You're kidding, right?" was Millay's response when Olivia called her.

"No, I'm not. We must get to know this woman quickly. Rawlings will look into her alibi, but she's already been deceitful by omission. I doubt she'll volunteer anything of significance to the police. After all, she failed to mention that she was Violetta's sister."

"She's *what*?" Millay asked, and Olivia knew she was hooked. "Fine. But I don't exactly blend in with the soccer moms, you know."

"They don't matter. Only the storytellers do, and you're on the road to becoming a published novelist. That's sure to impress them. You all tell tales. Yours are just in print form." Olivia opened the Range Rover's back door and gestured for Haviland to jump in. He did his best to look offended when Laurel sat in the passenger seat.

"I'll meet you there, but I'm not talking up my book to these people," Millay said. "And I'm only coming because Violetta was awesome and I'm pissed off that she was killed. Nothing else would convince me to spend a Monday afternoon in a store filled with kids. I'll be there in ten." She hung up.

"My turn?" Laurel dialed the chief's number while Olivia waited for a break in the traffic. Seeing her chance, she shot out in front of a pink VW Beetle convertible being driven by a young woman balancing a cell phone against her steering wheel. As they drove down the street, Olivia darted glances at the Beetle in her side and rearview mirror. More than once, she saw the car drift over the double yellow line and back again.

At the next stoplight, Olivia's eyes were locked on the young woman. The top half of her face was hidden behind the brim of a tennis visor and a pair of bug-eyed sunglasses, but judging by the frantic movements of her fingers, she was busy texting. When the light turned green, the driver behind her lightly honked his horn to encourage her to move. In response, the woman raised her middle finger and accelerated. She swerved around Olivia and floored it across a pedestrian crosswalk, causing an elderly couple to jump backward in alarm.

Olivia growled and Haviland mimicked the sound. The traffic grew thick again near the Methodist church, and Olivia found herself trailing the pink bug. This time, the Beetle was fading to the right, coming dangerously close to clipping the side mirrors of the cars parked along the street.

Laurel was too engrossed in her conversation with Rawlings to notice the angry set of Olivia's jaw, but when she deliberately passed the turn leading to Through the Wardrobe, Laurel put her hand over the phone and whispered, "Where are you going?"

"I just need one red light," Olivia said. "Don't worry, we won't be late."

At that moment, the pink car edged into its neighbor's lane, forcing a minivan to abruptly swerve away. The driver honked and shook his fist. Olivia noticed a pair of car seats in the back of the van, and her anger escalated.

"Yes!" she exclaimed when the next traffic signal turned red. Jerking her gearshift into park, she leapt out, jogged up to the pink convertible, and yanked the rhinestone encrusted cell phone from the young woman's hands.

"Hey!" the girl shrieked, and Olivia instantly recognized her. It was Estelle, Harris's annoying ex-girlfriend. "Give me that!"

Ignoring her, Olivia jogged over to the sidewalk and

dropped the phone in a trashcan. "You know that expression 'hang up and drive'?" she shouted at Estelle as she headed back to her car. "Well, *now* you can drive."

"I'm going to call the police!" Estelle threatened, her cheeks flushed pink with indignation.

"With what phone? Oh, wait, my friend is talking to the chief right now." Olivia pointed at Laurel. "Would you like to speak with him? Explain how you've nearly killed two senior citizens? How every time you send a text you're inches away from getting in an accident or committing property damage?"

"You're just doing this because I broke up with Harris!" Estelle yelled.

The signal turned green, and Olivia paused before getting in her car. "I did it because you're an idiot. And Harris broke up with you. Probably because you're an idiot. Now get out of the way, or I'll give the chief your license plate number."

After calling Olivia a string of choice expletives, Estelle drove off.

Next to her, the minivan driver, a handsome man in his midthirties, began to clap. His kids joined in and so did Laurel.

"Bring on the puppets." Olivia grinned.

When they arrived at the bookstore, however, there wasn't a puppet in sight. Flynn had cleared the children's area of its usual assortment of pint-sized chairs and bean-bags, leaving the rectangular alphabet-block rug free for the children to sit on. In addition to the rainbow-colored kites suspended from the ceiling, a sign welcoming the storytellers was hanging from the basket of a papier-mâché hot air balloon.

"I didn't know you were so crafty," a woman in a plaid golf short teased Flynn as she pushed her child toward the rug.

"I'm not. Jenna made the balloon. She also designed the 'Stories Take Us to Other Places' poster. We're selling them for ten dollars apiece." Flynn gave the woman his most charming smile.

She responded instantly. Touching him on the arm, she said, "I'll take two."

"He's got the soccer moms eating out of his hands," Millay said, coming up behind Olivia, Laurel, and Haviland. "I can't believe you used to date him."

Olivia frowned. "Flynn wasn't like that with me. He's an incorrigible flirt, but only when he thinks it will lead to a sale."

"So what's the plan?" Laurel asked. "Rawlings said to simply observe Amabel's demeanor. He'll be picking her up for additional questioning when this event is over. I got the sense he was in the middle of something when I called."

Olivia wondered if the chief had decided to have another talk with Lowell. Looking around the familiar bookstore, she felt some of the weekend's tension ebb a little. She truly loved this place. Flynn had replaced nearly all of the traditional bookshelves with antique wood wardrobes. He'd refinished each one by hand and lovingly polished them with lavender beeswax. The store always smelled of books, beeswax, and coffee.

Upon spotting Olivia, Flynn extricated himself from the clasp of another female customer and came over. He held out his hand to Haviland, who carefully placed his paw onto Flynn's palm. "Hello, sir. Care for a treat?"

Flynn had begun keeping a small jar of organic dog treats next to the register. Olivia knew that he was catering to Haviland because she was one of his best customers, but she didn't mind. Though she'd avoided Through the Wardrobe for several weeks following her breakup with Flynn, she and her former lover were now back on amiable terms.

"How's Diane?" Olivia always asked after Flynn's girl-friend, who also happened to be Haviland's vet.

"She's probably at home burning pictures of me." Flynn drew a finger across his throat. "We're not seeing each other anymore. She wanted to move in together and I wasn't ready." He shrugged. "Guess I'm just one of those confirmed-bachelor types. I don't suppose you and the chief have had to tackle that issue yet. But get ready, Olivia. Eventually, it'll come up. At our age, it always does."

Recalling her late-night conversation with Rawlings, Olivia averted her eyes and tried to think of something to say. Millay saved her from having to respond by slinging an arm over Flynn's shoulder. "Are you going to make me sit on the rug, Mr. McNulty?"

"With all the leg you're showing in that miniskirt? Not a chance. Every male in the room would be staring at you instead of focusing on the performers." He glanced in the direction of the stockroom and then checked his watch. The show was scheduled to begin in five minutes. "These story-tellers are good, too. Theirs is a different type of perfor-mance than Violetta's, but . . . well, there's nobody like her . . . she was one of a kind." His face darkening, he turned to Olivia. "I know you can't tell me anything, but at least give me hope that the cops have a lead on her killer."

"I honestly don't know anything, Flynn," she said. "I wish I did."

He accepted her answer with a solemn nod and was silent for a long moment. However, it wasn't in his nature to be glum, so when Laurel's twins, Dallas and Dermot, arrived, he exchanged a complicated series of playful high-fives, knuckle knocks, and chest bumps with the pair.

Laurel sat near her boys on the rug while Steve settled into one of the folding chairs positioned in a semicircle behind the kids.

"I think it's time," Flynn said with a smile and then glanced over Olivia's shoulder. "Ah, your niece and nephew are here. Now we can definitely get started." He winked at Olivia and headed for the back room.

Olivia saw Caitlyn rushing toward her and immediately opened her arms to receive the little girl's embrace.

"I didn't know you were coming to the show, Aunt Olivia!" Caitlyn broke away to hug and kiss Haviland.

Kim was carrying Anders. The baby was dressed in a darling sailor suit and white socks covered by tiny blue anchors. He smiled at Olivia and then stuck his fist in his mouth and gurgled. "I think he's getting another molar," Kim said. "He chews on everything, and he's been drooling like a bloodhound."

"A fine breed, the bloodhound," Olivia said, caressing the baby's chubby cheek. "Affectionate, loyal, and gentle. Sounds just like my sweet niece and nephew."

"You've never seen either of them throw a tantrum. You think they're perfect, and you spoil them rotten," Kim scolded.

Olivia knew her sister-in-law didn't really mind. "Haviland's spoiled too, but it hasn't affected him adversely."

At that moment, a drum began to beat from somewhere in the back of the store, and Flynn came out of the storeroom wearing an American Indian headdress. He danced forward until he stood at the edge of the alphabet rug and then froze. "Who wants to hear a story?" he asked in a dramatic whisper.

"We do!" the children shouted in unison, and Olivia sensed this wasn't the first time they'd been entertained by Flynn.

"We have two special guests here today. One of them is from the mountains like me, and the other guest was born in South Carolina. Have any of you been to South Carolina?"

Hands shot into the air. "Daddy took us to the giant peach water tower!" a boy declared. "My brother said it looked like a huge butt crack!"

Laughter erupted from the audience, and even Millay, who looked like she hadn't gotten much sleep lately, couldn't help but smile.

Instead of shushing the boy, Flynn pretended to be very interested in his comment. "I don't believe Mr. Rapson is going to share any stories about enormous butt cracks, but then again, he just might. Let's see what happens, okay?"

The kids giggled and nodded in agreement.

The drumbeats continued, and a man and woman emerged from the back room. The man held a gray wolf mask in front of his face. Its mouth was set in a toothy snarl, and some of the children stiffened at the sight of it. The second wolf was white and appeared to be grinning. Both of the storytellers wore black clothes and long tails made of mop heads.

"This is the story of two wolves. It is called 'The Two Wolves Within,'" the woman began in a booming voice.

"It comes from Cherokee legend," the man said, lowering his mask. "I am the grandfather and this is my grandson."

The woman put her mask aside and squatted. She rubbed her hands together and held them out as if she were warming herself at a campfire.

The grandfather sat in a chair and mimed smoking a pipe while his grandson complained about a boy who'd been mean to him that day. Olivia recognized it as a tale about bullying, and she could see that many of the children identified with the grandson. Many of them shook their heads or frowned over the cruelty inflicted on Amabel's character. It was obvious that they no longer saw her as an adult woman. To them, she'd become another child.

Olivia studied Amabel carefully. She was an attractive woman with molasses-brown hair and eyes the color of deep water. Her face was so expressive that Olivia could read each of the grandson character's emotions perfectly, and when she told the grandfather that her heart was filled with hate, her eyes burned with such a cold light that Olivia had to repress the urge to shudder.

Millay leaned over and murmured, "She's creepy."

"If you hold on to hate, it will poison your heart." The male storyteller spoke in a slow, deep voice. He sounded ancient and wise. "I have an angry wolf inside me too. We all do. Listen." He held up the mask and growled, startling several of the children. A little girl climbed into her father's lap and hid her face.

Amabel raised her mask. "I know that a kind wolf also lives inside you and me. He doesn't like to fight. He tries to get along with everyone." She *woofed* like a playful cub and then moved the mask again. "But how do you decide which wolf to listen to, Grandfather?"

"The wolf I feed will control me," he said. "So if you stay angry, you feed the angry wolf. He grows strong and powerful, and will take over."

"He'll control me?" Amabel asked, sounding a little afraid.

The grandfather nodded.

"Then I will only feed the gentle wolf. I won't fight with the boy who was mean to me."

"That is good," the grandfather said and handed his mask to Amabel. "But he still lives in you. You cannot change that. We all have two wolves within us. Feed the gentle wolf and starve the angry one."

And with that, Amabel raised the snarling mask and growled quietly while Greg Rapson took the grinning wolf face, hopping around in a circle, howling. His antics made the children laugh, and eventually, Amabel crept away.

Shedding their masks and mop head tails, the pair told

several more stories, each longer and more elaborate than the last. Greg tried to dominate the performance, but Amabel's facial expressions were more engaging than his theatrics.

As she watched the two of them, Olivia couldn't help but wonder why people who competed against one another for prizes and grants would come together once a year to share tricks of the trade. Flynn had explained that the annual retreat was held in different locations and that having the members of the Southern Storytellers Network come to Oyster Bay would be a boon for his store and for the town, but Olivia hadn't realized how much the gathering mattered to the performers The entire notion seemed odd to her, but perhaps the bookstore event was an example of how they needed to work together in order to earn money.

When the performance was over, Flynn showed the children a display of picture and easy-reader books he'd set out as a tie-in to the afternoon's experience. There were tall tales and legends, fairy tales, Cherokee stories, a biography of Paul Bunyan, fables, nonfiction works on wolves and forest animals, and many more.

After clapping loudly, the children rushed the table. They grabbed armloads of books before racing back to their parents with cries of, "Can I have this? Pleasepleaseplease!"

Laurel tried to fend off double entreaties from her twins while Olivia beckoned Caitlyn to join her at the table where the storytellers sat handing out fliers listing their school programs and other regional events.

"That was fun," Caitlyn told Amabel, who rewarded her with a smile and a paper wolf mask to color. Caitlyn hurried off to show her mother her prize.

"I'm sorry for your loss," Olivia told Amabel softly.

Amabel drew back, immediately wary. Instead of

acknowledging the remark, she merely thanked Olivia for coming and turned to look at Millay again.

"I think you guys were better than she was," Millay muttered quietly. "You're out here in the middle of the day. No stage. No special lighting. Only a few simple props. You two are the real deal."

Amabel and Greg were both clearly pleased by the compliment. "Have you been to many of our events?" Greg asked.

Millay gave a noncommittal shrug. "I'm into stories. Mine are the written kind. Not to brag or anything, but I just signed with a literary agent, so I know what it takes to put everything you've got into your work." She looked at Amabel. "See, most people can't understand why you do this when you already have a totally respectable job. It's not about the money, right? For me, it's about getting people to listen. Moving them with words. Kind of being in charge of them. TV, movies, the Internet—all that stuff uses bells and whistles. It's a trick. It's not art."

"Where have you been all my life?" Greg asked, and Olivia peered over the edge of a flier to note that his ring finger was bare. He was staring at Millay as if he wanted to memorize every part of her.

Millay's mouth curved into a suggestive smile. "Right here. Waiting." She then turned her attention to Amabel. "Seriously, I'd love to hang out with you guys. The bummer is that I have to work. The bills keep piling up, you know, and my writing hasn't paid crap so far. But I'd like to buy you a round if you're free tonight. I'm a bartender, and I can do whatever I want behind that counter."

Greg immediately accepted, but Amabel hesitated. "I'm supposed to get together with some of the other storytellers," she said. "Our annual retreat is a chance to find out which schools and libraries still have enough money in their budgets to hire people like us. And I'm not sure if tomorrow's any better. A group of us, including Greg here, have plans to meet at The Bayside Crab House for dinner. We all have coupons for half-priced entrées."

"Then we're all in luck because I work at The Bayside Crab House." Keeping a straight face, Millay gestured at Olivia. "So does she. The food's awesome and the coupons will go a long way, but sitting at the bar will help even more. Isn't that true, Olivia?"

Olivia nodded. "Absolutely. I can reserve seats for you if you'd like."

The offer was too sweet for the storytellers to refuse. Amabel told Olivia to expect a party of six for dinner and drinks.

"See you tomorrow night," Millay called sweetly. She and Olivia then joined those waiting in line to check out.

At Olivia's insistence, Caitlyn selected a book of Jack tales and an easy reader about a group of problem-solving mermaids. She'd also picked out a *Rainbow Fish* board book for Anders. Clasping all three books against her chest, she danced from foot to foot, clearly impatient for the line to move faster. Olivia guessed her niece was eager to get home, to fly down the hallway into her room, and spend the rest of the day reading in the pink beanbag chair Olivia had given her for her birthday. Olivia had had a special reading place when she was a girl too. She liked to sneak a book up the lighthouse stairs and through the door outside to the balcony. There was a full-time lighthouse keeper back then, and he'd reprimanded her once or twice, but after a while, he pretended not to notice the skinny child with the freckles and large sea-blue eyes. After all, she didn't say much—just smiled shyly and then buried her face in her book.

"Ready?" the cashier asked, recalling Olivia to the present.

"You caught me gathering wool." With an apologetic smile, Olivia placed the books on the counter and turned to Millay. "What about Fish Nets?"

"I'll tell my boss I'm sick," she said. "The guy I split my shifts with needs the money, and I only blow off work when something really important comes up. Some lies are necessary."

Olivia accepted the bag of books from the cashier and handed them to her niece. Caitlyn thanked her, kissed her on the cheek, and went to show her mother her new acquisitions. Olivia led Millay to the corner where the free coffee station had been placed. Ignoring Flynn's watery bookshop blend, she touched Millay on the arm. "We all tell lies, but there are times when the truth is best." She lowered her voice. "I talked with Harris last night and he is miserable. I'm not trying to interfere, but one woman to another, it's time to fish or cut bait."

A shadow crossed Millay's face. "What's going on between me and Harris is more complicated than a fishing metaphor."

"Crossroads always are," Olivia agreed. "Trust me, I'm standing at one myself. And I don't like it at all. I was perfectly content with the road I was on."

"Well, that's better than anyplace I've ever been. Contentment sounds pretty nice." Millay picked up a plastic coffee stirrer and twisted it between her fingers. "I'm never happy for long. I don't know why. I just can't seem to hang on to anything good."

Olivia didn't know what to say to that, so she remained silent. Laurel signaled to them from the back of the line, and they joined her while she tried to wrestle a 3-D pirate bookmark from Dermot's hand.

"Should we hang around?" she asked. "See if anything happens?"

Olivia shook her head. "It's not like the storytellers will show their true colors in front of this crowd. Besides, I expect Rawlings or one of his men to show up any minute now."

Laurel tried to get the bookmark away from Dermot again, but the little boy was too quick.

"Guess what I heard when I was paying for my books?" Olivia whispered theatrically, and Dermot stopped wriggling long enough to listen. "I heard that any child who doesn't listen to his mother won't get one of the really cool masks they're giving away. You can pick the calm wolf or the angry wolf. Which one would you choose, Dermot?"

Instead of replying, Dermot sprinted to the bookmark spinner, returned the 3-D pirate bookmark to its proper spot, and stood straight as an arrow at Laurel's side.

"I didn't realize you were the Child Whisperer," Laurel teased. She gestured to where Steve was trying to get Dallas to clean up the pile of books he'd strewn across the floor. "Want to work another miracle?" She kissed Dermot on top of his head. "Go tell your brother about the mask."

He ran to the next room and grabbed his twin by the straps of his overalls. Dallas was about to protest when Dermot pointed at the storyteller's table. After a long pause, in which Dallas seemed to be weighing whether he'd rather have a mask or further annoy his father, he picked up the books.

The twins were the last in line to meet Amabel and Greg, and Laurel let them rush off to show Steve their masks before shaking the storytellers' hands and showering them with compliments. They spoke with her warmly enough, but the moment she walked away, Amabel's eyes followed her distrustfully. Greg couldn't stop shooting lecherous glances at Millay.

"As if he'd ever have a shot," Millay said under her breath. "I'm cool with older guys, but not older guys who

are thinking X-rated thoughts in a room full of kids. That's just nasty."

The two women tarried by a set of shelves filled with Outer Banks and coastal Carolina books. Olivia leafed through a book on indigenous flora and fauna wondering if Oyster Bay would ever turn green again. She missed the purplish pink of the large swamp flowers, the cheerful yellow buds of Saint-John's-wort, and the star-shaped petals of the dotted horsemint. Even the fiery blossoms of the gaillardia, which the locals called the Indian Blanket, were no longer sprinkling the dunes with color. Only the sea oats, with their thin stalks and brown, featherlike heads, flourished.

Eventually, only the storytellers and a handful of customers remained in the store. Olivia covertly observed Flynn's interaction with Amabel and Greg. He thanked them both for coming and vigorously shook their hands. They chatted for a moment and then Greg left. Amabel lingered behind, but Flynn had turned away to speak with a customer.

As soon as he was free again, Amabel shouldered her purse and walked up to him. She leaned in, put her palm flat on his chest with an intimacy that clearly surprised him, and whispered into his ear. His eyes went wide, and she laughed at his reaction. She walked out of the bookstore, and he watched her cross the street. Flynn's body was still as a stone, but Olivia craned her neck so she could follow Amabel's progress. A police cruiser was parked at the end of the block.

"What was that about?" Millay said, having witnessed the odd interaction.

Suddenly, Olivia remembered how Flynn had introduced the storytellers. She drew in a sharp breath. "Flynn told the audience that Amabel was from the mountains. He said, 'one of them is from the mountains *like me*.'"

Millay frowned in confusion. "I thought Flynn moved to Oyster Bay from the Raleigh area."

"Me too. But where was he before that? Does he know some of the storytellers he invited here?" Olivia studied Flynn as he shook himself free of his trance and began straightening a table of new hardcovers. Glancing down at the floor, he bent over to pick up one of the white paper wolf masks. He straightened and eyed it thoughtfully, his expression unreadable. "Which wolf are you, Flynn McNulty?" Olivia asked in a low and troubled voice.

Chapter 9

*The unread story is not a story; it is little
black marks on wood pulp.*

—URSULA K. LE GUIN

Olivia took Haviland to the dog park and sat on a bench
in the shade while he chased squirrels and sniffed the
base of every bush and tree. When he was panting heavily,
Olivia poured water into his travel bowl and watched him
lap it up while she wondered what to do next. She had plenty
of time to dwell on the riddle of Violetta's death, which
seemed to grow more complicated with every passing hour.

After Haviland cooled down a little, Olivia told him to
heel and headed to Circa, Oyster Bay's antique shop. The
proprietor, Fred Yoder, had become a friend of hers, and she
often stopped by to browse his wares or to join him when
he took Duncan, his Westie, to the park.

Inside Circa, Fred was busy showing a sword belt to a
customer. "It's in amazing condition," he told a middle-aged
man in khaki pants and a polo shirt. "The belt plate shows
the seal of Virginia, the state motto, and the two brass hang-
ers are intact. The leather has been repaired here, below the
wreath, and it was skillfully done."

The customer was obviously interested in the belt. He couldn't stop touching it. "I was supposed to be looking for an eglomise mirror. My wife will kill me if I come home with this instead."

Fred smiled. "Well, we can't have that. Take your time looking around. I'll be right back."

"Where's Duncan?" Olivia asked when he came over to greet her.

"Asleep in the kitchen. He's gotten so lazy that he no longer bothers to get up when the bell above the door rings." He took Haviland's paw and shook it respectfully. "Some guard dog, eh?"

Haviland rolled his eyes, which was the canine equivalent of a shrug. Fred laughed and gave him a hearty pat on his back.

Olivia gestured at the man examining the belt. "I don't want to interrupt," she whispered. "I can see that you've got a fish on your line."

Fred waved off the notion. "It's best to give people space where they're trying to make a decision. And that isn't an inexpensive item. Can I offer you a cup of coffee?"

"I'd better not. In truth, I stopped by to ask if you could think of an antique specific to the Appalachia region. Something very valuable."

Frowning, Fred rubbed his chin and gave the matter serious thought. "Appalachian antiques? Nothing of note comes to mind. When I come across things from that area, they're usually quilts, woven rugs, and other textiles. Old farming equipment, tools, household goods like lanterns or tins, but nothing like that sword belt over there. Nothing to give a shop owner the tingles." He glanced around his establishment. "Honestly, when I think of that part of North Carolina, I think of coal."

"Me too," Olivia said. "What about silver coins?"

Fred considered the question. "Possibly. Silver was a common form of currency before paper bills came along. They were probably circulated even longer in remote parts of the country, but the mountains aren't known for being caches of rare coins. I've always had the feeling that the people of Appalachia had to use every cent they could lay their hands on just to get by. It's a hard place, isn't it?"

"I believe so, yes. That's why I keep hitting a wall. I'm trying to figure out what might have been passed down from generation to generation in a mountain family—something that was valuable a long time ago and still worth a notable sum today. But I can't think of a single object."

At that moment, the customer turned to Fred and grinned. "What the hell? I'm going to get it! I might spend a few nights in the doghouse, but it's worth it."

"Sure thing, sir. I'll be there directly." Fred smiled and looked at Olivia. "Give me some time to think about your question. Maybe the family had ancestors who lived in a city or immigrated to Appalachia from another country. Maybe that relative brought a prized possession from another area with them. That's the only theory I can come up with at the moment, but I'll post a query on my antique forums and see if I get a nibble."

Olivia thanked him, accepted a treat for Haviland, and drove home.

In the spacious silence of her house, she did something she often did when she was having a hard time solving a problem.

Opening her hall closet, she selected one of dozens of jumbo glass pickle jars from the shelf. She carried one from five summers ago to the Aubusson rug in the living room and got down on her knees. Unscrewing the jar lid, she inhaled a wisp of salt water and then overturned the contents onto the rug. She ran her fingers over shotgun shells, rings, coins, and belt buckles as names passed through her mind. Greg Rapson, Amabel Hammond, Lowell Reid, Dewey Whitt, and Violetta Devereaux.

"Would Greg really commit murder because he was jealous of another storyteller? He must have a better motive to be viewed as a realistic suspect. Money, perhaps? I wonder how much college professors take home?" Olivia addressed her comments to a battered wheat penny. "After all, there's no guarantee that he'll win future competitions even with Violetta out of the picture."

Olivia let the penny drop and reached for a ball-shaped earring. "And Flynn? Why would he kill a woman he'd invited here to perform? Unless there was another reason he wanted her to come to Oyster Bay. But what would that be?"

Tossing the earring aside, she caressed the smooth surface of a brass buckle and considered Lowell. "What about the thief? Was he biding his time? Waiting until this performance to make his move? Did he want information or was Violetta carrying something on her person? Was he hoping Dixie would hide him after he'd gotten what he wanted?"

She drew the buckle closer. There were too many questions surrounding Lowell Reid. And then there was Amabel. A poor girl from the mountains with the kind of innate intelligence that won her academic scholarships and the chance to escape her family's hardscrabble lifestyle. Later, after Violetta was already gone, Mabel became a full-time college professor and part-time storyteller. But was the girl named Mabel truly gone? The girl who'd lived in her younger sister's shadow for years. The girl who had probably fought to be seen and heard in a house haunted by the memory of her brother.

Olivia assigned a shotgun shell to Amabel, believing she was probably a volatile and unpredictable creature. She might be cool and smooth on the outside, but surely some part of Mabel still existed inside Amabel's calm and collected casing. If not, why take up storytelling at all? Why cling to a past that was Mabel's if Amabel wanted to deny her existence?

Dewey's symbol was a silver St. Christopher's pendant because Olivia pictured the mountain guide as someone who had the ability to lead travelers to safety. Even on a snowy night. The question was, did he lead Hicks where he wanted to go or did he lure him to his death?

"What was up there, Professor Hicks? What did you hope to find?" she asked the assortment of beach trash and treasures, but the metal objects remained mute.

Scooping her collection back into the jar, Olivia screwed on the lid and stood up. She walked around the living room, hoping for insight, but her efforts had only created more questions. Coming to a stop in front of a Limoges pillbox on the bookshelf, she picked up the diminutive piece, smiling a little as she touched the tiny hand-painted poodle resting on a pillow of deep blue. The French words on the bottom of the box gave her pause.

"Devereaux is French. What did this French family do before they were forced to scratch a meager living from the land? Where did they start out?"

Returning the box to its precise place on the shelf, Olivia picked up the phone and dialed Harris's number.

"I hope you're about to tell me about some incredible Happy Hour specials. I could definitely use a Happy Hour right about now." Harris sounded out of sorts.

"How about coming to my house? I have beer and wine. Well, there's a decent supply at the lighthouse keeper's cottage anyway."

Harris hesitated. "We usually go there to solve problems, don't we?" he said absently, as if he'd forgotten that Olivia was on the other end of the line. "Okay. Yeah. We'll have a drink, and then I can tell you what I found. I spent my lunch break researching Violetta and her family. It wasn't enough, but I did come across a few interesting tidbits."

"Then quit teasing me and get over here. I might even have some cheese in the fridge, and I could rustle up a package of crackers. I don't know how fresh they are—"

"Just dump everything you have on a plate. You know I'll eat it. I'll be there in ten."

Olivia and Haviland walked the short distance from the main house to the cottage, keeping their faces lowered against the heat of the late-day sun. The gravel crunched beneath their feet and clouds of dust trailed in their wake like diaphanous tumbleweeds.

Olivia had just arranged a platter of food when Harris burst into the cottage. He tossed his briefcase on the sofa, yanked his tie loose, and kicked off his shoes. "It's hot," he complained. "And no matter how much I drink, I still feel thirsty."

"That's how the drought affects your body. Here. This should help." Olivia handed him a beer in a chilled pint glass.

He took a greedy swallow. "So *this* is what Nirvana tastes like."

Olivia tried to be patient, but she was eager to learn what Harris had discovered. Edging closer to him, she drummed her fingertips on the countertop.

Harris watched her and grinned. "Okay, I can see that you're in no mood for small talk, so here's what I found." He pulled a few sheaves of paper from his briefcase. "Violetta's family hasn't always been from Whaley. In fact, her grandfather wasn't born there. Her grandmother was, but Grandpa Quentin moved down South from New York City."

"New York?" Olivia hadn't expected that.

Harris nodded. "Yep. I found a record of his Whaley land purchase. He married Virginia Bumgarner pretty soon after that."

Olivia winced. "I can see why she took his surname."

"Quentin was fifteen years older than her too, the sly devil. I found all kinds of results using an online database, including birth records for their children and Josiah's children. And a bunch of death certificates. Between the two generations there were three kids who didn't make it past the age of eight." He put the papers down and drank more beer. "It was really depressing to look at those documents. To read their names and wonder how they died. Did they get sick? Did they have an accident? One of the certificates listed the cause of death as 'Drowned.' A single word."

"That's terrible." A chill crept into the room, accompanied by the first shadows of the evening. "What about Josiah's children? Did you find Elijah's death certificate?"

"Yeah. The cause of death was cited as 'Unknown illness.'" Harris sighed. "And someone, the doctor I guess, wrote a line underneath about the deceased having blue lips and face. That seemed like a strange thing to make a note on. After all, Elijah died in the middle of winter and who knows how much time passed before anyone outside the family had the chance to examine the poor kid."

Olivia hesitated and then folded her arms over her chest. "Harris, I'm going to tell you something in confidence. You cannot breathe a word about this to anyone. Got it?"

Harris straightened. "Whenever you look at me like that I want to curl up and hide. But I'll keep my mouth shut. Scouts honor."

"No one knows this, but Violetta was blue skinned."

"That's not really a secret, it is?" Harris was clearly disappointed. "I mean, she was strangled."

Olivia shook her head. "Asphyxiated, but that's not what I'm saying. She had a blood disorder. A rare one, I assume. She was blue *everywhere*."

"Whoa." Harris opened his eyes wide. "Seriously? Cool." He grabbed his laptop from his briefcase, flipped up the lid, and began to type. "You ready for this mouthful? The condition is called Methemoglobinemia. And I'm only saying that right because there's a pronunciation guide on this page."

"I'm still impressed," Olivia said.

Grinning, Harris continued to study the screen. "Basically, once you translate the fancy med speak, it's a condition in which a person's blood has a higher amount of a particular hemoglobin than normal. It's called methemoglobin, and it can't release oxygen. This gives people a bluish tinge. It can be a hereditary genetic condition or an acquired one."

Olivia's brows shot up. "You can catch it?"

Harris nodded. "From repeated exposure to certain antibiotics, nitrates, and anesthetics. The second kind is worse because it comes with other symptoms. If you inherit it, you look like a Smurf, but if it's acquired, you can also suffer from fatigue, headaches, and shortness of breath."

"Grumpy's parents described Josiah as being pretty reclusive. Maybe he had the condition too. And if so, was it passed down to only Violetta or to her siblings as well?"

"Depends if the mom was a carrier, I guess." Frowning, Harris kept reading. "Even if Elijah had Methemoglobinemia, I don't think it killed him. Unless he and Violetta were both exposed to the same nitrates or antibiotics. Maybe they both got sick, but she recovered."

Olivia considered this. "The Devereaux kids did sell wild plants to drug companies. Maybe they traded the plants for antibiotics. We'll have to find out from Violetta's sister." She told Harris that Rawlings had probably spent the latter part of the afternoon interviewing Amabel.

At that moment, her stomach issued a loud gurgle, and Harris gestured at the nearly empty plate in front of him. "Cheese? Cracker?"

"No, thanks. I'm in the mood for a Florentine Pizza. How about you?"

"Hey, if you're ordering, I'll take a ham and pineapple." Harris gave his flat belly a pat. "I'm more than willing to drown my sorrows in an extra-large pizza, a few bottles of beer, and this investigation."

Olivia didn't want to talk about Harris's relationship troubles, so she sifted through the take-out menus in the kitchen until she came across Pizza Bay's neon-pink menu. "I can't believe I don't have this number memorized by now," she said.

"Ask them for one of their magnets. Then you can hang some of Caitlyn's artwork in this kitchen," Harris suggested and turned back to his computer.

He'll make some woman very happy one day, Olivia thought. She wished that woman could have been Millay because Harris was good for her. Perhaps she'd realize what she'd had in him once he'd moved to Texas, but Olivia doubted it. Millay wasn't one to dwell on the past. She shut it in a box and walked away without looking back.

Olivia phoned in the order and poured herself a drink while Harris pivoted his laptop to show her images of blue-skinned people.

"There's such a range in hue." She leaned closer to the screen, fascinated. "That man has just a bluish tinge while that woman is a deep indigo."

"And here I thought having braces, acne, and rosacea was rough." Harris's face was full of sympathy as he scrolled through the images. "You know, none of these photos are recent. Look at the dates. However, most of the American ones were taken of families living in Appalachia."

Intrigued, Olivia carried her tumbler of Chivas Regal over to the sofa. "I wonder why."

Harris's eyes flew across the text of an article on Appalachian history. "Interbreeding. That's the answer, pure and simple. The mountain communities were really isolated. Cousins marrying cousins wasn't uncommon back then. It didn't carry the stigma it does now."

Olivia nodded. The mountain people wouldn't have been the first to follow this custom. Throughout history, dozens of secluded societies passed down unique and often detrimental genetic traits as a result of too much intermarriage within a small population. "Josiah found a good place to hide his condition. It was probably a good place to hide his children's blue skin too. I wonder if that's why his father left New York. Maybe he was exposed. Even if his skin color were only a little off, he'd have trouble finding work or renting an apartment. Not many people would accept a man who looked so different back then."

"I know you're thinking aloud here, but there's no way I'm going to be able to track down that kind of needle-in-the-haystack detail. I'd be totally thrilled to find out what street Josiah lived on or where he worked during his years in New York." Harris finished his beer and carried it to the sink. After he rinsed the bottle and tossed it into the recycling bin, he froze. "Violetta mentioned a curse in the opening of her act. I bet she was talking about having blue skin. Look what it did to her. To avoid being stared at like a circus freak, she had to wear makeup and move around at night like some kind of vampire."

Olivia sipped her drink and stared out the window. The stretch of beach was white. Nearly all of the brown and yellow had been bleached away by the sun. The sand was hot enough to scorch. Looking at it now made her think of her closet full of pickle jars. Her treasures. Very few of them were valuable—a handful of old coins or pieces of gold jewelry—and yet she kept things most people would consider trash.

"What if Violetta's treasure was sentimental?" Olivia suggested. "Something that only had value to her?"

Harris touched the top of his chest near his shoulder. The scar from his bullet wound was there, hidden beneath his shirt, and he often rubbed it when he was troubled or lost in thought. "I don't know. She said the clues were in her stories. Why toss out bread crumbs if you don't want someone to follow your trail? I think she saw someone in the audience that night at the library—a threat, an enemy, a sister, a person from the past, who knows—and she was, like, taunting them."

Outside, Olivia heard the crunch of car tires on gravel. "That must be our supper," she said and got up. However, she didn't open the door to a young man wearing a Pizza Bay delivery shirt. Instead, she found Rawlings standing on the welcome mat.

"Am I interrupting?" He smiled wryly and jerked his thumb at Harris's car.

Olivia knew he was teasing, but she chose to ignore the jest. "Drink?"

"I'd kill for a beer."

"You won't have to get violent. I think Harris left you one or two." She touched him on the arm. "Come on in."

He followed her into the cottage and greeted Harris with a tired smile and a firm handshake. After telling Olivia to forgo the pint glass, he took a long pull of beer right from the bottle and sighed. "Now if only I had a slice of pizza, I'd be a happy man."

At that moment, the Pizza Bay delivery car pulled in

front of the cottage. "Hot damn," Rawlings whispered and stared at his beer. "Is there a genie in this bottle?"

Olivia and Harris laughed. Olivia paid for the pizza and gave the gawky teenage delivery boy a generous tip. The trio then settled down to eat, and Olivia refrained from peppering Rawlings with questions until he'd had at least one slice of ham and pineapple. Harris, on the other hand, didn't grant the chief the same luxury.

"How was your interview with Amabel?" he asked.

Rawlings chased a bite of pizza with a swallow of beer. "She's a hard one to read. When I asked why she hadn't come forward and identified herself as Violetta's sister, she told me she didn't think the information was relevant."

Olivia served him a slice of Florentine pie. "Where was she following Violetta's performance?"

"In the lobby," Rawlings said with a hint of annoyance. "At one point, everyone was in the lobby, and so every person I interview can use that answer and someone will collaborate it. And it's not like the attendees were checking the time or paying attention to whether someone slipped off down the hall or not. The restrooms are there, so even if someone went missing for five or ten minutes, it wouldn't seem unusual."

Harris pointed his pizza crust at Olivia. "Especially considering how you women chitchat in the ladies' room. What exactly are you doing in there?"

"Talking about you men, naturally." Olivia grinned and then turned to Rawlings. "Go on."

"I asked Amabel about her childhood, her schooling, her career, you name it. She kept her answers as terse as possible, and I had no cause to press her. I only saw a flicker of genuine emotion when I mentioned Elijah's name."

Harris got up, grabbed his laptop, and brought it back to the table. He showed Rawlings the image of Elijah's death certificate. "This is all I could find on him. This and his birth certificate."

Rawlings stopped eating. He gazed at the screen, his pond-green eyes solemn. "In the end, is that all we are? A life described on two pieces of paper? That little boy was more than a pair of documents."

His words hung heavy on the air. Olivia couldn't help but picture Anders—round, rosy, and dimpled. She imagined so many different futures for him, each more wonderful than the last. And she was just the boy's aunt. Olivia couldn't begin to comprehend what it would feel like to be a parent, to be forced to watch a life so full of promise ebb like the outgoing tide. She wondered how Ira and Josiah had handled such agony. How anyone could handle it.

"Did Amabel react when you mentioned the treasure?" she asked Rawlings.

"Not so much as a twitch. She said that Violetta was not only fanciful, but enjoyed manipulating people as well. Created a persona using her stories and her condition." He explained Violetta's medical condition to Harris, who managed to look completely fascinated all over again. "The ME told me the actual term, but it's about twenty syllables long."

Harris tapped a few keys and showed Rawlings his screen. Olivia could read the word "methemoglobinemia" just above the arrow-shaped cursor. "This it?"

"That's the one," Rawlings said. "And as interesting as the condition is, I have no idea if it's relevant to my investigation. What I need and what I'm lacking at this point is a motive." He stared at the images of the blue-skinned people on the computer screen and then gently closed the lid. "We've gone through Violetta's room at The Yellow Lady. Everything appears in order. Lowell still had her props and makeup kit in his car and has given us permission to search and fingerprint the lot."

Olivia was surprised that Rawlings was being so open about the case. He must truly be stymied, must genuinely be in need of help. "What about Hicks? Any anomalies in the file you got from the sheriff?"

Rawlings hesitated and then seemed to come to a decision. "In fact, there was something in the report that troubled me. A few days after Hicks's death, the head of his department at Western Carolina asked that his research be sent to the university. I think they were hoping to find something worthy of publication." He flipped the pages of the notebook he always carried in his shirt pocket. "According to the sheriff's findings, there were no journals or papers in the cabin Hicks was renting, and his computer had disappeared."

Olivia could feel the food sticking in her throat.

"What does that mean?" Harris asked.

"I believe Lowell saw something on that mountain that night. Something that frightened him," Rawlings said with a quiet fierceness. "If I were a betting man, I'd wager that Hicks recorded all of Violetta's stories and pored over them until he believed he had discovered the location of the treasure. And I think he was killed because of his discovery."

Harris snorted. "By a ghost?"

"By Lowell or Dewey Whitt?" Olivia said.

"Then it has to be Dewey," Harris declared. "Violetta pointed out into the audience. The ghost was in front of her. Lowell was behind her."

Rawlings rubbed the bristles on his chin. "Whitt's supposedly on a fishing trip in West Virginia. I spoke with his wife, but I won't cross his name off my list until I talk with him directly. He doesn't carry a cell phone, so I have to wait until he comes home."

Harris ran his hands through his ginger-colored hair. "Well, if the bad guy isn't Dewey, then who stole the professor's research?"

"The same person who came to Oyster Bay to get answers from Violetta," Olivia said. "Someone who couldn't solve the riddles the way Hicks did." She put a hand on the chief's arm. "I know the last thing you need is another fly in the ointment, but Flynn's also from the mountains. He said so at the children's program at Through the Wardrobe." She went on to describe the odd exchange she'd observed between Flynn and Amabel as she was leaving the bookstore.

Rawlings took a few notes and then got to his feet. "I need to get back to work. I only stopped by to spend a little time with you, Olivia." He smiled at Harris. "Having you here was a bonus. Being able to bounce ideas off both of you has given me fresh insight. Do me a favor, Harris, and put that massive brain to work on behalf of the citizens of Oyster Bay. Find me some details on the Devereaux family's heritage, no matter how small."

"I already tracked down a few things," Harris said with false modesty. "I can tell you about them on our way out."

"Good man. Thanks for the meal and the company." Rawlings leaned over and gave Olivia a peck on the cheek. He then ruffled the fur on Haviland's neck and strode from the cottage. Harris collected his things, waved to Olivia, and followed him.

Olivia cleaned up after their meal and walked back to her house. Feeling restless, she paced around the ground floor. The rooms felt empty all of a sudden. They had never felt empty before.

I wish Rawlings had stayed, she thought. *I wish we could sit together and talk until we were both too tired to think. I wish I could fall asleep to the sound of his breaths.*

Taking a notepad and a fresh cocktail out to the deck, she stood at the railing as Haviland trotted over the dunes. The sun had lost some of its intensity, and a low bank of clouds was moving in from the Atlantic at a sluggish pace.

"Could we actually see rain?" she asked the ocean and sniffed the air. It smelled gritty and dry. "Something's got to give," she said darkly, wondering if she'd been talking about the weather or the investigation.

Uncapping her pen, she wrote a list of names on the paper: *Amabel, Lowell, Flynn, Greg, Dewey* and then added the word, *Motive*.

She couldn't think of any reason for Flynn to kill Violetta, so she moved on to Lowell. Money was the most obvious motive, but why would he wait until Violetta was in Oyster Bay to murder her? It made no sense. Perhaps Amabel or Greg was guilty. Maybe they'd chosen this place solely because it was where the retreat was being held. But what of Dewey? Was he really on a fishing trip or was he here? In Oyster Bay?

"Violetta called it her Gethsemane." Olivia set her notepad down and went inside to fetch her mother's Bible. After examining the index, she turned to the fourteenth chapter of the Book of Mark and skimmed to verse thirty-two. Twilight descended as she found the verses about Jesus in the garden. Tracking the red font with her index finger, she read his prayers and the words he spoke to his disciples. She said the last line of the passage aloud: "'Here comes my betrayer!'"

Closing the Bible, she stroked the soft leather cover and stared out at the horizon.

"People don't usually betray strangers," she mused quietly. "In order to betray someone, the person you betray has to trust you. There has to be an existing relationship between the two of you." She thought of Judas's kiss. "You may even love each other."

Something about the Biblical passage evoked an image of Violetta onstage, the blue light shining around her head like a crown of glowing stars. Olivia recalled the power and majesty of her voice and her incredible ability to transport her listeners directly into her stories.

"Who did you love, Violetta? Who did you trust? Who came to kiss you on the cheek before killing you?" Olivia's questions floated away on the dry air.

Far off in the distance, lightning flashed over the water. Olivia saw Haviland abruptly raise his nose and then turn back toward home. When he reached the deck, he gave a vigorous shake of his fur and then pawed at the mat, asking to be let inside.

Olivia slid the door open but did not follow him into the house. She sat on the deck, witnessing a storm gather far offshore. Unfortunately, it was too far away to bring her town any relief.

As night fell, Olivia sipped her scotch, watched the lightning burn the sky, and thought about betrayal.

Chapter 10

Thunder is good. Thunder is impressive. But it is lightning that does the work.

—MARK TWAIN

The next morning Olivia woke to an empty bed. She didn't expect Rawlings to be there, but Haviland wasn't curled up in his usual spot at her feet either. The room felt uncomfortably cold.

Outside her window, the sky was overcast. The pale light leaking through the haze made the water look dull and sluggish. Remembering the storm front that had gathered offshore during the night, Olivia gazed down at the sand, hoping to find it damp from a strong rain, but it was dry and dusty.

As she walked through the hushed house, Olivia found Haviland waiting by the kitchen door. He thumped his tail in greeting and nudged the doorknob with his nose. She let him out, and he spent less than a minute doing his business before sitting on his haunches next to the Range Rover and issuing a single bark. Olivia shook her head.

"Come back inside, Captain. There's no Grumpy's today. You've had way too much pork lately. It's chicken, rice, and veggies for you this morning."

Haviland snorted and turned away from the door. He put his paw in his food bowl and tipped it over in protest.

"After breakfast, we're going to take a walk. We haven't found a single thing for this summer's pickle jar in nearly a month. Something has to be out there."

Olivia fed Haviland and then let him out again. She drank a cup of coffee while perusing the *Gazette* and ate a bowl of Greek yogurt mixed with fresh berries and granola as she listened to the weather report on TV. She dismissed the meteorologist's prediction of a possible afternoon shower, turned off the set, and dressed in sweatpants and an old T-shirt. Grabbing her metal detector and backpack from an exterior storage closet, she headed down the path leading to the water's edge.

As she crested a dune, she paused to inhale a deep lungful of air. It had a slight metallic tinge, and Olivia sensed the only thing the storm had given the town had been this acrid odor and a night filled with flashes of lightning. She was disappointed that the rain had remained out to sea, having wanted to wake to a freshly washed world. Instead, the dust and grit continued to cling to every surface. It would be another day of brown hues and feelings of unquenchable thirst.

Once she and Haviland had walked a mile beyond the lighthouse, Olivia unshouldered the Bounty Hunter and switched it on. Its clicks and beeps sang through her headphones and then immediately fell silent.

Sweeping the device back and forth as she moved over the sand, Olivia wondered if Rawlings had made any progress in the investigation. Her mind then drifted to thoughts of Flynn McNulty. She marveled over how little she truly knew him, even though they'd been lovers for months. Olivia wasn't one to volunteer details about her past, and Flynn hadn't seemed at all curious about her life before he became a part of it. At the time, she'd found his lack of interest refreshing. Living for the moment was all both of them wanted. But now she couldn't help but dwell on his history. Had his beginnings been as humble and difficult as Violetta's? Olivia doubted it. Flynn was always so cavalier. He didn't behave like someone who'd survived hardship. He bore no visible scars.

"So why is he more intriguing now that I know he's from the mountains?" she asked aloud. "Because he might be connected to Violetta? Am I still in her thrall even though she's dead? Was her spell that powerful?" Olivia knew there was no sense denying it. Thoughts of the storyteller were never far from her mind.

Suddenly irritated, Olivia glared at the metal detector's display. It continued to remain stubbornly mute. Once again, the trench shovel she carried in her bag would remain folded. She wouldn't unpack her sieve, and Haviland wouldn't be called to help her dig. The pickle jar would stay empty.

"You always send things for me to find," she complained to the sea. "Why are you holding on to your treasure now?" The regular rhythm of the waves breaking onto the shore told her nothing. Sighing in frustration, Olivia turned back for home.

Haviland jogged ahead, raising his nose every now and then as if the air were still charged with electricity. As he passed beneath the shadow of the lighthouse, he abruptly stopped and pawed an object in the sand.

"Are you after some poor crab?" Olivia drew up alongside Haviland and saw that he was sniffing what appeared to be a tubular-shaped piece of stone. She leaned over and grabbed it with both hands.

"It doesn't feel like a rock," she told Haviland. "More like a shell."

Pivoting the object this way and that, she marveled over

its contrasting textures. The interior was bubbly and glassy, while the exterior felt like sandpaper. Slipping it into her bag, Olivia hurried back home. She filled a glass with ice water and settled in front of the computer to research the mystery object. "It's a fulgurite," she told Haviland excitedly. "Lightning glass. The lightning strikes the sand, fusing the grains together into a tubular form in less than a second. The shape of the lightning is left imprinted in its surface."

Opening her bag, she drew out the fulgurite and cradled it in her palm. One of the ends was jagged, as if the point of the lightning bolt had been forever captured inside. "Petrified lightning," she said, touching the rough exterior in awe. "It just goes to show that everything can be imprisoned. Even something six times hotter than the surface of the sun." She held her treasure for several minutes, fascinated by the way it felt beneath her fingertips. Finally, she rolled her prize in bubble wrap and placed it in her handbag.

Thirty minutes later, Olivia had showered and dressed in a navy cotton sundress. The color reminded her of the deepest parts of the ocean. She usually brightened her ensemble with a necklace of fat silver beads, but the shiny jewelry seemed out of place in the wan daylight, so she left it sitting on the bed.

She'd barely pulled out of the driveway when her cell phone rang. Seeing that it was Rawlings calling, Olivia eased the Range Rover to the shoulder and put the car in park. Haviland barked at the unexpected stop, but Olivia shushed him and answered the phone.

"I wish I had some of your good Kona coffee to start my day," he began.

Olivia admitted that she'd missed having him there that morning and then said, "Any breakthroughs?"

"I'd planned on asking Leona Fairchild a few more questions yesterday, but she was in no shape to answer any. That's why I'm calling, Olivia. Mrs. Fairchild had a heart attack yesterday afternoon. She's stable," he added hastily. "But I know you're fond of her and that you'll probably want to visit her."

Olivia ran her fingers over the fur on Haviland's back. "I'm heading to the hospital now." She was about to hang up and then hesitated. "How are you, Sawyer? Did you sleep at all?"

"A few hours," he said, his voice gravelly with fatigue. "But we've made some progress. For example, we found an interesting connection between Greg Rapson and Lowell Reid."

"Oh?" Olivia fumbled with her headset and, after she finally got it to work, pulled back onto the road.

"Greg taught a class called Human Resources Development to inmates at the jail where Lowell was incarcerated. The purpose of the class was to teach prisoners how to apply and interview for jobs."

Olivia tried to remember if she'd seen Rapson after Violetta's performance, but she'd had no idea who he was at the time, so she was unable to bring forth an image of him in the library lobby. "Was Lowell in the class?"

"He was. We have copies of his transcript."

Olivia was too worried about Leona to process these new facts. All she could think about was that the older woman's health had probably been affected by the stress of having had a murder occur in her beloved library. "I thought Rapson and Amabel were both college professors. And that Rapson didn't live near Violetta. What was he doing teaching a class to convicted criminals?"

"Mr. Rapson teaches at the community college level," Rawlings said. "The pay is lousy, and he takes side jobs whenever he can. Performing is one of them. Teaching inmates is another."

"And did he ever mention that Lowell had once been his student?"

Rawlings snorted. "No, he didn't. Just like Amabel failed to tell us that she was Violetta's older sister. These storytellers certainly keep things close to the chest."

"And Flynn?" Olivia couldn't help but ask. "What's his dark secret?"

"I'm still working on that."

As she was nearing downtown, Olivia knew she had to wrap up their conversation. "Most of the storytellers will be at The Bayside Crab House this evening. Millay's tending bar, and I hope to ingratiate myself enough to get a sense of who these people really are."

Rawlings was silent for a moment. "Your schemes have gone awry in the past, Olivia. Dare I suggest you maintain a safe distance this time?"

"You can suggest it, but I won't listen. Sawyer, I can't. These people tell lies for a living. They jump from one character's skin to another like a troupe of shape-shifters. Millay and I might just be able to peek beneath their masks, and we all have to work together to find Violetta's killer. If we don't, Dixie could be my next friend to suffer a heart attack."

"And I suppose Millay will be pouring with a liberal hand."

Olivia couldn't tell if the chief was amused or irritated. "A very liberal hand."

Rawlings sighed. "In that case, I'd better get back to work. If I solve this thing in time, I can have you to myself tonight and stop you from trying to do my job."

He rang off, and Olivia nabbed a parking spot in front of Decadence. The desserterie was very busy. Inside, patrons sat at little café tables sipping pots of chocolate and enjoying buttery croissants or diminutive cinnamon buns. The room was redolent with the scents of baking bread and the sounds of relaxed chatter.

Shelley Giusti stood behind the counter filling a white box with peanut butter brownies. She looked up from her task and waved at Olivia. The customer waiting for the brownies turned and smiled in delight. It was Jeannie, Rawlings' older sister.

"Olivia!" she exclaimed. "You've caught me giving in to my guilty pleasure."

"We all have them," Olivia said gesturing around the shop. "And no one here looks too unhappy about it." Her eyes roamed over the items in the display cases. Everything was beautifully made and artfully arranged.

Jeannie watched her. "I'm glad you cave in to a temptation from time to time. With your figure, it's hard to imagine you eating a whole box of brownies. Me, on the other hand, I'll eat half of those the second I get them home." She laughed heartily.

Olivia grinned. She was quite fond of Jeannie. Sawyer's sister was one of the most cheerful, easygoing, and kindhearted people Olivia had ever met. She was also fiercely loyal to her family, and Olivia admired the older woman's combination of sweetness and steel. Jeannie laughed loudly, ate with gusto, and was friendly to everyone she met.

"How can I help you today, Ms. Limoges?" Shelley asked, handing Jeannie her purchase.

"I need the biggest box of assorted chocolates you have," Olivia said and pointed at the menu tacked to the wall. "That one called Versailles should do it."

Jeannie hooted. "There's over a hundred pieces in that gold box! Are you and Sawyer having a special evening?" She put her hand over her heart. "Oh, I sure do hope so. He needs you, hon. Sawyer's been alone for far too long, and we all know that men are lousy at being alone."

"That's absolutely true," agreed Shelley amiably and put on a fresh plastic glove. "Which chocolates would you like?"

Olivia gave her a plaintive shrug. "Would you choose? They all look wonderful." She fidgeted impatiently while Shelley placed pieces of chocolate into the box, handling each one with the utmost delicacy.

"This is my new favorite," Shelley said putting two samples on a doily. "Dark chocolate blended with dried cherries and minced pecans, finishing with a note of chipotle."

Jeannie immediately popped hers into her mouth. Seeing Olivia hesitate, she elbowed her in the ribs. "Go on, girl. Jump in with both feet. Laugh too loudly. Sing in the shower. Eat the chocolate. Live a little!" She giggled. "I'm messing with you because you already feel like one of the family. And I hope you will be a Rawlings someday soon!" She squeezed Olivia on the arm, winked at Shelley, and left.

Blushing, Olivia bit the chocolate in half before Shelley could ask any questions. She barely noticed the creamy bittersweet chocolate or the sweetness of the cherries followed by a hint of heat. She couldn't stop thinking of how she'd feel about being called Olivia Rawlings. Clearing her throat, she tapped the counter to get Shelley's attention. "Actually, you'd better make up two orders of the Versailles."

Shelley raised her brows in surprise. "That *is* decadent."

"I'm bringing them to the hospital. A friend of mine had a heart attack."

"I'm so sorry," Shelley said with genuine sympathy. She then glanced at the golden box in her hand. "I don't want to dissuade you from parting with your money, but will she be allowed to eat these?"

"Oh, they're not for her. They're for the nurses. I want to make sure she has the best care possible."

Pausing in the middle of arranging the last chocolate in

the box, Shelley said, "Ah, that's clever. Very clever. The whole staff will be tripping over themselves to see to your friend's needs. She's going to be treated like a queen." Shelley examined her handiwork and frowned. "Maybe I should take out all the ones flavored with liquor."

Olivia knew she couldn't stay at the hospital long. Haviland wasn't allowed inside, and even in the shaded parking garage with the Range Rover's windows cracked and a full water bowl at his disposal, the poodle would quickly grow uncomfortable in the summer heat. It took forever to find someone who could provide her with Leona's room number, so she was already irritated by the time she had to wait while the elevator doors were held open for some sort of robot to drive itself into the cab.

"That's Roxie," said a man in blue scrubs when he saw Olivia staring at the robot. "She delivers meds on all the patient floors. She's basically a moving set of drawers."

Roxie was about the height and width of the trashcans lining Oyster Bay's sidewalks. With the exception of a single lock, the front of her cabinet was smooth. On her back, she displayed a sign cautioning people not to share the elevator with her.

Olivia pointed at the sign. "Should we leave?"

The man shook his head. "Nah. They just don't want anyone to tamper with her."

"Please do not get too close," Roxie announced in a no-nonsense monotone as she boarded the elevator. "I like my personal space."

That made Olivia smile. When the elevator came to a stop on the third floor, Olivia and the man in scrubs disembarked while Roxie warned people to keep their distance.

Olivia went straight to the nurses' station and asked to see Leona.

"You can go right in," the nurse said, pointing off to the side. "Down that hall. Fourth door to the left."

"Are you her nurse?"

The woman nodded. "Janet and I are on until seven."

"How's she doing?"

"Ms. Fairchild's recovering nicely. And we love having her on the floor. She's the perfect patient. Wish they were all like her."

Olivia sighed in relief and presented the woman with the chocolates. "These are for you and Janet and anyone else who takes care of Leona. She's a special lady."

The nurse's eyes went wide when she opened one of the boxes. "Lord have mercy! We'll be in an insulin coma after this." Despite her comment, she was clearly thrilled over the gift. "I promise to share, but only after I pick out my favorites." Thanking Olivia, she carried the boxes into the break room, humming as she walked.

Olivia approached Leona's door with less confidence. She disliked hospitals and her bedside manner was lousy, so she was pleased to find Leona sitting up in bed with an open book on her lap. She looked quite normal for someone who'd just had a heart attack.

"Knock, knock," Olivia said, hesitating in the doorway.

Leona pulled off her reading glasses and grinned. "Why, Olivia! What in heaven's name are you doing here?"

"What are *you* doing here?" Olivia said in return. She entered the room and took a seat in the chair near the bed. "You're not supposed to have a heart attack. You're supposed to reign behind that circulation desk for the next hundred years."

Leona gave a wry chuckle. "It's hard when the people

you've known all your life start getting old. Makes *you* feel old, doesn't it?"

Olivia considered this. "I don't have an issue with aging. It's the way time seems to be passing too quickly. Like it speeds up every year."

Leona nodded. "That's why you have to savor those little moments of beauty now. You have to spend as many hours as you can with the people that make you laugh."

"No wonder you only want to have dinner with me once a month," Olivia joked. Leona chortled, but the humor vanished almost instantly from her face and she reached for Olivia's hand. "I'm glad you're here. Not only because you came to visit a silly and stubborn old woman, but because I need to tell you something."

Olivia curled her fingers around Leona's, doing her best to avoid the IV lines. "Okay."

"It's about the other night." Leona had to pause and start again. "When Violetta was killed."

Saying nothing, Olivia nodded in encouragement.

"I've thought of little else since then. That's probably why I'm wearing a paper gown that doesn't cover a quarter of my ample backside." She tried to produce a smile but failed. "You see, Chief Rawlings asked me to think about where I was twenty minutes after the performance's conclusion. I've reviewed my actions over and over since giving my statement, and nothing seemed significant. But yesterday, I was feeling restless and out of sorts, so I took a walk and that's when I remembered an unusual detail."

Leona fell silent, and it was clear to Olivia that she was gathering herself to say something that had the potential to alter another person's fate. The words, once spoken, couldn't be retracted, and Leona wouldn't inflict that kind of damage upon someone without hesitating first. And that's when

Olivia realized that she must know the individual in question. Otherwise, Leona would have just come right out and said what she'd seen.

Olivia squeezed Leona's hand gently. "You can't help what you bore witness to. You were just there."

"That's right. I just happened to be at that place at that moment," she agreed and sighed heavily. "It was Flynn McNulty. That's the person I saw. He was entering the men's restroom about twenty minutes after the rest of the audience had relocated to the lobby. I only know how much time elapsed because of how quickly the crab cakes had disappeared. Spotting the empty platter on the buffet table, I checked my watch, thinking that the town's highbrow residents were greedy little pigs, and went back to the kitchen to inform the caterer."

"And then?" Olivia could feel her skin turning clammy, especially where her flesh touched Leona's, but she couldn't have moved her hand if she wanted to. Her body was frozen, waiting. Olivia was certain that after Leona spoke again, she would no longer be able to view her former lover as a harmless, easygoing bibliophile. In another moment, Flynn McNulty was about to transform into something else. A stranger. Perhaps even a killer.

"The detail I keep fixating on is this: Flynn didn't go into the restroom from the direction of the lobby. He entered from the other end of the hallway. The part leading to the conference room."

"Did he see you?"

Leona shook her head. "He was fiddling with his tie, and to say that he looked distressed is an understatement. Considering how successful our big-ticket event was, he should have been glowing. But there was a shadow hanging over him. I know that sounds like a phrase from an Edwardian novel, but it's an accurate description."

Olivia couldn't speak for a full minute. She could think of nothing else but Flynn's tie. Had he used it to hold a plastic bag in place around Violetta's neck? Had he stood behind her, his arm muscles stretched and taut, as her lungs burned and her body bucked and twisted? "The chief needs to hear this," she said eventually.

Leona nodded gravely. "Would you call him? And stay with me while we talk? I know it's asking—"

"Very little," Olivia assured her. "But I'm going to get in touch with him on my way to the parking garage. I'll put the A/C on for Haviland until Rawlings arrives. I don't want Haviland to overheat in the car. Is that all right?"

"Of course. I know how you dote on that animal." Leona tightened her grip on Olivia's hand. "Your mother and I always thought you'd grow up to become like one of our favorite heroines from classic literature, but you're more complex than any of them. Don't stop your character development now. Let my health scare be a lesson to you. Take a risk, my girl. While you have the time, take the biggest risk of all."

Olivia escaped before Leona could continue.

"Is the entire town colluding to get Rawlings to move in with me?" she mumbled in the hallway, nearly bumping into Roxie in her haste to reach the elevator. "You'll have to take the next one," she told the robot and closed the doors on the machine.

In the parking lot, she called Rawlings and told him what Leona had seen. "I'll be there in forty minutes," he said, which meant he was leaving immediately. Oyster Bay wasn't large enough to support a hospital, so the residents traveled to New Bern for their major medical needs.

Olivia used the time to take Haviland to a pet boutique on Middle Street. She bought her poodle a generous amount of Sam's Yams, a package of Buddy Biscuits, and for waiting patiently in the car while she visited Leona, he was also treated to a granola "Pupcake."

After a brief walk, Olivia returned to the hospital parking lot. Haviland had exercised and snacked, and Olivia hoped he'd take a nap while she was with Leona and the chief. She sat right next to Leona's bed while the librarian gave her statement to Rawlings. He stood near the window and listened without interrupting. When Leona was done, he asked her a few questions and then told her he'd like to have an officer type up her statement when she was feeling better.

"I know that was difficult for you and that you and Mr. McNulty are friendly," Rawlings said, gazing at Leona kindly. "Thank you for speaking with me, especially in your current condition."

"With this new stent, my condition's just fine," she said, brushing the notion aside. "Though I confess that I'm very tired now that I've unburdened myself to you."

Rawlings got to his feet. "That happens. But you've done the right thing, so rest now because I hope to see you back at the library soon. You're one of Oyster Bay's institutions. We couldn't do without you."

"Nonsense," Leona protested but looked pleased all the same. She waved them both out of her room, and Olivia promised to call the next morning.

Rawlings walked Olivia to her car.

"Do you think Flynn is capable of murder?" she asked, opening her door and peering in to check on Haviland.

Rawlings leaned on the doorframe and studied her. "You're more qualified to answer that question than I am," he said. "I don't know the man, and one of my officers took his statement on Saturday."

"Apparently, I don't know him either," she said, feeling suddenly defensive. "What we had—we didn't peer below the surface, okay? What about your research into his background?"

"So far, we've made two relevant discoveries. The first is this: in his midtwenties, Mr. McNulty worked for Dexter Pharmaceuticals in Banner Elk, a town less than an hour from the Devereuxes' home. Five years later, he was promoted to a sales position at Dexter's headquarters in Research Triangle Park. He worked there until an elderly aunt died, leaving him the majority of her money. Retiring from Dexter at the ripe age of forty-five, McNulty used his savings and the boon from his aunt to buy Through the Wardrobe and his house in Oyster Bay. His financials indicate that the shop is operating in the red. He's in danger of losing it if he doesn't make a significant payment to the bank soon."

Olivia winced at the unwelcome news. Suddenly, there was too much of that. Too much negativity and doubt. She didn't want the bookstore to be in trouble. She didn't want her former lover to be a killer. She didn't want Rawlings to call Flynn "Mr. McNulty." He only used surnames when referring to suspects. Normally, she admired the way he treated everyone with equal respect, but right now the formality angered her. "So that's his motive, I suppose. The sinking ship that is our town's only bookstore."

"Nothing's clear at this point," Rawlings said gently. "If Violetta had been in possession of something truly valuable, then yes, perhaps we'd have a motive. But at this point, the theory that she owned some sort of priceless treasure is nothing more than that. A theory. A story."

Olivia felt herself growing more incensed. "If she wasn't killed over the treasure, then what? She was a storyteller, for Christ's sake. An entertainer from the sticks."

"She was also very beautiful," Rawlings reminded her.

"Yes," Olivia agreed after she took a moment to calm

down. "Enchantingly so." She stared at Rawlings, willing her anger to abate. "Did Violetta sell plants to Dexter Pharmaceuticals? Did Mabel? Has Flynn known them all along?"

Rawlings shook his head. "I don't know yet. Two of my officers are with Amabel now. They have orders to—" He was interrupted by the ringing of his cell phone. He answered it, and Olivia watched as tension stole the color from his face, thinning his lips and causing the muscles in his jaw to contract. "I'm on my way."

"What is it?" Olivia demanded. She gripped the steering wheel until her knuckles turned white, waiting for what she sensed was more bad news.

"It's Dixie," he said. "She says that Lowell's gone. Not gone as in he's fled, but gone as in—"

"Missing," Olivia finished for him. "He's gone missing."

Chapter 11

~~~~~~

Drinking is a way of ending the day.

—ERNEST HEMINGWAY

Olivia followed Rawlings as he pulled out of the hospital parking lot, his cruiser's light bar sparkling like a beacon in front of her. He drove above the speed limit but didn't use the siren. As soon as he passed the sign welcoming visitors to Oyster Bay, he turned the lights off and slowed down.

Behind him, Olivia banged the Range Rover's wheel in exasperation. "Come on, Rawlings! This could be an emergency!"

But then she saw the line of cyclists riding on the shoulder adjacent to a group of mothers pushing jogging strollers and knew the chief had been prudent to reduce his speed. On a beautiful summer day in July, tourists were everywhere. They drove their rental cars at a sluggish pace, looking for street signs or parking spots, and waited patiently while a gang of teenagers wearing earbuds and sunglasses sauntered across the intersection without bothering to check for oncoming traffic.

Haviland barked at the teens as Olivia drove past, and a

few of the boys lifted their heads and howled in response. This sent Haviland into a tizzy, and he barked in indignation while Olivia drove around in search of a parking space. In the end, she pulled into the loading zone a block away from Grumpy's.

When she and Haviland finally burst into the diner, it was eerily quiet. The Closed sign had been hung, and the lights in the dining room were off. Dixie was perched on a counter stool with a cup of coffee in her hand and a vacant look in her eyes. Grumpy stood behind the counter, still wearing his stained apron. The brim of his "Made in the USA" baseball cap was pulled low over his brow.

Olivia took the empty stool next to Dixie and, without speaking, gave her a fierce, one-armed hug.

"Let's start with what we know. Mr. Reid was supposed to meet your boys two hours ago?" Rawlings asked. "At your house?"

"Yes," Dixie said in a hoarse voice. "The fishin' gear was laid out and all ready to go. Lowell even bought live bait. That's the main reason my kids thought somethin' was wrong. The pail of minnows was tipped over, and every single one of them was dead. Lowell was pretty cheap, but he said he was gonna go all out for the boys today. He packed a cooler with sodas and sandwiches, but that was spilled too. The ice was all melted. Everythin' went to waste."

Rawlings took a note. "Was anyone else at home with Mr. Reid?"

Grumpy shook his head. "The older kids have summer jobs. The youngest two, the boys, have been at the YMCA camp since school got out, but we told them they could skip the afternoon session to go fishing with their uncle. They went home on the Y bus, but he wasn't there to meet them."

"Was Mr. Reid acting peculiar? Either yesterday evening or this morning?" Rawlings wanted to know.

"Please call him Lowell. And yes, my cousin's been a nutcase since Saturday," Dixie said without hesitating. "Looks out the window every other minute like someone's comin' to get him. He's made me a nervous wreck." She pinched her thumb and index finger together. "I came this close to shippin' the kids off to friends' houses for the week, but Lowell promised to sleep out in the woods to keep any danger away from the rest of us."

Grumpy made a dismissive noise. "He pitched a tent right next to the dog kennel, but he's barely used it. He was on the sofa when I got up this morning."

"What about the dogs?" Olivia asked. "Did the boys mention how the dogs acted?"

Dixie glanced at her in surprise. "We've been lettin' them run loose. Grumpy thought they should have free range for as long as Lowell stayed with us. You know, just in case someone came pokin' around. But they didn't have a piece of some strange guy's pants hangin' out of their mouths, if that's what you mean." She turned back to Rawlings. "The boys said that Lowell's stuff is still in his car, and the keys are under the visor. It's just him that's gone."

"And his cell phone?"

Grumpy produced his own. "We've both called him a bunch. No answer."

Rawlings studied his notepad. "I think we're dealing with two possible scenarios. The first is that Mr. Reid, uh, Lowell, got into a car belonging to someone he knows and that the dogs are responsible for the spilled bait and cooler. The second possibility is that he was taken against his will."

Dixie put her hands over her eyes, but Grumpy gently pulled them off. He held her small hands in his massive ones and forced her to meet his gaze. "No chance he was grabbed with the dogs out, Dixie. They know he's family." He looked at Rawlings. "Lowell had to have gone by choice. He'd had to have told the dogs to back down. And we've got a loaded shotgun behind the front door. All of our kids know how to use it and so does Lowell."

"But who does he know in Oyster Bay?" Olivia asked and glanced at Rawlings. "Do you think he drove off with Greg Rapson?"

Dixie frowned. "Who's that?"

"One of the storytellers in town for the retreat," Rawlings explained. "He taught a class at the jail where Lowell was incarcerated. Your cousin was one of Mr. Rapson's students."

"Lowell's been to more than one jail, Chief," Dixie grumbled. "Was this the most recent place? In the western part of the state?"

Rawlings nodded.

"That's when he promised he was gonna straighten up." Dixie sighed. "He took all kinds of classes, read books, and when his sentence was up, he landed that job with Violetta. I thought he was gonna be okay. That everything would be okay. Until he came here. Until he brought somethin' evil to our door . . ."

"Let's go back to your place," Rawlings suggested and slid off his stool. "I'd like to take a look around. In the meantime, I'll call this in and have my officers keep an eye out for Lowell."

Olivia noticed that he didn't try to comfort Dixie or offer her any assurance that Lowell was all right. His failure to do so told Olivia that he took Lowell's disappearance seriously.

"I'll lock up real quick," Grumpy said and went into the kitchen, Dixie's untouched coffee cup in his hand.

Olivia followed Rawlings to the door. Haviland lingered, nudging Dixie's leg with his nose. She buried her face in his fur, running her hands along his strong back. "Are you going to call Greg Rapson?"

"No," Rawlings said. "I need to examine the scene first. Grumpy's right. Between the dogs and the gun, it would have been very difficult to have taken Mr. Lowell against his will."

Olivia felt chilled. "And yet you're calling their home a scene."

Rawlings waved his hand in dismissal. "Only out of habit. The man could be anywhere, Olivia. For all we know, he could be hanging out in a bar with the other storytellers. He must know quite a few of them after working with Violetta."

"You don't believe that he's having tea and crumpets with them any more than I do," Olivia said softly, not wanting Dixie to overhear. "Lowell was scared. He wanted to run, to hide. Because he poses a threat to someone. He saw a killer that night on the mountain, and he must know something about Violetta's treasure or whatever you want to call it. She trusted Lowell with the secret of her blue skin, right? So what other secrets did she trust him to keep?"

Rawlings considered her words. "The manner in which Violetta was killed makes me believe that her attacker wanted her to be aware of the fact that she was about to die. He might have pretended that she would live if she did as she was told or provided him with information. But he came prepared with that plastic bag. He was always going to murder her. If Mr. Reid knows something of import, then he was a fool not to tell me, because Violetta's killer has had time to prepare for a second interrogation. *If* that's what's going on here. Right now all I have are a few dead minnows."

Olivia pictured the tiny fish flopping about on the brittle grass, their gills pulsing as the last of their precious water was sucked into the thirsty ground. "What should I do?"

"Stick with your plans for this evening. Find out how the storytellers spent their afternoon. Find out which of them know Mr. Reid. Listen to their gossip and banter and watch their faces. And when they've had plenty to drink, ask them about Violetta. And the treasure." He held up a warning finger. "But don't leave the restaurant before calling me first. I don't want you going back to your place alone."

Olivia nodded and then glanced over her shoulder at Dixie. "Find Lowell, Sawyer. Find him alive. For her sake."

"I'll try," he promised and left the diner.

Too restless to go home, Olivia bought an iced coffee from the frozen yogurt shop and then took Haviland to the park. He chased squirrels and other dogs while she sat on a bench and thought back on Violetta's performance. Using the small notebook she always carried in her purse, she wrote down any phrases she could remember that weren't from the Jack tales.

Olivia recorded the part in which Violetta spoke of her father's warning not to tell a certain story and of how she would soon be turned into a ghost. "She seemed to accept that fate," Olivia murmured to herself. "To welcome it even. Why?" Fixing her gaze in the middle distance, she was transported into the dark room again. She could hear Violetta's powerful voice and see the blue light shining on the beautiful woman with the raven hair.

"The last story had the most clues," she mused as Haviland barked a hello to a familiar golden retriever. "The one about the man who acted like a bear. The man who hid his treasure in the hollowed-out tree trunk."

Suddenly, she froze. "The trunk. What if it's not a tree at all?" Digging through her purse, she pulled out her cell phone and called Rawlings.

"I can't talk right now," he said without preamble.

Ignoring him, she demanded, "What's happened? Is it Lowell?"

Rawlings didn't reply, and the white noise coming through the phone indicated that he was moving. "I'm at the hospital again. Mr. Reid was found in the marsh south of the docks. A fisherman saw his body half submerged in a cluster of cattails. Luckily, the man works as a volunteer firefighter and administered CPR. After coughing up a lungful of water, Mr. Reid was able to breathe on his own, but he hasn't regained consciousness."

"Jesus." Olivia sagged against the bench. "How's Dixie? Should I come over?"

"Please don't," Rawlings said tersely. "There's enough confusion as it is, and I need to speak with the Weavers one-on-one."

Olivia hated not being able to act. She also hated the image of Dixie pacing the waiting room while a medical team worked on her cousin. Even with Grumpy positioned like a silent sentinel at her side, Dixie would feel scared and alone. "Will Lowell live?"

"I don't know. His condition is serious." There was another rustling through the phone speaker. "I need to go, Olivia."

"Wait! I called because I wanted to know if you still have Violetta's prop trunk at the station."

"We do. Why?"

For a moment, Olivia wondered if her idea was ridiculous but decided there was nothing to lose by voicing it. "What if the hollow where the treasure was hidden wasn't inside a tree trunk at all? What if the clue refers to Violetta's wooden trunk? The one holding her props and makeup?"

Rawlings spoke over a cacophony of sounds including the ringing of phones and a voice crackling through the hospital's intercom system. "It's possible. I'll call and have someone check it out."

"Are you going to question Greg Rapson?"

"I have no cause to bring him in at this time," Rawlings said. "Unless Mr. Reid wakes up and can talk about what happened or his medical team provides me with tangible evidence that another person was involved in his near drowning, I have to treat this as a case of misadventure. If Mr. Rapson shows up at The Bayside Crab House tonight, perhaps he'll tell you how he spent his afternoon."

The implication was clear. If Rapson had anything to do with Lowell's so-called accident, then she and Millay would have to find out what he'd done.

"Call me when you can," she said. "And tell Dixie—"

"She's all right," he interrupted. "Her kids are here, but I'll let her know you offered to come." And with that, he was gone.

Olivia called for Haviland to heel and then strode to her car with an angry, determined gait. She didn't like being told what to do, even though she knew Rawlings was right. Her place was at the restaurant and his was at the hospital. They each had their duty to perform if they wanted to catch a killer.

At home, Olivia took her second shower of the day. She tried to force her simmering fury down the drain with the dirt and the dust, but it clung to her like a second skin. She dressed in a gauzy white skirt and a low-cut silk top the color of persimmons, and practiced her smile in the mirror. Though her mouth curved upward and her teeth showed, the smile never reached her eyes.

"It'll have to do," she told her reflection. "For once in your life, you need to be charming."

Just before leaving, she made a call to Fred Yoder. Though she hadn't known the antique dealer long, she trusted him implicitly. She also wanted another person present who could help her figure out if Violetta's treasure was real or fictional. Fred had heard dozens of stories about hidden valuables, and she sensed that he'd be better able to tell if Violetta's grandfather had brought something with him from New York or if Violetta had merely been spinning another tale. That is if any of the other storytellers knew more about the mystery of the treasure than she did. Like Amabel, for instance.

"I thought Violetta's performance was spellbinding," she explained to Fred after they'd exchanged pleasantries. "But to some of the other storytellers, and perhaps even to her sister, she used her talent to bend people to her will."

"Isn't that what all skillful entertainers do?" Fred asked with a laugh. "In any case, I'd be glad to help. I haven't had much luck coming up with an obvious answer as to what the Devereaux family treasure could be, but my best guess is that it's rare coins, stamps, or jewelry. Loose gemstones perhaps. Something portable and easy to hide."

Once again, Olivia thought about Violetta's prop trunk. She wondered if Rawlings had had one of his men examine its interior. Fred would have proved useful in that regard as well. When he sat down next to her at the bar at The Bayside Crab House, she told him about her theory, and he immediately shared several anecdotes about finding secret niches in furniture, boxes, and canes.

"You said that the trunk has a domed lid and was lined with some sort of velvet fabric, right?" When Olivia nodded, Fred grew more animated. "Many of the old steamer trunks were lined with paper. If the material you saw was in really good condition, then chances are it's not the original lining."

Olivia thought back on what she'd seen. "It was a deep blue velvet. The same color as Violetta's eyes."

"Then it's probably newer than the trunk itself," Fred said and smiled as Millay came over to take their order.

Fred asked for a beer on tap, and Olivia requested a glass

of Perrier. "But make it look like a gin and tonic. I have to appear to be boozing it up." She glanced up as a group of people approached the hostess stand. "Ah, the storytellers have arrived. Time for me to relocate to a table. Fred, I'll ask you to join us after they've had a couple of drinks. When we're ready to raise the topic of treasure, I'll pull up a chair for you."

Fred gave her a little salute. "Until then, I'll be happily watching the baseball game and enjoying this excellent microbrew."

"Look. Rapson's with them," Millay muttered to Olivia, her gaze locked on the storytellers. "If he's the one who went after Lowell, then he's got stones of steel coming here for booze and crab legs a few hours later."

Fred raised his brows. "Stones of steel?"

"Millay has a way with words," Olivia quipped, pasted on her best smile, and went to greet her guests.

Altogether, there were six of them. Olivia recognized Amabel and Greg, and during the short walk to their table, she learned that the woman who'd worn the turquoise caftan to Violetta's performance was named Sue. She worked at an animal shelter and was the mother of three. The man who'd held the carved walking stick that same evening was a dental hygienist from Florida. He'd never met Violetta before this retreat, and his eyes filled with tears when Olivia mentioned her.

"She was amazing," he said after a waitress served him a drink. "Let's raise our glasses to Violetta Devereaux!"

Olivia watched the rest of the group as they lifted tumblers or martini and margarita glasses. Amabel's mouth was pinched at the corners, and Greg's eyes were veiled and impenetrable. Both Sue and Kenneth, the dental hygienist, wore solemn expressions. The other woman, who introduced herself as Mariah and reeked of marijuana, swayed in her chair and started to hum.

"Please, Mariah," said the man sitting next to her. He wore a tight T-shirt that accentuated his enormous biceps and sculpted chest. "Don't start singing 'Lucy in the Sky With Diamonds' again."

"But Violetta was the girl with the kaleidoscope eyes," Mariah protested dreamily.

Olivia silently agreed. Violetta had an otherworldly quality about her, and her blue gaze had been filled with starlight.

"She was an entertainer. A fine one I'll grant you, but she wasn't a saint or an angel or a goddess," the man argued good-naturedly. "Now get that drink down your throat before it melts."

Mariah took a gulp of her piña colada.

"A goddess?" Amabel scoffed, rubbing the salt off the rim of her margarita glass with her pinkie. "That's how the media will portray her. She was always a media darling."

The conversation turned from Violetta to newspaper reviews, and by the time the storytellers had started in on a second round of drinks and a platter of calamari, Olivia discovered that the man seated beside Mariah was a personal trainer named Ian. Ian lived in South Carolina and claimed to be Violetta's biggest fan.

"I've followed her all over the country," he admitted outright. "She's the reason I got into this crazy life in the first place. I see hot women all the time in my line of work, but none of them could hold a candle to her."

Millay appeared. After serving the storytellers their third round of drinks, she took a seat. "I'm officially on break," she announced and gave them a conspiratorial wink. "And no worries about the tab. It's taken care of. This is your night to be treated like kings and queens."

"That'll be a first," Amabel groused, but her cohorts clapped and hooted, and Olivia was pleased to see that

Millay's heavy-handed pouring was having the desired effect. The group was becoming less inhibited. Greg openly leered at Millay's cleavage, Mariah pulled out the chopsticks holding her hair in place, freeing a mass of wild auburn curls, and Ian challenged Kenneth to an arm-wrestling match.

"Aren't you supposed to be working?" Amabel asked Olivia, her gaze sharp despite the fact that she'd already tossed back two shots of whiskey.

The woman can hold her liquor, Olivia thought grimly. "I'm one of the managers. Trust me, this isn't the first time I've spent my shift in the bar. It's one of the few perks of being in the restaurant business. When interesting people come to town, I hang out with them and make sure they're given the best possible service." She gave Amabel a little smile and then reached for a calamari.

Olivia fell silent and let Millay work her magic. She plied the storytellers with questions about their craft and subtly flattered each of them in turn. She even pretended not to notice when Greg brushed his elbow against her arm or breast, skillfully steering the conversation back to the topic of Violetta again and again.

"But who would have killed her?" Millay asked Greg, her dark eyes guileless. "Did she sleep with the wrong guy or something?"

A shadow passed across Greg's face, and he immediately shifted his body away from Millay's.

Ian gave a theatrical sigh. "She was so beautiful that she could have had any man she wanted. But she never got married or brought a guy to any of our retreats. And I didn't see her hanging out with anyone special here."

"But *I* did," Mariah declared triumphantly. "Well, I didn't see him, but I *heard* him. Violetta had a man in her hotel room Thursday night." Her speech was slightly slurred.

"And he didn't come to talk either. My room's right next to hers so I got an earful. Violetta's lover was *very* passionate. Lots of stamina." She stroked Ian's huge bicep and gave him a suggestive smile.

"Who was her mystery man?" Millay asked.

Mariah shrugged. "She didn't exactly call out his name, sweetheart." Giggling, she took another sip of her drink.

Olivia decided she'd better have some food brought to the table or the storytellers would become too inebriated to talk. She signaled a waiter who returned to the table several minutes later carrying servings of roasted shrimp cocktail with a spicy orange-tomato dipping sauce. By the time the shrimp cocktail was gone and the group had been given a salad tossed with fresh avocado and mango, Olivia still couldn't tell if any of the men at the table had been with Violetta Thursday night. Not one of them had given themselves away with a guilty glance or a fleeting look of anguish.

If not them, then who? Olivia thought. *Lowell? Had he been his boss's lover? Or had Violetta invited someone from her past to her room? Grumpy? Flynn?*

Olivia didn't want to imagine either scenario, but she knew she and Millay had stumbled upon a significant detail. Violetta had been with someone two nights before her murder.

"So she had sex with someone," Olivia said to Millay. "Big deal. Some guy wanted her and she wanted him. The real question is, who *didn't* like her? Who hated her enough to make sure she'd never tell another story?"

"That's what I don't understand," Kenneth said with feeling. "She was the best of us. Who'd want to silence her?"

Amabel dropped her fork against her salad plate. "The best of us? Please. She had a voice that carried and a nifty blue light. That's about it. Any of us could do what she did. As a matter of fact, I intend to do just that."

"You do have the same eyes," Greg pointed out, and Amabel shot him a dirty look before tossing back another shot of whiskey.

"Wow, that's true!" Sue exclaimed. "You could almost pass for her sister."

Amabel glared at the other storyteller. "Yeah. Almost."

"You didn't like Violetta, did you?" Mariah pointed her bread knife at Amabel. "You're just oozing negative energy. Are you one of those women who can't handle it when another female rises to the top?"

Olivia could have kissed Mariah.

"If the woman deserves to rise, then I'm all for it," Amabel said, sneering. "If she's not worthy of her laurels, then I tend to be resentful. And Violetta wasn't worthy."

"Why not?" Ian wanted to know. "She was a poor girl who made good."

"She was as cold as a winter night," Amabel whispered. "She stepped over people on her way out of those mountains. She broke people and never looked back to see the damage she'd done."

A hushed silence fell over the group. Olivia and Millay exchanged excited gazes, and Olivia found that she was holding her breath. They were on the cusp of a revelation, she was certain of it.

But before anyone else could speak, Amabel's attention was drawn to the hostess stand. Olivia followed her gaze and saw Flynn McNulty give the hostess a friendly pat on the shoulder before heading in their direction. His gait was awkward and his eyes glinted dangerously.

"He's hammered," Millay said softly.

When Flynn walked right over to Olivia and threw his arms around her, she knew that Millay was correct. Flynn smelled like the inside of Fish Nets at the end of a long, hot Saturday night. She tried to pry his arms off, but they wouldn't budge. "Olivia! Gorgeous, sexy, brilliant Olivia!" He kissed her on the cheek. Once. Twice. Wet, sloppy kisses. "Do I owe you my thanks for the grilling I was given by your boyfriend? For two hours! Hm?" He traced the line of her jaw with his finger. Olivia jerked her head away and managed to extricate herself from his embrace.

"Stop it, Flynn. You're drunk. Now sit." She shoved him toward the chair Millay had pulled out.

He dropped into the seat with a laugh. "So what are you doing with these fine folks? Conducting a little undercover work for the Oyster Bay Police Department?"

Amabel stared at Olivia suspiciously. "I thought you worked here."

Flynn threw back his head and let out a humorless laugh. Helping himself to Greg's drink, he finished it in three swallows and then pointed at Olivia. "She owns the whole place, Amabel. This is Olivia Limoges. Restaurateur. Socialite. Heiress. Patron to the arts. Girlfriend to the chief of police." Looking around at the storytellers' shocked faces, he chortled. "Oh, she didn't mention any of those things?"

"I'm trying to find out who killed Violetta," Olivia said simply, never taking her eyes from Flynn. "You only care about yourself, but—"

"What do you know?" he asked, roughly grabbing her arm. "What the hell do you know?" His fingertips pressed into her flesh, but she refused to let him see that he was hurting her. "I loved her," he whispered so softly that Olivia barely heard him.

And then Fred was standing over Flynn. He put his hand on Flynn's shoulder and spoke in a loud, clear voice. "I think you should let go of the lady now."

Surprised, Flynn looked down at Olivia's arm. "Yeah . . . sorry . . . I didn't . . ." He held out his hands in surrender. "Sorry."

Shoving his chair back, he got up, took a moment to steady himself, and then lurched toward the hostess stand. A young woman holding a stack of menus darted out of the way just as Flynn stumbled over the base of the sign reading, "Please Wait to Be Seated."

Luckily, a tall ginger-haired man caught hold of Flynn before he completely lost his balance.

Millay swore under her breath. "As if we didn't have enough drama, in walks Harris."

Chapter 12

Where you used to be, there is a hole in the
world, which I find myself constantly walking
around in the daytime, and falling in at night.

—EDNA ST. VINCENT MILLAY

Everyone at the table watched as Harris helped Flynn regain his balance. Once he stood upright again, Flynn clapped Harris on the back, produced a wobbly smile for the customers waiting to be seated, and strode out of the restaurant. After a moment's hesitation, Harris followed him.

As soon as the two men were gone, Amabel turned to Olivia. "How dare you?" she hissed, furious. "We came here tonight thinking we were being treated to a meal by a fan of our art form. Instead, you invited us to dinner in order to spy on us for the police?"

"I'm not ashamed of my actions," Olivia replied heatedly. "A woman has been murdered. Violetta Devereaux was invited to Oyster Bay to attend the same retreat as the rest of you." She waved her hand, incorporating all the storytellers in the gesture. "Now she's dead, and inexplicably, none of you seem to know a thing about it." Her eyes blazing, she stared at Amabel. "Her ending was a cruel one too."

"Aren't you guys worried about your own safety?" Millay

demanded. "No one's been taken into custody, so the person sitting next to you could be a killer. If it were me, I'd be propping furniture against my hotel room door at night."

Mariah squeaked and Ian patted her hand. "Nothing's going to happen to you."

Sue looked from one storyteller to the next. "I never thought about any of us being in danger. Who'd want to hurt me? I'm just a performer."

"Isn't that all Violetta was?" Olivia asked.

Ian shook his head. "No. She was larger than life. Everyone knew her name. Some college professor even wanted to write a book about her."

"Alfred Hicks," Olivia said. "Was he a colleague of yours, Amabel?"

Amabel took her purse off the back of her chair and got to her feet. "I'm done being cross-examined by you, Ms. Limoges. Why don't you do us a favor and mind your own business?"

Olivia felt a searing rage course through her. "This is *my* town. My mother worked in the library where Violetta was killed. The current librarian has suffered a heart attack over this tragedy. I'm not some bored socialite looking for a thrill. I want to restore peace to Oyster Bay and to its people, so this *is* my business." When Amabel opened her mouth to speak, Olivia held up a warning finger to silence her. "And yes, I'm fully aware that it's not my place to investigate. I'd gladly step back and let the police handle this mess, but wherever they turn, they're met with lies, half-truths, and omissions. The clock is ticking." She looked at the other storytellers. "You'd think Violetta's own sister would be interested in seeing that justice was done, wouldn't you?"

Mariah glanced from Olivia to Amabel and gasped. "That's why your eyes remind me of hers. You're Violetta's sister?"

"Allow me to introduce you to Mabel Devereaux," Olivia said. "I don't know why she's kept her connection to Violetta a secret, but I suspect she's made a habit of keeping secrets."

"Don't we all?" Greg said blandly and tossed his napkin onto the table. "Thank you for a most entertaining evening, Olivia. I think I'll turn in." He was about to bid Millay goodnight when Harris came up behind her.

Sensing his presence, Millay swiveled in her chair. "This is not a good time."

"Let's just get it over with," Harris said, ignoring her. "I'm sick of our breakup happening bit by bit. You won't rip the Band-Aid off, so I will."

"Harris—" Millay began.

"She doesn't love me," Harris informed the stunned storytellers. "Nothing I can do about that, right? So I might as well face facts."

Kenneth offered him his microbrew. "That's rough, man. Want my beer? I'm on my way out."

"We all are. Jesus. What kind of backward town is this?" Amabel gave Olivia, Millay, and Harris a disgusted glare and strode off, but Greg no longer seemed inclined to leave. In fact, he seemed to take pleasure in Millay's discomfort.

It suddenly seemed to dawn on Harris that it was uncouth to discuss his relationship in front of an audience. Blushing from his neck to the roots of his hair, he looked at Millay and jerked his thumb toward the bar. "Should we continue this over a drink?"

"Hasn't he had enough?" Sue murmured to Kenneth, but Olivia knew that Harris hadn't had a drop of alcohol. Pain had caused him to behave out of character. Pain and heartbreak.

Millay was about to get up when Greg put a hand on her forearm, preventing her from moving. "So this is your man, eh? What's wrong? He's not good enough for you anymore?

Not rich enough? Isn't the lead singer of some indie rock band? No, he's just a regular Joe, isn't he? Decent, hardworking, but he's missing that something you can't even put your finger on, right? That edge. You women want to pigeonhole us. Try to control us. Freaking geld us." He pointed at Harris. "Don't let her try to change you, buddy. She's the one who needs to change."

"Jackass." Millay shoved Greg's hand away and headed for the far corner of the bar. Olivia looked at Greg, marveling over his ability to flirt with a woman one second and verbally abuse her the next. She sensed his speech was personal and had little to do with Millay and Harris at all.

Instead of replying to Greg, Harris apologized for interrupting the party, performed an awkward little bow, and walked away.

The rest of the group gathered their belongings in preparation to leave. Mariah drained the rest of her cocktail and raised the empty glass. "No hard feelings, Olivia. You were just trying to help. And here's my advice to the police: find out who loved Violetta." She shrugged as if the problem were easily solved. "Take those two young lovers." She indicated Harris and Millay, whose heads were bent together as they exchanged vehement whispers. "Is there any force in this world more powerful than the emotions they're experiencing right now?"

"Ian loved Violetta. Are you accusing him of murder?" Greg appeared amused by the thought.

"No," Mariah answered quickly. "Unless he was the man in Violetta's room Thursday night."

Everyone looked at Ian. "I wish," he said. "Seriously, I wish it had been me. Maybe she'd still be alive. But Violetta never gave me the time of day. I was just another guy who mooned over her. And even though I can perform in front

of hundreds of people, I couldn't talk to her without sounding like a total idiot."

"It doesn't seem like it was easy to get to know Violetta,"
Kenneth said in an obvious attempt to console Ian. "If she
didn't hang around to socialize at the end of the big events
or during annual retreats, then who could have ever gotten
to know her? Who among us could have anything useful to
tell the police?"

"You'd think her own sister would," Sue said.

The rest of the storytellers nodded. In silent unison, they
stood up. With the exception of Greg Rapson, they politely
thanked Olivia for the meal and left. Greg stared at Olivia
for several uncomfortable seconds and then departed without saying a word.

The moment they were all gone, Olivia headed for the
manager's office. Haviland greeted her with loud thumps of
his tail, and she was tempted to drop down on the floor and
lay her head against his warm, soft belly. Instead, she took
a bottle of Chivas Regal out of the file cabinet and poured
two fingers' worth into her empty glass. After a fortifying
swallow, she checked her cell phone for messages. Rawlings
had called an hour ago to let her know that Lowell's condition was unchanged. He told her that while Lowell's vital
signs were stable, he was in a coma.

"He may not come out of it. Even if he does, he might
not be the same," Rawlings said solemnly. "It's possible that
his brain was cut off from oxygen for too long. There could
be permanent damage, but as of this point, no one knows."
After a pause he continued. "Dixie and her family have gone
home. She asked for you to get in touch with her tomorrow.
And there's one more thing. Lowell had something in his
back pocket—a scrap of paper with a list of typed words.
It's incomplete because it's been torn, but I've sent you a

text of the four we have to see if they mean anything to you or to your guests. Call me before you head home."

Clicking on her text message icon, Olivia read the words, "silver, moonlight, stones, and heart."

Easing back into the supple leather of the desk chair, she kicked off her shoes and put her bare feet on the blotter. She spoke the four words aloud, repeating them over and over, but the only image they called to mind was of the moonlit night Lowell had described. The one in which Alfred Hicks had been pushed to his death. Closing her eyes, she saw the silver-blue snow blanketing the pine trees, and the moon casting shadows on the sharp outcrops of rock.

Unable to think of anything useful, Olivia forwarded the words to the rest of the Bayside Book Writers and asked them to recall if they'd heard them during Violetta's performance. She ended her message by suggesting that they meet tomorrow after Laurel and Harris were done with work.

"I doubt Harris or Millay will even notice my text. Not tonight anyway," she said to Haviland and drained her glass.

Since she hadn't eaten dinner, she headed to the kitchen and watched as Hudson prepared her a filet of tilapia in lemon-garlic sauce. He served the fish with a side of asparagus risotto and steamed vegetables.

"And here's a piece of salmon for Haviland," Hudson said, offering her a plate. "Now get out of my kitchen. I've got too many orders to fill. If I stand here talking to you, I'll fall behind." He pretended to swat at her with his dish towel.

Olivia thanked him and carried the meals back to the manager's office. As she ate, she stared at the words Rawlings had sent and reflected on what she needed to tell him before the night was through.

On her way out, Olivia peered into the bar and saw that Millay and Harris were still sitting together. They weren't talking. Each of them seemed lost in their own thoughts.

Though they sat inches apart, Olivia could sense the chasm that had opened between them, and she felt a deep sadness wash over her. Their little group was about to be irrevocably changed.

Dejected, she called Rawlings and was unsurprised when she reached his voicemail.

"I'm going home," she said. "Come over whenever you're done. It doesn't matter how late. Just come."

During the drive home, she pushed away thoughts of Millay and Harris and concentrated on Flynn. Had he been the man in Violetta's room Thursday night? Had she heard him correctly when he'd said that he loved Violetta? Did he have it in him to commit murder? To put a bag over Violetta's head and wrap something around her neck as she clawed at him with her gloved fingers?

Olivia was so caught up in this image that she didn't immediately notice the car parked in her driveway. Because she recognized the car, she was disturbed to see it at her house. It belonged to Flynn.

As if her thoughts had conjured up the man, there he was, sitting on the steps leading to her back door. His elbows were propped on his knees and his eyes were dark hollows.

"You shouldn't be driving after all you've had to drink," she chided as she got out of the Range Rover, encouraging Haviland to walk in front of her.

Haviland approached Flynn warily, and Olivia let him take the lead. Every part of her was tensed for action. She'd never considered Flynn a violent person. Only a few days ago, the notion would have made her laugh. Not anymore. She didn't know the man sitting on her steps. Even Haviland behaved as if he were a stranger.

"You and I worked because we didn't go probing each other's wounds," he said softly, holding out his hand, palm up, for Haviland to sniff. "I knew you'd been dealt a bad hand, but I didn't want to hear the details. And what was the point of telling you that I was incapable of love? That I didn't have a heart to give away?"

"Because you'd already surrendered it to Violetta Devereaux?" Olivia asked. She stood just out of his reach, keeping Haviland between them.

Flynn didn't answer. He sifted through the dirt for pebbles and flung them one by one into the dry grass.

"How long ago was this? When you worked for Dexter Pharmaceuticals?"

Flynn lifted his gaze. "I see the chief has been talking about me. I guess I should be flattered."

Olivia sighed. "Aren't you here because you want to tell me something? Perhaps convince me that you didn't kill Violetta? Because I'm prepared to listen. I'm still your friend, Flynn."

"Are you?" His voice was heavy with booze and fatigue. "You'd think I'd have learned to distrust women by now, but apparently, it hasn't sunk in because here I am."

Olivia was tired of waiting for Flynn to reveal the purpose of his visit, but she wasn't about to invite him inside. She shifted on her feet and said, "Start at the beginning."

"It was a Wednesday afternoon in the late spring," Flynn said. "Back then, she didn't slink around in the night like some kind of vampire. When we first met, she wore this hat with a really low brim. It covered most of her face, but not all. It was only some old straw thing, but I thought it was glamorous. Mysterious. She and Mabel came to sell plants together, but Vi always waited outside." He rolled a pebble around his palm. "For a while, I didn't care that she didn't come any closer. Mabel was pretty enough. She and I were the same age, and we flirted like crazy. I kissed her a few times, but eventually, I began to wonder why her sister wore that hat and kept her distance. I started daydreaming about Vi until one day, I snuck up on her."

"Where was Mabel?"

Flynn shrugged. "Probably collecting the money we owed her for the plants." A little smile played at the corners of his mouth. "I stole around the building so I could come up behind Vi, and when I said, 'There you are,' she didn't jump or scream like most girls would. No. Not her. She didn't make a sound. Just slapped me across the face."

Olivia laughed. "Atta girl."

"Yeah, I deserved it. I would have let her hit me again and again if it meant more time with her. She didn't wear concealing makeup then—she couldn't afford it—and I thought she was the most remarkable creature I'd ever seen. Her blue skin, those electric eyes, that black hair. She was like something out of a storybook. A nymph. A siren. Something magical. Exotic. Utterly unique."

"What did she think of you?"

Flynn shook his head. "I have no idea. After the slap, she just walked away. I yelled after her that she was the most beautiful girl I'd ever laid eyes on and that I'd do anything to see her again, but she didn't turn around."

"That's a pretty good line."

"It wasn't a line. I meant every word. The next time she came, I asked a friend to stall Mabel while I brought Vi a bag of peaches. She still didn't talk. Just grabbed the bag and took off running. For months, I offered her little treats like that. The first words she ever spoke were to tell me how much her brother loved the bubble gum I'd given her. And then she smiled, and man, I was a goner."

Olivia could tell that Flynn was miles and years away.

"She started telling me stories about her life," he continued. "We never had much time, so this all happened over a long period, though I'd fallen in love with her the moment I saw her. The more I got to know her, the stronger my feelings grew. Vi worked so hard and had experienced so little in the way of pleasures. The rest of the girls I knew were shallow and silly. Not Vi. She was as deep and unfathomable as a cave lake."

"You became lovers?"

Flynn nodded. "We were together when Elijah died. Vi might have married me if that boy had lived. My whole life would have been different. Damn her father. Damn that man to hell."

Olivia kept her gaze on Flynn's clenched fists. Very gently, she said, "What happened?"

"I don't know exactly. Vi came to me a few weeks after the funeral and totally broke down. She didn't just cry. She wailed. She raged. Chunks of her hair were missing, and there were scratches on her cheeks and chest. When she calmed down enough to speak, she said that her daddy had a treasure hidden away—one that could have saved Elijah. A treasure so valuable that it could have given them all a different life, but her father wouldn't touch it. He said that Elijah's fate was in God's hands, not man's."

Now Olivia was certain that the treasure was real. Violetta wouldn't make up a story in the midst of such intense grief. "What was so valuable?"

Flynn grunted. "All I know is that she didn't have it. Otherwise, she wouldn't have asked me for a loan. I gave her everything I had. She promised to explain why she needed the money when she came back from wherever she was going. But she never came back." He relaxed his hands and laced his fingers together. "I tried to find her. For two years, I thought about nothing but her, but then the company offered me a promotion and I decided to get on with my life. I moved to Raleigh and did my best to forget her."

"And did you two ever meet again? Before this retreat?"

He nodded. "I went to one of her performances shortly before moving to Oyster Bay. When she came onstage, it was like I'd been sleeping for years and had been waiting for the sight of her face, the sound of her voice, to bring me out of my trance. I hung around until the end of the show and then followed her out to her car. She looked at me as if I were a stranger. She told me that I was part of her old life—that *that* Violetta Devereux was dead. She wore lots of makeup and was dressed like you saw her Saturday night, but I only saw the young woman I fell in love with. I knew then that I'd never stopped loving her. Never would."

Olivia considered her feelings for Rawlings. He was the only man she'd ever known who was just the right fit for her. With him, she could let down her guard. She trusted him with her heart, and in return, he treated it with the utmost tenderness. She'd found love in her middle age. Flynn had found his as a very young man. Olivia knew that love didn't abide by anyone's rules. It came along unexpectedly, tiptoeing like a thief, and changed everything. It was obvious that Flynn had been terribly wounded by love. The question was, had his feelings for Violetta turned black and bitter? Had he sought vengeance against the woman who'd run off with his money and his hopes for happiness?

"Were you the man in Violetta's hotel room Thursday night?"

A noise rose from deep in Flynn's chest, somewhere between a growl and a moan. It took Olivia a moment to recognize that the sound was the word "no."

"Flynn, if you know who wanted Violetta dead or sought the Devereaux treasure, you should tell me. Don't you want to see her killer brought to justice?"

Flynn stared out into the night. "What if it was me? What if I couldn't stand to be ignored? Why do you think I set up this whole retreat? I wanted her to come to Oyster Bay, to come to me. I called Lowell and arranged everything. She came to perform, to receive the adulation she craved, but did I get what I wanted? No. In the end, she turned me away. She turned me away. Again."

Olivia remembered what Leona had said about Flynn the night Violetta was murdered—how he'd gone into the restroom looking distressed. And that his tie was loose and askew. Was he in turmoil because he'd just killed the only woman he'd ever loved?

Before she could ask him anything else, Flynn got to his feet. "Believe what you want about me," he said wearily. "It doesn't matter now."

Flynn stepped around Haviland, who watched him with wary eyes until he was halfway between Olivia and his car. The poodle edged closer to Olivia, his ears raised and his body alert and ready for action.

"You shouldn't drive!" Olivia called when Flynn opened his car door. Ignoring her, he slid behind the wheel, turned on the ignition, and backed slowly down the driveway.

She waited until the beam of his headlights had been swallowed by the darkness before going inside.

Rawlings found her on the deck an hour later. She was wearing a white cotton nightgown and sipping very slowly from a glass of sparkling wine.

Pulling a chair closer to hers, he sank into it and took her hand. "Hi."

Olivia turned and gave him a tired smile. His hand felt good in hers. Warm and strong and solid. "Flynn was here a little while ago. I don't know if he was confessing to murder or to something else entirely."

Rawlings went rigid. "And you let him in? Seriously, Olivia. This is yet another reason for us to live together. Dangerous men wouldn't show up at your door if they knew it was my door too."

"I didn't ask him in for tea and crumpets," Olivia snapped. "He was sitting on my steps when I got back from the restaurant, and I maintained a safe distance the whole time. Besides, Haviland was here."

Rawlings released an exasperated sigh. "Haviland can't protect you from everything."

"Neither can you," Olivia said. "And I'm not looking for a protector. Never was."

They both fell silent. Olivia tried to quell her frustration and allow the gentle whisper of the waves to ease the tension growing between her and Rawlings.

Eventually, Rawlings withdrew his hand, but not before giving hers an apologetic squeeze. "How did things go at the Crab House?"

Olivia refilled her wineglass and passed it to him. "Prosecco. Not my usual poison, but it's very refreshing. I feel completely dried out and the wine helps. And you'll need it because this is going to take a while."

While Rawlings drank, Olivia told him everything that had happened at The Bayside Crab House and at her place afterward.

When she was done, he didn't speak, and she knew he was processing every detail, trying to form a clear picture in his mind. "A man was in her room at The Yellow Lady," he said. "A lover. Why didn't anyone come forth with this information before?" He stared angrily at the ocean. "I don't think the man was Flynn. He was a part of a past she wanted to forget." He paused. "No. 'Forget' isn't the right word. She wanted to deny it. And that would mean denying him."

Olivia nodded in agreement. "And so he was spurned again. His plans and hopes dashed. What would that do to a man?"

"Nothing good. Mr. McNulty is definitely a suspect in my book, but we have to consider who might have been with Violetta on Thursday. Did she ultimately reject him too? Are the other storytellers covering for him?" He frowned.

"You'll be busy tomorrow. Interviews at the B&B, another round with Flynn, and then there's the subject of the treasure. It must exist, but what is it?" When Rawlings didn't answer, Olivia followed his gaze. She willed the sea to calm her, but the multitude of thoughts churning in her head wouldn't be still. "Did you find anything in Violetta's trunk?"

Rawlings gave her a thin smile. "Your instincts were spot on, Olivia. There was a space behind the velvet lining. When Officer Cook peeled the material away, he found an old photograph of a little boy. I'm guessing it was Elijah."

The triumph Olivia felt over having her theory proven correct vanished when she pictured Violetta hiding the image of her beloved brother under the velvet so she could carry him with her everywhere she went. Olivia's eyes filled with tears. "That was all?"

"Yes." Rawlings sighed. "It would have been wonderfully convenient had there been a solid clue, but there wasn't. And I'm not sure why she hid the photo. Why not keep it in her purse? Did she feel guilty about his death?" He set the wineglass on the deck rail and turned to Olivia. "I need to get some sleep. I have an early start tomorrow."

"Me too. I want to see Dixie before the diner gets busy. I've also sent a text to the rest of the writer's group asking them to mull over the words you found in Lowell's pocket." She paused. "Has there been any change in his condition?"

Rawlings shook his head. "No. And he was definitely the victim of foul play. A nurse showed me a bruise on his back likely caused by someone kneeling on him. There's other physical evidence that he struggled while his assailant held his head underwater. He has mud under his nails, and his palms are covered with cuts and scrapes, as if he tried to unseat his attacker by pushing off the bottom."

"God, that's awful." Olivia shuddered. She hesitated for a long moment and then said, "Maybe he'll . . . heal as he sleeps. Now that he's in a safe place. Maybe he can rest for a while."

Rawlings reached for her. She got up and came to him, lowering herself onto his lap and resting her head against his sturdy chest. "Keats would have agreed with you," he whispered. "He wrote:

> *'O soothest Sleep! if so it please thee, close,*
> *In midst of this thine hymn, my willing eyes,*
> *Or wait the amen, ere thy poppy throws*
> *Around my bed its lulling charities;*
> *Then save me, or the passed day will shine*
> *Upon my pillow, breeding many woes.'"*

Olivia put her arms around Rawlings' neck and ran her fingers down his bristly cheek. "You never cease to amaze me, my chief. Let's go inside and forget about our many woes for a brief time."

Rawlings responded by holding her tightly against him. "I'm shooting for more than a brief time. How about the rest of our lives?"

Olivia stood and held out her hand. The moonlight fell over her shoulders and set her white nightgown aglow. "No more talking. No more thinking," she murmured. "It's our turn to hide away. If only for tonight."

Nodding in surrender, Rawlings took her hand and followed her inside.

Chapter 13

*And when I breathed, my breath was
lightning.*

—BLACK ELK

Olivia woke before dawn. A splotch of pale pink hovering over the ocean hinted at daylight, but the world beyond her window was still hushed. The gulls hadn't started crying, and the sandpipers had yet to emerge from their nests.

Creeping downstairs, Olivia found Rawlings and Haviland already in the kitchen. Rawlings sat at the table with a cup of coffee and a pad of paper in front of him, and Olivia could see that he'd covered an entire page with notes. Haviland, who was stationed by his empty food bowl, glanced over his shoulder at her, doing his best to look deprived.

"How long have you been up?" she asked Rawlings in a hushed voice.

"An hour or so. I jerked awake and started thinking about the search warrants I'll need and the teams I have to send to The Yellow Lady and to McNulty's house. I want to get inside all of the storytellers' cars too. I got the ball rolling on most of this stuff yesterday, but I have to do this by the book. No mistakes. And the time for polite chats over coffee is finished."

Olivia nodded. The storytellers had been told that they weren't free to leave town, but Rawlings couldn't keep them in Oyster Bay indefinitely. Eventually, he'd have to charge someone or let them all go. The clock was ticking. Olivia knew that Rawlings had to solve the riddle of Violetta's murder and apprehend Lowell's assailant soon or the killer might never be caught.

Standing behind Rawlings' chair, Olivia leaned over and wrapped her arms around him. She placed her smooth cheek against his rough one and closed her eyes. The two of them stayed that way for a moment, wordlessly strengthening and supporting each other. Then Rawlings capped his pen and got to his feet. He put his coffee cup in the sink and gave Haviland a parting scratch behind the ears.

"It's too early to visit Dixie," he said, scooping his keys off the counter. "Will you go back to bed?"

Olivia shook her head. "Michel wants to increase our shrimp order, so I'm heading to the docks. If I'm lucky, I'll catch them before they leave for the day."

Rawlings stared down at the pad of paper in his hand. "I envy those men. They go out each day, casting a wide net into the water. They know exactly what they hope to catch. I feel like I'm fishing in the dark with an unbaited hook."

"Those guys aren't so different from you," she said. "They trap the wrong fish all the time and end up having to throw them back into the sea. It takes endless patience and perseverance for them to come home with a filled hull. And like you, they must pay attention to a hundred different factors. The wind, the weather, the tides, and most of all, their instincts."

Smiling, Rawlings opened the back door. "Well, I'm off to cast my net in the murky waters. But unlike your fisherman friends, I'm not looking for shrimp or grouper. I'm hunting a shark."

Thirty minutes later, Olivia pulled into a parking spot at the docks and let Haviland out of the car. The poodle grinned happily as he jogged on the rough wood jutting into the water like a thick arm, glancing this way and that. Olivia sensed that he hoped to locate the source of the tantalizing smells and be rewarded with a snack of fresh fish.

"You're going to be disappointed," she told Haviland.

Captain Fergusson was coiling a length of rope as Olivia approached *Clara Sue*, his trawler.

"Permission to come aboard?" she asked.

Fergusson made a noise of assent and offered her a scarred, calloused hand to help her up the wobbly gang-plank. Once she had both feet on the deck, he removed his battered baseball cap and said, "Morning, Miss Olivia. You're up mighty early today."

Olivia watched Haviland trot across the gangplank, his nose quivering in excitement. "I couldn't sleep. Something about the pink sky made me think of you. So here I am."

"It's a shrimp sky," Fergusson said, lifting his weathered eyes to the horizon. "A good omen. We'll bring home a fine haul today."

"That's excellent news for my customers. They'll be served the freshest fish in all of North Carolina tonight. Speaking of which, I'd like to add to my original order."

While she and the captain talked business, two other men prepped the boat for departure. One of them bore a close resemblance to Fergusson.

"Is that your son?" Olivia asked the captain. She'd never seen the young man before.

A sadness surfaced in Fergusson's eyes. "Aye. He's joined the family business. Not by choice, by God. Not by choice."

Olivia sensed the subject was fraught with emotion, so she didn't reply. Instead, she took the piece of lightning glass she'd found on the beach out of her purse. Peeling away the bubble wrap, she handed it to Fergusson. "Have you ever seen one of these?"

"Once. They don't come along too often." He turned the fulgurite around and around. "The one I saw was black. A wicked-looking thing—all burned and jagged. You could still feel the lightning trapped inside. Belonged to a man who used to work for me, but I wouldn't let him bring it aboard."

"That's because you're insanely superstitious," said a voice from behind the captain. It was Fergusson's son. He smiled indulgently at his father and then turned to Olivia. "Hi. I'm Toby."

He and Olivia shook hands. Close-up, she realized that he couldn't be more than eighteen or nineteen, which meant that Fergusson was old enough to be his grandfather.

"He's our youngest by a decade," Fergusson said, answering her unasked question. "A late-in-life surprise."

"That's me." Toby grinned. "The impressive product of a cold night and a few shots of whiskey."

"Mind your tongue, boy," Fergusson growled, but his eyes glimmered with amusement.

Olivia took an immediate liking to Toby. "Why haven't I seen you before?"

"I was away at college," he explained, a cloud passing over his face. Gesturing at the lightning glass, he asked to hold it. He ran his finger over the gritty exterior and whispered, "Beautiful. I know a few professors who'd kill to see this." He looked at Olivia. "I was studying to be a meteorologist." He jerked a thumb at his father. "Growing up around this guy, I heard about the weather twenty-four/seven. But now I'll get to see how it affects us firsthand."

"Go on back to work now, son," Fergusson commanded, but not unkindly.

When Toby had moved off to the stern, Olivia touched

the old fisherman lightly on the arm. "That time in Fish Nets, when we were discussing a possible drought, you told me that words have power. Remember? You also said that words could be dangerous. Do words have something to do with why Toby is on this boat?"

Fergusson's eyes darkened with anger. "A lady cousin on my mama's side passed away a few days before I saw you at the bar. Promised to leave enough money for Toby to finish college. He'd have been the only Fergusson to do that, but I guess we didn't grovel enough, because my cousin gave all her money to a bird sanctuary. She wrote a letter saying that Toby would waste her money just like all us Fergussons waste money. She finished off by writing that Mary and me had been too old to have Toby and that we'd have to live with our mistake and not expect her to fix things for us."

"How nasty," Olivia said.

Fergusson clenched his jaw. "My boy heard every word of that woman's poison. We never considered him a mistake. He's been nothing but a blessing, but she made him doubt the truth of that. I hope the devil's poking her in her bony ass with his sharpest pitchfork."

Olivia shook her head in disgust. "No one can hurt us like a family member. I'm sorry. For both your cousin's cruelty and for the interruption of Toby's education. Are there any scholarships or grants available?"

Fergusson shrugged, shamefaced. "I don't know about that kind of thing. I reckon Toby hasn't looked into it because he thinks we need him on the boat. But we'll be fine. We're always fine. I want a different life for him. I want him to get out of this town and live big. His smarts are wasted on this boat. He's meant to be more."

Olivia was moved by the captain's distress. "Would you allow me to make a few phone calls on Toby's behalf? See if there's any money sitting around that your son might claim? He doesn't even need to know unless I can come up with something useful."

Fergusson hesitated, and Olivia sensed he was wrestling with his pride. Finally, he gave her a single nod and walked off.

Olivia watched Toby work for a moment, but her mind drifted to thoughts of other children: two sisters named Mabel and Vi who'd clawed their way out of the poverty of a small mountain town. How many disappointments had they known? How many dangerous words had they heard and repeated? How many had they turned into stories?

On impulse, Olivia walked to the stern and handed Toby the lightning glass. "I'd like you to have this. For luck."

His eyes went wide and then dropped to the fulgurite. "The heat required to make this is incredible—it's the kind of pressure needed to produce a diamond. A fulgurite is better than a diamond to a weather freak like me. Thank you, ma'am. I'll take good care of it."

Olivia waved good-bye as she and Haviland disembarked.

Halfway to the car, Olivia came to an abrupt halt. "Could it be?" she said out loud, her brows furrowed. And then she turned to stare out over the water. After a long moment of reflection, she hurried to her car and drove away.

Grumpy's Diner was quiet when Olivia and Haviland entered. A few men sat at the counter fueling themselves for a long day of manual labor with sausage, eggs, hash browns, toast, and Dixie's famous coffee, but all the booths were empty.

Olivia barely recognized Dixie when she skated out of the kitchen with a basket filled with paper napkins and silverware. There was a noticeable absence of hot pink, glitter, frills, stripes, or lace on her outfit. She wore a denim skirt, tube socks, and an Atlanta Braves T-shirt.

"Hey," Olivia said, making no move to sit at her usual

booth even though Haviland had already settled on the vinyl cushion and was gazing out the large picture window.

Easing the basket from Dixie's hands, Olivia pulled her friend close and put her arms around her. Because Dixie was on roller skates, the embrace ended up being more forceful than Olivia had intended.

"No need to mug me!" Dixie scolded, pushing herself backward. Her grim face looked a little brighter, however. "You manhandle the chief like that?"

Olivia smiled. "Whenever I get the chance."

Dixie pointed at the basket. "You gonna set the tables?"

"Yes, I am. I'll work while you talk." Olivia placed four napkins at each booth and was in the middle of putting forks down when Dixie touched her on the arm.

"There's isn't much to report. Lowell's not gettin' better."

Olivia stopped what she was doing and looked at her friend. "I imagine it'll take time for his body to recover. From what Rawlings told me, he came awfully close to . . ."

Dixie held out her hand. "Don't say it." She gestured at the utensils. "Keep on with this. I'm gonna grab you a coffee." She jerked her head in Haviland's direction. "And a few scrambled eggs for the handsome gentleman in the window booth. You know I like 'em furry."

When Dixie returned, Olivia had finished setting the tables and had taken a seat across from Haviland. She watched as the men at the counter left en masse, thanking Dixie on their way out. One of them lingered behind. Hands in pockets, he said, "We're all praying for your cousin, Dixie. If you find out who's responsible, you let me know. We'll see that justice is done."

Dixie nodded. "Thanks, Bill."

When he was gone, Dixie sat down next to Haviland and served him a platter of eggs. "Don't worry," she said to

Olivia. "I'm not gonna let them form a lynch mob. Those fellows mean well, but they're not the sharpest knives in the drawer. Shoot, they'd probably rough up the wrong person. The mayor or a minister or some homely-lookin' grandma." She grinned briefly and then quickly grew solemn again. "Have you learned anythin' new? About Violetta or those storytellers?"

In between sips of Dixie's fortifying coffee, Olivia told her everything that had happened the night before.

When she was done, Dixie shook her head in disbelief. "Flynn? You think you know a person and then—Jesus!" She shook her head again. "But he wouldn't hurt Lowell. Why would he?"

"For the treasure," Olivia said. "I have no doubt that it exists. I also believe that Alfred Hicks was killed because of it. And none of the likely suspects—Flynn, Amabel, and Greg—have cast-iron alibis for the night Hicks died. As for where they were when Lowell was attacked? Rawlings is looking into that. He was up while it was still dark this morning, making a list of what he had to do to put an end to this mess."

"I've been thinkin' about Lowell's story," Dixie said. "I didn't believe it at first, because it just sounded crazy. A ghost? Come on! But I was leafin' through a catalogue last night—a hunter's catalogue that Grumpy gets—and I think I might know how a man could turn himself into a ghost." She took a sheaf of thin, glossy paper out of her apron pocket. "I was gonna show the chief, but I want you to tell me if there's somethin' to my idea first."

Olivia accepted the paper. It took her a moment to understand what she was looking at, but when the image became clear, she exclaimed, "Oh, I see it now. Yes." She glanced from the picture to Dixie and back again. "Yes! Especially with the snowfall and the moonlight. There would have been shadows everywhere, so the pattern shown here is perfect. And it also speaks of premeditation," she added softly.

"Snow camo," Dixie said. "The killer would've had to be watchin' the weather. He knew when Hicks was goin' up the mountain. He knew that it'd be after sundown and the group would get caught up in a storm."

"You're brilliant, Dixie." Olivia scanned the product description. The white coat and pants, which were covered with irregular black and dark brown markings, were called "Ambush Gear." The outfit was designed to protect the wearer against bitterly cold conditions and was guaranteed to blend into most hunting environments. "Do you want me to bring this to Rawlings?"

Dixie nodded. "Please. It's hard for me to get out of here before two, and I wanna go to the hospital right after we close." She pointed at Olivia's empty mug. "Refill?"

"How about a pair of take-out cups? I think I know where to find Rawlings, and I want him to see this right away."

"Thanks, 'Livia. No matter what happens, I know that you did all—"

"None of us will give up until someone's behind bars, Dixie. Not the chief, not me, and not the Bayside Book Writers. And don't you give up on Lowell." She tapped her temple. "He's in there, fighting. They say one should talk to coma patients, and I've never met anyone who could out-talk you."

Dixie threw her head back and laughed. It was the most wonderful sound Olivia had heard for days.

Armed with the best coffee in Oyster Bay, Olivia made her way to The Yellow Lady. The maize-colored mansion, with its wraparound porch and lavender front door, was known for being an oasis of green grass, colorful blooms, and charm. But not today. Olivia hadn't been to the B&B for a long time. When she'd last visited, her purpose had also been tied to a murder case, so the three police cruisers parked in front of the quaint Victorian brought back a host of unpleasant memories.

After telling Haviland to wait on the porch, Olivia walked into the lobby, half-expecting to see the former owners, Roy and Annie Kraus, stationed behind the mahogany concierge desk. However, the person leaning on the leather blotter was an ashen-faced young woman. She stared blankly at Olivia and then seemed to suddenly remember that she was the innkeeper.

"May I help you?" she asked, her voice a tremulous whisper.

Olivia produced her friendliest smile. "Hi there. I'm looking for Chief Rawlings."

The woman was on the verge of answering when the sound of a heavy footfall echoed down the stairwell. A moment later, Officer Cook appeared at the bottom of the stairs. Seeing Olivia, he frowned.

"Officer Cook. I know you're busy, but I need to speak with the chief. Is he here?" Olivia did her best to sound cordial. She and Cook had never really gotten along, but over time, Olivia had had to admit that the young officer was dedicated to his profession and deserved her respect. In turn, Cook had grudgingly accepted the fact that not only was she the chief's lady, but she and her writer friends had proved to be useful during past investigations.

Cook shook his head. "The chief's overseeing interviews at the station." Glancing at the paper in her hands, Cook asked, "Can I help?"

Olivia gestured toward the front porch. "Could we talk outside?"

The moment they were out of the new proprietor's

earshot, Cook folded his arms over his chest and gave Olivia his sternest glare. "We're in the middle of conducting a thorough search of the premises, Ms. Limoges, and—"

"Just take a look at this." She brandished the catalogue page. "I think this explains why no one saw Alfred Hicks's murderer. Someone wearing snow camo ambushed Hicks on the mountain. If you show this to the chief and he agrees with the theory, it might influence how he approaches the suspects or people of interest or whatever you call them."

The corner of Cook's mouth twitched in amusement, and then he straightened and threw back his shoulders. It was a posture he often used when Rawlings entered a room. Olivia didn't know whether Cook was mocking her or not, but he took the paper and said, "I'll contact the chief right away."

She thanked him and then pointed at the lavender door. "Is she the new owner? The terrified blonde behind the desk?"

He nodded. "That's Mrs. Kelly. Mr. Kelly's out of town for the week. He's gone to some nursing home in Florida. His mama's sick."

"Mrs. Kelly." The name wasn't familiar to Olivia. "Has she been helpful? Did she hear anything? See anything?"

Cook shrugged. "You can barely talk to her without her bursting into tears. She says she's been too busy to pay attention to conversations or to when her guests come and go, but I'm not totally buying that."

"Well, I'm sure she's worried about The Yellow Lady's reputation. Do you mind if I have a go? I could give her some pointers on running a business in a tourist town and maybe get her to relax long enough to open up."

"Be my guest. Our department is stretched too thin as it is. With a team here, one at Mr. McNulty's house, and a third at the station conducting interviews, we don't have time to coax things out of her. Not that I'm sure there's anything to coax. I just have a gut feeling that she knows more than she's letting on."

"You have solid instincts. They're worth paying attention to," Olivia said.

Cook arched a brow but didn't reply. Instead, he turned and headed for one of the police cars. Olivia went back inside the inn and introduced herself to Mrs. Kelly, whose first name was Bev, and then sat down in one of the guest chairs facing the desk. After assuring the young woman that the police wouldn't trash the place, she asked if there was anything she could do to lend a hand while Mr. Kelly was away.

Bev's eyes filled with tears. "I can't handle any of it. This whole owning-a-B&B-thing is just too much. And now *this* happens!" She gestured in the general direction of the upstairs guest rooms.

"You're not responsible for the behavior of your guests," Olivia said. "Not any more than I'm responsible for how patrons act in my restaurants. Not only that, but any media attention ends up being good for business. Do you know what else would be good?"

Sniffling, Bev looked at her and said, "What?"

"If you knew something that could help the police," Olivia said in a conspiratorial whisper. "I've been lucky enough to have done that in the past, and you should have seen how many newspapers and television stations jumped on the story. People drove to Oyster Bay from all over to eat at The Boot Top Bistro or The Bayside Crab House."

Bev didn't seem keen on the idea. "We have plenty of guests. That's not the problem. It's all the work. Getting up at five to do the baking and then spending the rest of the day doing laundry and dealing with the yard. Lee said this would be a break for us, but it's actually *breaking* us."

Olivia could see that Bev wasn't exaggerating. Her hands

were red and her fingernails were ragged and torn. She was too thin, her hair was limp, and the skin under her eyes was puffy from lack of sleep. "Can't you hire a few people? This place is too much for the two of you to manage, especially in the height of the tourist season."

"I can see that now, but we put every dime into buying it, and then our rainy-day budget got eaten up by new gutters and a paint job and . . ." she trailed off.

"Listen, I know that you don't want to make any decisions without your husband, but I can offer some friendly advice. If you'd like me to look over your books, I can at least suggest things that can be done to free up a little cash. You clearly need assistance with the cleaning and the laundry. How much are you charging for a standard room?"

When Bev told her, Olivia immediately shook her head. "Including breakfast? That's not enough. You should increase the rate by fifty dollars for all new bookings. That's a start. Now, one of my sous-chefs has a sister in need of work. Any kind of work. I've met her, and I think she'd be a perfect fit for this place."

With a hopeful expression, Bev grabbed onto Olivia's hand. "If I could just have some help, I might actually enjoy owning this yellow monster."

Olivia smiled. "Say the word and we'll review your expenses. I know all the local wholesale suppliers."

Bev's eyes went wide. "Really?"

"Hey, I've got plenty of time if you want to get to work right now."

Bev nodded. "I do. I really do. It'll keep me from focusing on the cops, and maybe it'll keep this place afloat. Oh, I am *so* grateful that you showed up here today."

Feeling slightly guilty for manipulating the naïve young woman, Olivia vowed to do her best to help The Yellow Lady turn a profit.

"Do you mind if I let my dog in while we work?" Olivia asked after Bev returned from her office carrying a stack of file folders and a pile of loose papers. "This might take a while."

Bev pulled aside the sheer curtain covering the nearest window and cried, "A poodle! I had one when I was a little girl. Pollyanna was the smartest, sweetest, most wonderful dog ever. By all means, bring her inside."

"Haviland's all male," Olivia corrected gently. "And he's very agreeable, so feel free to pet him."

Bev delighted in Haviland. She stroked and scratched him while Olivia reviewed the inn's finances. It quickly became clear that the Kellys could save money in several areas, thus enabling them to hire a part-time housekeeper and possibly a lawn service as well. When she was through, Olivia was too hungry to think any more, but she was loath to leave. If Bev knew intimate details about her guests, now was the time to ask her.

"I hate to leave during our moment of triumph," she told the younger woman. "But I have to eat something. I've been up since dawn and am running on two cups of coffee."

Bev's hands flew to her mouth. "Where are my manners? Please, come on back to the kitchen. I have tons of food left over from breakfast because, well, half of my guests had to leave with the police. Would a quiche, fresh fruit, and turkey sausage suit you?"

"Sounds delicious," Olivia said and meant it. She was starving. Not only that, but she hoped that by having gained Bev's trust and gratitude, she could get her to open up about the storytellers and Thursday night in particular.

It didn't take long. The women had finished their quiche slices and were enjoying a summer berry salad when Olivia broached the subject.

"I'm sorry that your current guests have been stressful,"

Olivia began. "I guess we can attribute it to their artistic temperaments. I hope they've been respectful to you at least."

"Oh, they've been very polite," Bev said. "In fact, they're so charming that I can't believe any of them could be involved in this murder."

"I guess the police will have their suspect as soon as they find out who visited Violetta's room Thursday night." Olivia lowered her voice even though they were the only people around. "I only know she wasn't alone that night because Mariah told me."

Bev speared a strawberry with her fork and pushed it around her plate. "I wish I knew who the man was, but our room's downstairs near the kitchen. The only thing I heard wouldn't help the police, so I didn't bother mentioning it."

"Oh? What was that?" Olivia asked casually.

"Well, even though I was exhausted Thursday, I had a hard time staying asleep. So I got up and went to the kitchen to make a cup of decaf tea. I like to drink it on the porch when there aren't any guests around—sometimes it's hard to share your house with a bunch of strangers—and that's when I heard a man talking to a woman."

Olivia pointed toward the front of the inn. "Near the check-in desk?"

"That's where the guests were, yes. I sat out by the kitchen door, which means I was right around the corner from them. I was already sipping my tea when they came out, and I didn't mean to eavesdrop, but I was too tired to move."

"After the workday you put in, I'm amazed you ever got up," Olivia said with a grin.

"Exactly!" Bev's relieved smile told Olivia that they were now confidantes. "But honestly, I don't think what I heard means anything. The man was just complaining. He kept saying, 'She used me *again*. Tonight. For the last hour. She used me and threw me away like I was trash. She took everything I had and turned her back on me. Do you know what that does to a man?'"

"Did he sound angry?" Olivia asked.

Bev nodded. "Definitely. The woman didn't say much. She just asked if he planned on doing something about his situation, and he said he was going to teach her a lesson. I didn't know who he meant by 'her,' and I started feeling like a creep so I went inside. I have no idea who these guests were, and I don't think their conversation would help the police, do you?"

"Maybe," Olivia said. "Do you mind if I tell them? I'm very close to the chief."

"It's fine with me." Bev's relief was palpable. "Thanks for everything. You've taken such a load off my shoulders."

"It was a fair trade." Olivia gestured at her empty plate. "Lunch was wonderful." After promising to send an e-mail with a list of recommended wholesale suppliers, Olivia woke Haviland from his midday nap and left.

The moment she was in her car, she called Rawlings. To her surprise, he picked up on the first ring.

"I hope you have Flynn in custody," she said without preamble.

"Why's that?"

Olivia hesitated. She was on the brink of condemning another person. A resident of Oyster Bay. A former lover. A friend. The least she could do was stop and recognize the gravity of the moment.

Finally, she closed her eyes and said, "Because I just discovered a piece of evidence against him. Something the owner of The Yellow Lady overheard."

"What kind of evidence?" Rawlings wanted to know.

In a leaden voice, Olivia replied, "The damning kind."

Chapter 14

Whether we fall by ambition, blood, or lust,
like diamonds we are cut with our own dust.

—JOHN WEBSTER

Olivia hurriedly told Rawlings what Bev Kelly had over-heard the Thursday night before Violetta was killed.

"Bev couldn't sleep so she got up after midnight. The man was complaining about how he'd just been used by Violetta. He must have been her lover. They'd had sex, and afterward she told him to leave. Hurt and angry, he turned to another woman for comfort. The man vowed to make Violetta pay for rejecting him," Olivia explained. "It has to be Flynn because Violetta's done this to him before. And it makes sense that he'd seek consolation from Amabel. They also have a shared past. And who knows? The two of them may have been in touch this whole time. That's just another question you'll have to ask him."

Rawlings grunted. "When I can locate him, that is. I'm afraid Mr. McNulty is nowhere to be found."

Olivia sucked in a sharp breath. "You have people at his house, right?"

"As we speak," Rawlings said. "There's no indication

that he's left town. His house is orderly, and nothing appears to be missing. I believe he's around. I just don't know where. And in light of what you've told me, I'm wondering what his intentions are."

"I don't like the sound of that."

"That makes two of us. Listen, Olivia, do not go back to your house without me," Rawlings commanded. "The last time you went home alone, an inebriated Mr. McNulty was waiting on your doorstep."

Olivia sighed. "Flynn could be on a boat to anywhere by now. Why would he go to my house?"

"Last night, he came to tell you his side of the story," Rawlings said. "He may have more to share. For whatever reason, he wants you to hear what he has to say, so you need to stay in a highly visible, public place until I can get to you. As soon as I have the chance, I'll drive you home so you can pack a bag. You're not sleeping at your place tonight."

"But—"

"I put out an APB for Mr. McNulty," Rawlings interrupted. "The men guarding Lowell's hospital room have also been told to watch out for him. Time is running out, Olivia. You must see that. All the players are growing restless, and someone's going to snap. Don't expose yourself to unnecessary danger. Just let things play out. We're close to ending this. I know we're close."

Olivia wondered what he meant by that. "Are you making headway with the interviews?"

"We're seeing cracks in the storytellers' composures. Of course, those who threaten to lawyer up will have to be released within the next few hours unless we find incriminating evidence in their hotel rooms or cars. I'm going to hold them at the station as long as possible. We have to keep at it. We've got to find something to break this case."

"All right, here's my proposed itinerary. I'll spend the afternoon at The Boot Top, and then I'm meeting with the Bayside Book Writers to go over the words you found in Lowell's pocket. That is, if you still need us to work on those?" She couldn't prevent a touch of petulance from entering her tone. No matter how much she cared for Rawlings, she didn't like being told what to do.

"Yes, please keep working on the word list. We haven't been able to make heads or tails of it, and though I can't explain why, I believe it's important." He paused. "Look, Olivia, I know you're cross because I'm asking you to stay put, but this town has suffered enough losses lately." He fell silent for a long moment and then continued, "I've lost enough already. And so have you. I just want to try to hold on to what we have. It's my . . . our . . ."

"Our treasure," she finished for him.

Rawlings released a gratified sigh. "Yes. That's why I want us to live together. And since you said what you just said, you can damn well expect me to raise the subject again as soon as this case is closed. But for now, I need to go."

Smiling a little over the tenderness permeating Rawlings' warning, Olivia murmured a good-bye and ended the call. She sat in the car for a moment, gazing at The Yellow Lady's grounds. Even in the midsummer months, when the heat and humidity were at their worst, the inn's gardens were usually a riot of colorful blooms. Not anymore. The drought-resistant flowers were wilted, their stalks and leaves edged with yellow and brown, their blooms stunted and sparse. Olivia reflected on what Rawlings had said about restlessness. He might have been describing the suspects, but it was how she felt as well. And when she thought about Dixie and the Bayside Book Writers, the word seemed to apply to them too.

"We need a storm," she said to Haviland. "Something to break the stillness."

Haviland thrust his head out the window and then looked back at her. Olivia knew that he wanted her to start driving so that the air would rush up his nostrils and into his mouth, introducing dozens of exciting smells and filling him with a sense of euphoria.

"I'm going. I'm going." Olivia turned the engine on and buckled Haviland's canine seat belt. "You're an addict. A scent addict."

The moment the car began to move, Haviland's tail started wagging, and his tongue lolled from the side of his mouth. Olivia smiled at him. "I'm glad one of us can be carefree."

Olivia headed to The Boot Top where she whiled away two hours answering e-mails and discussing menu details with Michel. During that time, she exchanged a flurry of texts with Millay, Harris, and Laurel. At Laurel's insistence the group agreed to meet at Decadence.

"I need chocolate. And to be home for the boys' bedtime," she said in a message.

Olivia read the text aloud and grimaced. "Milkshakes at five thirty? Ick. That's my cocktail time. What am I supposed to do?" she asked Haviland. "Eat a pound of whiskey-infused truffles?"

Someone rapped on the office door, and Haviland jumped to his feet, his brown eyes shining. Olivia knew the poodle was hoping to receive treats from Michel or the sous-chefs.

"*C'est moi*," Michel announced and entered. Leaning against the wall, he drew in a deep, theatrical breath, and released it. "I need to talk to you about diamonds."

Olivia gave a start. Ever since Toby had compared the making of a fulgurite with the creation of a diamond, she'd been devoting a great deal of thought to the precious stones. "Why?" she asked Michel.

"I'm going to ask Shelley to marry me," he said, his cheeks pink with joy. Before Olivia could speak, he held out his hands. "I know you're going to say that we haven't been together long enough, but you have to remember that she and I have history. It doesn't matter that I fell in love with her in culinary school twenty years ago. What matters is that I never fell *out* of love with her."

"Michel. You've fallen in and out of love with dozens of women," Olivia pointed out gently. "I'm not trying to put a damper on your plans. I just want you to be sure. Marriage is an institution based on monogamy. You're taking an oath to be with *one* woman for the rest of your life. Are you ready to make that pledge?"

Michel nodded vigorously. "*Oui!* In the past, I went for unavailable women. I think I deliberately chose unsuitable partners because I couldn't have the only woman who could ever complete me."

Olivia rolled her eyes. "If you're going to spout greeting-card poetry or quote lines from romantic comedies, then you need to turn around and go back to the kitchen."

Haviland groaned, as if in agreement, but Olivia knew he was just disappointed that the chef had showed up empty-handed.

"No poetry," Michel promised. "But you must help me, my dear friend. Shelley's been married. She's already had the solitaire diamond, the church wedding, and the white dress. I want to do something simple and intimate. Quiet. But I want still to sweep her off her feet."

"You? Simple? Quiet?" Olivia teased and then said, "I like it, Michel. How about an antique ring? It's unique and infinitely more affordable. Fred Yoder of Circa Antiques could help you pick one out."

Michel frowned. "A used ring? Sounds second-rate."

Olivia shrugged. "That's not how I view old things. I

think of them as being pieces of history. Of having their own story. You and Shelley aren't young lovers. You already share a past, so a vintage ring seems to fit you both better than one produced in some diamond factory."

"You're right! I *knew* you'd have the answer!" Michel seized Olivia's hand and planted a kiss on it. "After Shelley and I are wed, you and the chief should tie the knot. You're made for each other. You should ask *him*. That would be so modern." He rubbed his hands together in expectant glee. "Go on, take the plunge."

Olivia gave him her fiercest scowl. "I'll plunge *you* in boiling water if you plan to continue to flit about like a love-crazed cupid."

Beaming, Michel backed out of the office. "*Violà!* It's this passion that makes the chief so hot for you, *non*?" He ducked as a box of rubber bands sailed over his head.

"Go cook something!" Olivia shouted and then tried to focus on paying bills. However, she glanced at the clock on her computer screen so often that she made very little progress. Finally, she closed the accounting program and began researching the value of loose diamonds. She became so absorbed in this task that she was nearly late for her meeting at Decadence.

Leaving Haviland at The Boot Top, Olivia drove to the desserterie. Normally, she'd walk, but she'd barely make it there in time as it was. There were no parking spots to be found, so Olivia decided to look for a space in the alley behind the shops and was lucky enough to find one right next to Shelley's car.

"Where's Harris?" she asked upon joining Laurel and Millay at the table nearest the front door.

"Late," Millay said. "And so are you."

"I know, but I had an idea that I wanted to check out

before sharing it with you." She paused as Shelley came over with a root beer float for Millay and a creamy-looking martini for Laurel.

"It's a tiramisu martini," Laurel said. "They're utterly divine."

Olivia looked at Shelley uncertainly. "Can you recommend something lighter?"

Shelley suggested a peach Bellini, white sangria, or a mango mojito.

"A plain mojito, please," Olivia said, thinking of how refreshing the combination of fresh mint, limes, white rum, and soda water would taste. "Light on the sugar. Oh, and Shelley. I parked out back. Is that okay?"

Shelley waved her off. "Of course. Gives me the chance to show off my hibiscus to someone. It's actually blooming! Did you happen to notice?"

"I didn't," Olivia admitted. "I vaguely remember a parched twig in a pot from the night of your grand opening."

Shelley snapped her fingers. "Rats. And here I thought you might be my mystery gardener. Someone's been coming by every day to water that little tree. They even put one of those fertilizer sticks in the soil."

Olivia immediately thought of Flynn. He'd noticed her watering the plant the evening of the opening. Had he taken an interest in its welfare? "Was it watered today?" she asked Shelley.

"Sure was. The dirt was dry as sand when I came in this morning but was moist to the touch after lunch. This do-gooder is elusive, I tell you." She sighed. "I'd like to thank them with some chocolates or a cheesecake or something. So if you hear any rumors about a green-thumbed miracle worker, let me know, okay?"

Olivia nodded. "I will."

When Shelley left, Millay raised her spoon and pointed it at Olivia. "You had a lightbulb moment when she brought up that plant. What were you thinking?"

Glancing at the door, Olivia said, "I wanted to wait for Harris, but—"

"There he is!" Laurel interjected. The women peered out the picture window as Harris jogged across the street.

He burst into the shop, unslung his messenger bag from his shoulder, and sank into a chair. "That text you sent me earlier?" he said to Olivia. "I think you're on to something. I got a reply from this geological—"

"Hold that thought," Olivia said as Shelley arrived with her mojito. Harris eyed it appreciatively.

"Could I get one of those too?" he asked. "And a piece of that pineapple-kiwi cheesecake. I'm starving!"

Millay smirked. "You're feeling fruity this evening."

Before Harris could come up with a snarky reply, Laurel plunked her notebook on the table. "Can I have the floor, Harris? I think I discovered a pattern in Violetta's stories. Not the Jack tales, but the ones she made up."

"Go on," Olivia said excitedly.

"Millay e-mailed me all the sentences and phrases she could remember from Violetta's performance, and when I compared them with mine, I noticed that there were certain words that repeated in every story at least twice. All of those words were on the list the chief found in Lowell's pocket."

Olivia slid her drink over to Harris and beckoned him to help himself. She was too caught up in what Laurel was saying to bother with her mojito. "And?" she prompted, believing that Laurel was about to confirm the theory she'd come up with that afternoon.

"So if you and Harris remembered the same words, then we could be on to something. A pattern. A clue." Laurel sounded breathless with anticipation.

Hastening to pull his notes from his bag, Harris passed them to Laurel. Olivia followed suit, and they both watched, enraptured, as she got busy with a pink highlighter.

When Shelley returned with Harris's mojito, she looked hurt. "You didn't care for your drink?" she asked Olivia.

Olivia smiled at her, thinking how lucky Michel was to have won the affections of such a lovely woman. "No, no. I gave mine to Harris because he was so thirsty. I'll take the one you made for him." As soon as Shelley handed her the mojito, Olivia took a deep sip. The cocktail was cool and invigorating, and she sighed in contentment. "Perfection," she said. Shelley flushed with pleasure and moved off to chat with a young couple sharing an enormous root beer float.

Laurel capped her highlighter and put the pages in the center of the table. "We recorded all the words from Lowell's list. Each of those words appeared two or more times in her stories. Along with these." She circled a group of words written on her pad.

Millay leaned over and read them aloud. "'Secret, blue, curse, cold, Pa, ice, granddaddy, heart of trunk.'"

"If we combine those with Lowell's do we get a tangible clue?" Olivia asked hopefully. She quickly reviewed the words Rawlings had sent her yesterday: "silver, moonlight, stones, and heart."

"Half of these remind me of that annoying jewelry commercial we're subjected to every holiday," Harris said. "You know it, right?"

Laurel nodded. "Yes. The one that says that now's the time to invest in a diamond because investing in a diamond is investing in your future?"

Olivia was grinning so widely that when Shelley arrived with Harris's cheesecake she started to laugh. "Maybe I should fix you a pitcher of mojitos."

"They help me think." Olivia raised her glass to Shelley. "Keep 'em coming."

Harris's eyes went wide as he stared at his dessert. "Will you marry me?"

"I've already had two proposals today," Shelley said. "And like I told those other gentlemen, my heart belongs to another. That first taste of love . . . sometimes it remains for a lifetime," she mused dreamily and walked away.

Her remark made Olivia think of Flynn and Amabel. Flynn had clung to his affection for Violetta for two decades, and there was a possibility that Amabel had done the same thing. Flynn had admitted that he'd never recovered from Violetta's betrayal, but he'd wooed Amabel first and then unceremoniously dumped her in favor of her sister. She was a woman scorned. And perhaps a woman who still harbored feelings for the man who'd hurt her so long ago.

"Love or money. Which is the motive?" Olivia murmured, sipping her cocktail. She looked up to find her friends gazing expectantly at her. "Diamonds. I think the family treasure is diamonds."

Harris pushed his cheesecake aside and flattened a piece of wrinkled paper with his palm. "The genealogical info I got? It was about Josiah's dad—the one who moved to Appalachia from New York." When Millay gave him a hurry-up gesture, he frowned but continued. "Quentin Devereaux worked for Cartier Jewelers. And guess what happened the year he left New York? The store was robbed. It was one of the biggest jewelry heists in history, and the thieves were never caught."

Laurel whistled. "What does the chief always say about coincidences?"

"He doesn't believe in them," Millay said and studied Harris. "Were you able to find exactly what was stolen?"

"Loose gems, mostly. The thieves were in and out in a

matter of seconds." He passed Millay the printout. "That's why they got away. They weren't greedy."

"And they had an inside man," Olivia pointed out. "Quentin Devereaux."

Harris shrugged. "I have to agree, but he never fell under suspicion. He was a night-shift guard and was on duty when the robbery occurred. Was knocked out cold by one of the thieves. Must have been a convincing blow because he went back to work a week after the robbery. That's all I could find on him until he bought the land in Whaley three months later."

"He played it smart," Millay said with a hint of admiration. "And he was patient. They probably watched him like hawks for weeks, but he just did his job and went back home until his bosses were certain that he wasn't one of the bad guys."

Laurel drummed her fingers against the list of words. "Half of these could be used to describe diamonds. What about 'granddaddy' and 'Pa'? Do those terms refer to how the treasure's been passed down?"

"Possibly," Olivia said. "And I think 'blue' and 'curse' point to their blood disorder. The Methemoglobinemia was also passed down from Quentin to Josiah to Violetta and Elijah."

"And that only occurred because Quentin's Appalachian wife must have been a carrier too," Harris added. "Do you know how slim those odds are? They're like, ridiculously small."

Laurel shook her head. "I can only imagine how Quentin felt when Josiah was born with his blue skin."

"I'd say he felt cursed." Millay grabbed Laurel's hand and pointed at her wedding ring. "Maybe he thought his son was born blue because he ripped off the jewelry store. I seriously doubt the Appalachian docs could explain where the blue skin came from. I bet Quentin saw himself as a freak. But when his *son* wasn't normal, he probably thought he was being punished for his crime."

Millay's explanation struck a chord with Olivia. "Cursed. If so, it explains why Quentin hid his haul. And why Josiah never touched the diamonds either."

"I don't know." Harris was clearly dubious. "When Elijah got sick, Josiah already had two kids with blue skin, so why would he care any more? Why wouldn't he use the diamonds to save his son?"

"What if Mrs. Devereux was pregnant?" Laurel said. "How badly would the couple want to deliver a healthy, normal baby?"

Millay nodded. "For a blonde, you're pretty sharp. But someone tell me this: how does the word 'silver' fit into all these totally unfounded theories?"

"Or the word 'cold'?" Harris asked and picked up Laurel's list of words. "Alfred Hicks was out in the 'cold,' searching for the 'heart of a trunk' by 'moonlight.' And since Violetta's murder and Lowell's attack happened *after* Hicks was killed, there's only one explanation as to why the murderer hasn't stopped."

The friends stared at Harris until Olivia demanded, "And what's that?"

"Violetta had the diamonds on her. Whoever pushed Hicks off the cliff figured that out and followed her here."

Millay snorted. "Why would his killer wait six months?"

"Why indeed? Unless your store is going under, and you've arranged a storyteller's retreat in your own back-yard? A retreat that would bring an old flame and a fortune in diamonds into town," Olivia said and finished her drink.

"You think Flynn murdered Hicks? And then lured Violetta here for a second chance at the diamonds? There are some serious holes in that theory," Harris pointed out. "Then again, he's gone missing. That makes him look pretty guilty."

"Flynn." Laurel ran her hands through her hair. "I just can't see him killing two people for money. When I think of all the times I've taken the twins to Through the Wardrobe to listen to him read . . ." She swallowed hard.

"It's not only about the diamonds for him." Olivia wanted to phrase her next words carefully so as not to pour salt in Harris's raw wound, but there was no way to tiptoe around the subject. "Violetta broke his heart. It was hard for me to believe that he hadn't gotten over the pain after all this time, but if you'd heard him Tuesday night, you'd know that he hasn't. He never will."

Harris gave Millay an accusing stare as he muttered, "Betrayed with a kiss. Is that what Flynn did to Violetta before asphyxiating her?"

Olivia's mind instantly formed an image of Flynn's lips pressing a featherlight kiss to Violetta's blue skin before slipping the plastic bag over her head. She shivered and rubbed her bare arms.

"If he's the killer, then why did he go after Lowell?" Millay argued softly.

"Either Lowell realized that it was Flynn who pushed Hicks, or Violetta refused to tell Flynn where the diamonds were and he thought Lowell was wise to their location," Olivia surmised. "Dixie told Rawlings that the words in Lowell's pocket were typed using a font designed for Apple computers. Lowell has only used a computer in prison, and it wasn't an Apple. However, Alfred Hicks's missing laptop was a MacBook Pro."

Millay suddenly released a groan of frustration. "We're talking in circles here. It's totally creative of us to come up with all these stories, but can we stroll into the station with them and tell the chief that we know what happened to

Hicks, Violetta, or Lowell? No." She banged the table in frustration. "These words aren't evidence. We're cobbling a new tale out of a bunch of story fragments because we're totally desperate. We have nothing tangible to bring to Rawlings."

Her declaration silenced the group, and Olivia had to wonder if their meeting had been a waste of time. So what if they believed the treasure consisted of stolen diamonds? All signs pointed to Flynn as the killer, but no one knew where he was. Would raising the subject of the treasure change the statements Amabel and Greg had already given to the police? Olivia doubted it. Still, Rawlings would want to hear their theories. Any leads, even false ones, would give him a clearer picture of this convoluted case.

Olivia was just about to suggest that the Bayside Book Writers adjourn so that she could drive to the station when her phone, which was set to vibrate, buzzed. Glancing at the screen, she gasped.

"Lowell's awake!" she told her friends. "Dixie just got a call from the hospital. She's on her way there now."

"Oh, Lord, that is such good news!" Laurel's face flushed with joyous relief. "He can tell the chief who attacked him, and we can get on with our lives."

Harris darted a quick look at Millay and then put a hand on Laurel's. "Which makes this as good a time as any to tell you that I'm moving to Texas."

"What?" Laurel was clearly stricken, and Olivia felt her stomach lurch. She knew this would probably happen, but to hear Harris speak the words aloud was a blow. Everything would change now. Nothing would ever be the same.

"Just for six months. Unless I really like it there," Harris hastened to add.

Laurel gaped. "But why?" Confused, she turned to Millay. "I thought you two would work things out. I thought . . ."

She looked at Harris again, her blue eyes growing moist with unshed tears. "What about your writing?"

Harris shrugged. "I'm done. You guys have helped me so much that all I have left to do now is to polish the manuscript and see if anyone wants it. It's time for some new challenges, you know? In my writing and my job and, well, in other areas of my life too. I need a change of scenery."

Laurel grabbed both of his hands in hers and squeezed. "You have to come back, Harris. I need this group just the way it is now. I look forward to our meetings so much, and you're one of the reasons why. You're a funny, generous, brilliant, awesome guy. Don't stay in Texas. Please don't stay there."

Harris smiled. "I'll keep in touch. Promise. And I'll read and critique anything you want to send me."

"When do you leave?" Olivia asked.

"Two weeks," Harris said.

Laurel sighed. "I'd like to try to talk you out of this, but I have to go home." She leaned over and kissed Harris on the cheek. "No matter what you do, Harris Williams, know that your friends are in Oyster Bay. This group and my family are what make this town my home. So you go have your little adventure, but then you come home, you hear me?"

"Yes, ma'am." Harris saluted Laurel. She left, wiping her eyes, and Harris gathered his things. "I'll keep looking into the genealogical stuff," he said to Olivia. "And I'll mull over everything we know. Maybe some of the pieces will rearrange themselves in my head, and I'll think of something that could help the chief."

Olivia got to her feet and put a hand on his shoulder. "Thanks, Harris. And I echo everything that Laurel said. You're like a diamond in the rough, and personally, I like you that way. Don't get too polished. All of us are flawed. It's what brought us together. It's what keeps us writing. It gives us character. And you are an amazing character."

Unexpectedly, Harris turned and gave her a fierce hug. "Save my spot, Olivia."

A lump formed in Olivia's throat, and she was unable to reply. Harris wished Millay a good night and then left the desserterie.

"You're all going to hate me, aren't you?" Millay asked when he was gone.

"Never," Olivia said after she'd collected herself. "You told him how you felt, and he made a decision. That's better than stringing him along. And I know you're just as miserable as he is. You both need a new start, but don't you go running off to another state. If you do, I will track you down and drag you back here by the hair."

Millay cracked a smile. "That might be tough. I've been thinking about getting a Mohawk."

After Millay was gone, Olivia lingered behind to pay the bill. She hadn't stopped at the ATM for ages and had to use a credit card. After praising Shelley again for the refreshing mojito, she stepped out into the dusky evening. Because it was the height of summer, darkness wouldn't fall for hours yet, but a wall of clouds had blocked the sun and the hazy sky seemed gray and tired.

The alley behind the shops was deserted. Most of the merchants had gone home, and the only sound came from the radio in Shelley's kitchen. Olivia paused to look at the flourishing hibiscus tree on the patio. Its lacy blooms were a bluish lavender that reminded Olivia of Violetta. The plant was healthy and lush—a refreshing sight in a time of drought. The whole world seemed gray and beige, and yet here was a burst of periwinkle and bright green. The tree gave Olivia hope. She got in her car thinking that if a plant could survive hardship with constant care, then so could the Bayside Book Writers. They just couldn't give up on one another, no matter what happened.

And suddenly, Olivia desperately wanted to see Rawlings, to share everything the group had talked about at Decadence, but also to tell him that she was ready to open her house and her heart to him. Every part of her heart. She was terrified, but she was willing to take the risk.

But the moment she turned on her engine, a hand encircled her neck, and she released a garbled cry of surprise.

"I need to talk to you," Flynn said from her backseat. His voice was chillingly calm. "Don't do anything stupid. Just drive."

Olivia glanced in the rearview mirror. She hardly recognized the man behind her. His face was haggard, his hair was wild, and his eyes bored into her reflection. "Where?" she asked, hating how her hands trembled on the steering wheel.

"To the lighthouse," he whispered. "We're going all the way to the top. No one will interrupt us there. Trust me, Olivia, that's a good thing. Because I'm about to tell you the most memorable story you've ever heard."

Chapter 15

Olivia didn't follow Flynn's directions immediately. She risked several precious seconds weighing her options. Other than trying to call Rawlings on her cell phone or opening the car window to scream for help, she couldn't think of a surefire way to save herself. She doubted she could even reach her phone without Flynn noticing, and it was unlikely that Shelly or the Decadence kitchen staff would hear her shouts over the noise of the radio. And even if they did, how would Flynn respond?

As if in answer to her unspoken question, Flynn's fingers dug into her skin. "Don't do anything to keep me from telling my story. If you do, I'll be forced to use this."

Olivia felt the cold kiss of metal against her neck. She hadn't even known that Flynn owned a gun.

Glancing in the rearview mirror, she said, "I have to be able to move if you want me to back out. This is a tight spot, and I need to turn my head to see what's behind me." Her voice was surprisingly steady.

The hand on her neck fell away, but Flynn kept the pistol barrel pointed at her head. Olivia put the car in reverse and accelerated gently. Then, spying a cluster of garbage cans in her rearview mirror, she pressed down on the pedal, slamming the Range Rover into the cans. They made a dull crunch against her bumper and then fell over with a thud, but that was all. No one came rushing out of Decadence to see what had happened, and Olivia knew she'd failed to draw attention to her plight.

"That's the only free pass you get," Flynn snarled into her ear. "Screw with me again and Haviland will pay the price."

The words were more frightening than the gun or Flynn's hands around her throat. Olivia felt a wave of nausea wash over her, and she had to fight to keep the car in the middle of the alley. "How did you get to him?" she asked in a child-like quaver.

"Most folks don't know that Diane and I have called it quits. And since she's your vet and has watched your dog before, it didn't seem that strange for me to be picking him up on your behalf." Flynn smiled. "It's nice to know that Haviland still trusts me. He hopped in the car with his tail wagging. Gentle as a lamb."

Olivia stared at him in the rearview mirror. She saw the flash of his teeth as he smiled, and she wanted nothing more than to slam on the brakes and hope that his face would smash against the windshield. As Olivia drove out of town, she tried to think of how she could deliberately crash and still survive while killing Flynn or at least rendering him unconscious, but she had no idea how to accomplish such a feat. Not only was he shielded by her seat, but if she suddenly accelerated, he'd only jam the gun barrel against her neck. And he had Haviland. The thought had her clenching her jaw in fear.

Olivia tried to calm herself. She needed to be sharp and

lucid, to not be ruled by her emotions. But it was hard. So hard. She'd never felt such hatred toward another person before. Fury surged through her, white-hot and fierce. "If you so much as scratch him, I will kill you," she promised, her eyes dark in the mirror. "Go ahead and shoot me. I'll come back from the grave and haunt you. You'd better fire every bullet in that magazine because if you don't, I will end you."

"I don't want to hurt him, Olivia. You either," Flynn said, his tone morose and almost regretful. "Nothing will happen unless you force my hand."

Olivia drove out of the business district and turned onto the narrow road leading to the Point. There was rarely any traffic on this quiet stretch, and Olivia knew the chances of someone seeing Flynn in the back of her car were slim. Glancing out the passenger window, she noticed how the clouds had multiplied and darkened since she'd first gone into Decadence.

When she pulled in front of the lighthouse keeper's cottage, Flynn released a pent-up sigh. He then leaned over the seat, grabbed Olivia's purse, and threw it on the floor by his feet. "I just need you to listen to me for a little while, and then this will be over. Get out. We're going to the lighthouse."

Olivia did as she was told. Every time she was tempted to turn and fight, she pictured Haviland as she'd last seen him in her office at The Boot Top Bistro. Right now, she didn't even know where he was, and if anything happened to Flynn, she might not be able to find where he'd hidden her dog. Flynn had found her Achilles' heel. He knew that she would do anything to keep Haviland safe. It was the only thing that would have her walking so meekly alongside a madman with a gun.

Flynn was moving fast. He kept his hand on Olivia's lower back, pushing her forward so quickly that she nearly stumbled over the uneven sand. When they reached the lighthouse and Flynn discovered that the door was locked, he kicked it a few times and then, without the slightest warning, raised his gun and shot the lock. It flew into the sand, the metal twisted and blackened, and rested there like some kind of charred beetle. The gunfire echoed over the water, but Olivia knew that it didn't matter. Her closest neighbors were an elderly couple who suffered from hearing loss, and the rest of the beach was completely deserted. Even the birds had fled, leaving only the low, gray clouds and the incoming waves, which were hurrying into shore. The lazy curls of the past few weeks were gone. These waves seemed aggressive. Almost angry. The air was charged too, as if the sea and sky were in collusion. And yet, there was a certain still quality to the entire scene.

A storm is brewing, Olivia thought, and then Flynn propelled her into the lighthouse. They walked up and up the curving staircase and stepped out onto the balcony. The enormous beacon light rotated behind them, its bright beam scorching the dark sky.

"Sit down," Flynn commanded and waited for Olivia to comply before lowering himself to the ground. He then leaned against the wall and looked at her, the gun propped on his right knee. Half of his face was in shadow; the other half was illuminated by the blinding light.

Olivia expected him to speak, but he simply stared at her. Discomfited, she broke eye contact and examined the sky, unable to see either sun or moon behind the thickening clouds. A breeze touched her cheek and lifted strands of her hair. It carried the sea on its breath, and she drew strength from the scent.

"Where does it all start?" she asked Flynn, impatience winning out over caution. "With Hicks? Do you want to confess to his murder?" When her questions were met with a stony silence, she made herself speak more gently. "Tell me the story. Your story."

"I haven't killed anyone," he finally said and then looked down at his gun and frowned as if wondering how it came to be in his hand. "It wasn't me."

Flynn seemed to have become lost in the thoughts he'd seemed so keen on voicing. Olivia wanted to hear them. She needed to know the truth, to discern how dangerous he really was. This man she'd shared meals and books and nights in bed with. A man who'd been a stranger all along.

"Does it begin with the diamonds?" she asked. In a flash, Flynn leapt up and was at her side. He seized her wrist and pressed the gun against her sternum. On the other side of the bone, her heart hammered in terror.

"Where are they? Where are the diamonds?" Flynn asked, shaking her wrist. His eyes were wild, feverish.

Olivia shook her head. "I don't know. My friends and I were meeting at Decadence to talk about Violetta's treasure. We guessed that it had to be diamonds, and Harris confirmed our theory by tracing Quentin Devereaux's history." When Flynn didn't ease his grip, she repeated her first statement. "I don't know where they are!" She tried to jerk her hand free. "We thought you had them. That you lured Violetta to Oyster Bay to steal them from her."

Flynn abruptly let go, putting both hands to his head in astonishment. "Steal?" His voice turned cold with anger. "*Steal?* She owed *me*. All I wanted was what she owed me. If she'd just given me something . . ." He backed away, restoring the distance between Olivia and himself.

Olivia rubbed her sore wrist. "How could you be sure that Violetta would bring the diamonds to Oyster Bay?"

"Amabel told me she would. She guessed that Violetta kept them close at all times. To her, the diamonds had become a symbol of Elijah. The treasure that could have saved him became her personal talisman. Violetta took them when she left home, and Amabel's wanted them for herself ever since. Unlike her sister, Amabel was going to use them to change her life. And mine. She even roped Greg in on the scheme, though I wasn't aware of his involvement. I wouldn't have approved."

"Because your share would be further divided." Olivia tried to keep the disgust from her voice.

Flynn shook his head. "They were worth over two million dollars, Olivia. I did my research. I read everything I could find about the Cartier theft. I made phone calls to jewelers in New York's Diamond District. For decades, Violetta carried around that fortune, denying the rest of her family a brighter future. She was going to punish them all for the rest of her days. Even Amabel, who loved Elijah too."

"Do you know where Violetta hid the diamonds?"

"Unfortunately, Amabel couldn't tell me that, but she knew lots of useful details that could help me get my hands on them." Flynn averted his gaze. "Like how Violetta dressed in hunting gear and waited for Hicks to climb to the top of a cliff so she could push him off."

Now it was Olivia's turn to be astounded. "*Violetta?* But why?"

"Hicks's research wasn't just about folktales. He was a big fan of true crime, and when he deduced that Quentin Devereaux had been involved in one of the biggest jewelry heists in American history, he decided to make a name for himself writing about it. The storytelling angle was a foil, a way for him to get close to members of the Devereaux family. But he made a huge mistake. After interviewing Vi, he accidentally left his notebook behind. Vi read his outline. She read how he was going to expose the family medical condition and describe how all the Devereauxes stood by and let Elijah die. He brought back the past she'd buried.

And he planned to bring her oldest and worst nightmares to life and invite thousands of strangers to read about them. Violetta wouldn't stand for that. Never."

"And Amabel knew all of this?"

Flynn nodded. "Yes, but not until after Hicks's death. She wanted the diamonds too and had never realized that Violetta knew where they were. So she paid her younger sister a visit at another storytelling event in Charlotte. The two of them hit the whiskey, and Vi started boasting about how she'd woven landmarks into the stories she performed when Hicks was listening. Vi even had the gullible fool believing there were rocks in the riverbed that would only sparkle under a full moon, pointing a sharp-eyed observer to the tree trunk where the treasure was stashed. Hicks bought every word. And why wouldn't he? She could make-believe anything. It was her gift."

Olivia recalled Violetta's performance in Oyster Bay's library. "She was truly remarkable."

"And Hicks thought he was *so* clever for unraveling her riddle," Flynn said scornfully. "He went so far as to hire Lowell to accompany him that winter evening because he wanted someone to bear witness to what was certain to become a famous discovery. He promised Lowell that if he found the diamonds, he'd return the entire stash to Violetta right away. He didn't find the treasure. And Amabel was smart enough to know that the diamonds weren't out in the woods. She figured out that Violetta left a false trail for Hicks because she knew the real location of the gems—that she'd taken them with her when she left home all those years ago."

"So Lowell wasn't in on Violetta's scheme?"

"No," Flynn said.

Olivia studied him. "How can you be so sure?"

An expression of bleak remorse crossed Flynn's face. "I

overheard Vi and Amabel talking after the performance at the Oyster Bay library. Greg was there too. In that room behind the stage Vi was using as a dressing room." He put the gun down and laced his fingers together. "I wanted to see Violetta alone. She'd refused all my earlier attempts and I knew she'd be back there, so I left the party in the lobby. Apparently, Amabel and Greg did too. They wanted the diamonds. But I wanted even more than that. I wanted Vi to say she was sorry. And I wanted her to repay the loan from all those years ago. The bookstore's in trouble, you see." His glance pleaded for Olivia to understand.

"You should have come to me, Flynn. I would have helped. Gladly."

He waved off the notion. "No. Don't you see? She owed me."

Thoughts whirled in Olivia's mind like confetti in a shaken snow globe. "But Leona saw you going into the restroom looking distraught. She said your tie was loose and askew."

Flynn gazed out at the sea, which had turned as gray as the sky. "That tie was too tight. I felt like I couldn't breathe." His voice was barely a whisper. "Like I was the one who'd had a bag put over my head. But it wasn't my tie that went around her throat. It was Greg's."

The beam of light spun around and around, and Olivia closed her eyes against it, returning to the evening of Violetta's death. She saw the storyteller onstage, her face and eyes awash in that ethereal blue glow, her finger pointing accusingly at someone in the audience. Had she known that she had more than one enemy in the crowd? She must have looked at Greg, Amabel, and Flynn and seen something dark and lethal in all of their eyes.

She said that this place was her Gethsemane, Olivia thought. Violetta had known that someone she'd once been close to was likely to betray her, steal her treasure, and end her life.

"Greg was her lover," Olivia said aloud. "Greg was with her Thursday night. Not you. He was the man she used and then tossed aside like trash. He was the man who had a plan to make her pay for how he'd been treated."

Flynn was staring at Olivia mournfully. "That's how she went through life. People adored her, were spellbound by her, fell deeply in love with her, and could never touch her. Not here." He tapped the center of his chest. "She was as hard and cold as those diamonds. Greg made her pay for that. Amabel asked her over and over where the diamonds were hidden, and she responded by laughing at them. She laughed until the air was all gone."

Suddenly, Olivia realized what Flynn was saying. "You watched her die?"

He said nothing. She waited, and eventually, he gave a single nod.

"Why didn't you try to stop them?" she asked.

Again, he turned toward the ocean. A rumble of thunder reverberated over the waves and both Flynn and Olivia raised their eyes to the slate sky. The clouds appeared to be sinking, closing the gap between heaven and earth. A sheet of lightning lit up the horizon, competing with the lighthouse beacon.

"I just wanted Vi to give me something," Flynn whispered. "Amabel wanted it all. She hated that Vi and Elijah had a special bond. She hated that she hadn't been born blue and, therefore, wasn't special. She hated that her sister left home and never looked back. Never sought her out. Never cared that as sisters, they were supposed to share a bond too. Amabel wanted to be Violetta. Amabel thought that if her sister was gone and she had the diamonds, center stage, and me, then she'd finally be happy."

Olivia had to lean forward to hear him. The breeze was escalating into a bona fide wind. It whistled around the lighthouse, scattering fistfuls of sand and salt. "When did you and Amabel start talking again?"

"She called me after Hicks died. Of course, I had no idea Violetta pushed him to his death. Amabel only told me about that when she couldn't find the diamonds. She planned to get them away from Vi during her trip here, and we'd split them equally. I'd save the store, and she'd buy all the things she'd lived without her whole life." He shook his head. "I had no idea that she wanted to kill Violetta, and Amabel must have realized that I'd never hurt her sister. That's why she dragged Greg Rapson into her scheme."

"She was going to divvy up the diamonds with whoever helped her," Olivia mused aloud, horrified by Amabel's ability to plot her sister's murder. Olivia had sensed a coldness in her from the moment they'd met, but she had no idea that Amabel was so calculating, so utterly remorseless. To premeditate the murder of one's own sister . . .

Flynn was watching her. "I thought you might be able to explain it all to me. How can old wounds suddenly fester? How can the things we've shoved into the deepest pits of our souls claw and scratch their way out? Why couldn't Amabel lead her own life? Why couldn't I let go of Violetta? Why did someone else seeking the diamonds set off this sequence of tragedies? You have insight into this kind of thing. Can you tell me why this happened?" He swallowed hard.

Olivia fell silent, giving serious consideration to his question. "I don't know, Flynn. Some people are more adept at moving on. And then there are those who can't forget. Or forgive. Violetta had no problem leaving people after she'd gotten what she wanted from them. She must have known that eventually, she'd make someone so angry that they'd want to hurt her."

"And yet, it took Amabel years to act. After Vi left home, they never saw each other again until that night in Charlotte after Hicks died. Amabel didn't attend the same storyteller events as her sister, but the bitterness grew in her all the same. She couldn't go anywhere without hearing about the amazing Violetta Devereaux. She couldn't escape her younger sister's shadow." Flynn touched his chest. "And that shadow grew until Amabel's heart turned black."

"So their second reunion of the year occurred here? In our library? When Vi pointed at Amabel in the audience the night she was killed?" The notion chilled Olivia. "That's how Violetta knew her time had come. She looked into her sister's eyes and just . . . knew. And she didn't try to escape her fate. Why?"

Flynn gave her a wry grin. "Because she wanted her whole life to read like a story. An incredible and, more importantly, an unforgettable story. If she died of heart disease or went peacefully in the night, her name would eventually be forgotten. As Elijah's was forgotten. That's not the kind of ending she would ever accept. She feared obscurity more than anything else. By mentioning the diamonds during her performance, she invited her sister to act, guaranteeing herself more time in the spotlight. She continued performing, manipulating people and shaping her own story until her very last breath." He choked on the last word.

Olivia frowned. "I don't see how Lowell fits into this macabre picture."

"Greg was Lowell's teacher in prison," Flynn said. "But you probably know that by now. It was his idea for Lowell to apply for the position of Violetta's assistant. Greg thought he could get in her good graces if he put her and Lowell together. Greg Rapson's had a thing for her since he joined the storyteller circuit. And Lowell? He really was trying to go straight. Too bad he ended up right smack in the middle of something too tempting to resist. Cartier diamonds? The guy stood no chance."

Thunder rumbled again offshore, but the sound was closer now. Again, lightning burned the sky white, but only for half a heartbeat.

"So you really don't know where the diamonds are. The cops don't know where the diamonds are. And Amabel and Greg didn't leave town, so I'm assuming they don't have them. Does Lowell, I wonder?"

Flynn shrugged. "I hope he does. He might be a thief, but he's still a decent guy."

"Do you know who tried to drown him?"

"I'd guess it was Amabel or Greg or both. They'd already killed one person together, and they didn't get the diamonds from her or Lowell would have never been attacked. He may have figured out where Vi kept them. She tossed Hicks's laptop and notebook in a mountain lake, but Lowell might have kept one of the pages printed from Hicks's MacBook Pro. He's smarter than he lets on."

Olivia hoped Rawlings was with Lowell right now. If so, Lowell would tell him who'd held his head under the water, and the chief would immediately return to the station, fueled with a quiet anger, to coax a confession from Amabel and Greg. But she had no way of knowing what Lowell's ordeal had done to his faculties. She could only desperately wish that he was still the man he'd been before he was drowned and brought back to life again.

There was another round of thunder and lightning, and Olivia moved a little closer to Flynn. She saw despair in his eyes, as stark and gray as the sky. "What else, Flynn? What else do you have to tell me?"

"I watched them kill her, Olivia," he said. Tears slipped down his cheeks. "They didn't see me. I could have shouted. I could have grabbed them, but I couldn't move. She stared straight at me, and I felt the old rage. I've felt it for most of my life. Part of me reasoned that she deserved what she was getting." He wiped off his tears, but fresh ones followed. "She didn't struggle. Not until the very end. And the whole time, she looked right at me. Right through me. As if I didn't exist. As if I *still* didn't matter. And so I did nothing. I crept away without making a noise like the ghost she'd turned me into all those years ago."

The wind ruffled his hair and the sleeves of his shirt. The thunder boomed and in the distance, a new sound floated up to the lighthouse balcony. The sound of sirens.

Rawlings. He's coming for me, Olivia thought, her heart lifting.

Flynn heard the sirens too. He slowly got to his feet and took hold of the gun again, the barrel pointing at the floor. "This was never for you," he told her, gesturing at the weapon with his free hand.

Olivia wasn't sure if she believed that. "What about Haviland?"

"I suppose he's wherever you left him," Flynn said. "I'd never hurt him, Olivia. Or you. I just wanted someone to listen. It's the last story I'll ever tell."

It took a moment, but when the meaning of his words sunk in, Olivia cried, "Flynn, no! I can help. I can hire the best lawyers in the state. I'll pay off the loan on your shop. This isn't the way. Let me be a friend to you."

He gaped at her. "Why would you help me? I'm despicable. I let a woman die, Olivia. I kidnapped you at gunpoint."

"You've made mistakes, but you're still one of us," she said over the whoosh of the wind. "Don't do this, Flynn. You're one of us."

The thunder was so loud that it blotted out his reply. He pivoted away from the lighthouse beam, plunging his face in shadow. "Go on now. I don't want you to see this."

Another flash of lightning. Olivia cast a frantic glance around, searching for some way to stall Flynn until Rawlings arrived.

The noise of the sirens was louder now. Rawlings wasn't far. She knew it and Flynn knew it too. He gestured at the door leading back inside. "Go."

She shook her head. "Don't. Please don't."

"*Go!*" Flynn bellowed over a crash of thunder. The storm was moving inland, and it was coming fast.

Olivia heard someone call her name. It was Rawlings. He was probably outside the lighthouse keeper's cottage.

He'll come here next, she thought.

"Go to him," Flynn said. The emptiness in his voice tore at Olivia's heart.

She began to cry. "I can't. I can't leave you here."

"When they get close enough, I'm going to do it. For Christ's sake, I'm trying to spare you, Olivia. Won't you let my last act be a decent one?"

"*Olivia!*" Rawlings shouted, his voice carried by the wind.

"This town has lost enough already," Olivia spoke as if she hadn't heard Rawlings. "I've lost enough." She was aware that she was repeating Rawlings' words from earlier that day, but they felt right. "Please. I'm still your friend. You're not alone in this."

Flynn smiled at her. She recognized gratitude in that smile, but it was too tainted by despair and resignation for her to dare hope that she'd changed his mind. "I've been lost since the day I first saw her," he said, his voice a hoarse croak. "I mean to find her again." He pulled the pistol's hammer back and looked at Olivia. His eyes pleaded with her. "Go."

There was a crash down below, and Rawlings called to her again. She heard fear in that call, and she wanted to assure him that she was okay. Acting on impulse, she moved toward the stairs. She only meant to yell, "I'm here!" before returning her attention to Flynn, but she never got the chance. The second she left the balcony, a crash of thunder was immediately followed by a sharp blast. Olivia gasped and clutched at her chest as if she was the one who'd been shot.

"*Olivia!*" Rawlings' shout was filled with anguish. Olivia heard him racing up the stairs, and then her knees buckled and she sank to the floor. She could feel the storm gathering behind her, gaining in power and force. She could sense the waves rising and smashing against the shore, and imagined that they were a harsh contrast to the slow, steady ebbing of Flynn McNulty's lifeblood.

She didn't know when Rawlings reached her. She stared at him, unseeing, as he spoke to her, shook her gently by the shoulders, and checked her for injuries. Then his hands dropped away, and he stepped out onto the balcony. Olivia watched him bark commands into his radio while she pulled her legs into her chest. She suddenly felt so cold, as if winter had crept into her body and turned her bones to ice.

Rawlings got down on the floor and held her to him. He rocked her slowly and stroked her hair, whispering "shhhh, shhhh," like she was a child who'd woken in the middle of the night because of a nightmare.

Eventually, other men and women in uniform appeared and began to transform the lighthouse into a crime scene. Dully, Olivia observed them unpack their equipment. She shut her eyes to keep from seeing the camera flash and thought about all the times she'd snuck into this building as a child, climbing up the stairs with a book tucked under her arm. She'd spent so many afternoons on that balcony, savoring an apple as she read. Every now and then, she'd have a pimento cheese sandwich that she'd share with the seagulls. Whenever she finished a book, she'd hold it on her lap and gaze out at the endless water, dreaming of all the places she'd visit when she was grown. She especially loved to read on the balcony after supper. The moon would rise over the ocean, creating a gleaming path of white-gold light. Olivia vowed that one day she'd follow the moon road to a magical place, a place where a skinny, freckled girl could find love and friendship.

She'd found those things here in Oyster Bay, where her journey had begun. But there'd been no straight path for Flynn to follow. Neither the lighthouse beam nor the lightning held still long enough to guide him. Yet he'd gone forth into the darkness all the same.

Rawlings murmured a few orders to his team and then led Olivia downstairs and over the dunes to the keeper's cottage. When he moved to open the door, she hesitated and held out her hand, palm facing skyward. A fat drop of rain splashed against her skin. Another drop followed. And another.

She raised her face, inviting the water to fall on her. She wanted it to wash her salty tears away, but they stuck fast to her skin.

"Come on, love," Rawlings whispered and slid an arm around her waist. "It's over now. Come on inside."

Olivia let him lead her into the house. He made her lie down on the sofa and then covered her with a blanket. He brewed a cup of strong coffee and stirred in a dollop of whiskey with the cream. All the while, he said nothing.

He sat with her while she sipped her coffee. Outside, the rain fell harder. The sound of it hitting the roof was a beautiful symphony to Olivia. It muffled the gunshot that kept going off again and again in her head.

"Would you open the windows?" she asked Rawlings. "All of them?"

Nodding, he got up and moved around the cottage. When he was done, the snug house was filled with the cacophony of a summer storm. It was unexpectedly comforting.

Olivia knew that Rawlings was waiting for her to speak—that he had an urgent need to know everything she'd heard on the lighthouse balcony. She would tell him of course. She would repeat every word, recall every terrible detail, if it meant helping him put two murderers away.

But just for a moment, she wanted to lose herself in the storm. After weeks of drought and dryness and heat, she wanted to close her eyes and drown in the rush of water.

A short while later, while Rawlings held her hand and the tempest raged outside the cottage, she began to speak.

Chapter 16

The minute I heard my first love story I started looking for you, not knowing how blind that was. Lovers don't finally meet somewhere. They're in each other all along.

—RUMI

Rawlings listened without interruption. He asked her to pause a time or two while he wrote something in his notepad, but Olivia recounted the last conversation she would ever have with Flynn McNulty with disturbing quickness. She was surprised by the lack of emotion in her voice. It was as if the storm was reacting on her behalf, battering the earth with wind and rain and handfuls of sand while she talked.

"And then you were there," Olivia said when she was done. "You found me."

"I'll always find you." Rawlings gazed at her tenderly for a long moment and then glanced at his cell phone. "Cook's called me a dozen times. He texted that it's urgent."

Olivia had images of Cook frantically dialing the chief's number to report that Amabel and Greg had somehow escaped, but knew she was being ridiculous. However, as she watched Rawlings' reaction to Cook's news, she sensed that the investigation was far from over.

"It's Lowell," Rawlings said after ending the call. "He's

gone. A nurse entered his room to find it empty." He pushed the phone in his pocket and turned toward the door. "Violetta's murderers may be in custody, but Mr. McNulty's confession must be corroborated. Our suspects might panic when they hear that Flynn bore witness to their crime, but unless I can get them to admit to the killing, I need Lowell. He has to press charges against Amabel Hammond and Greg Rapson."

Shoving the blanket off her legs, Olivia stood up. "Did anyone talk to Lowell after he woke up? Did he realize that he wasn't in danger anymore?"

"I have no idea," Rawlings said. "New Bern PD had an officer stationed outside his door, so I don't know how he slipped out to begin with. Two of my men are en route to the hospital and should arrive any minute now. They'll report back on his condition when he disappeared, but we must find him without delay." He checked his watch. "Cook will lead the search. As for me, I need to convince one of our murder suspects to talk."

"Dixie might know something about Lowell," Olivia said, following Rawlings to the door. "She sent me a text while I was still at Decadence saying that he was awake." Picking up her purse, she checked her phone, only to find that the battery was nearly dead. "Stupid little machine," she muttered and then froze.

"What is it?" Rawlings waited by the open door. His body was tense with impatience, but he looked at her as if he had all the time in the world.

"I think I know how Lowell snuck out," she said. "In fact, he might still be in the hospital—on another floor or hiding somewhere. He can't leave without a change of clothes and some cash, right? Or a ride."

Rawlings tapped on his radio. "Tell me and I can pass on the info to my men."

"When I went to visit Leona, I shared the elevator with

a robot. It delivered medicine from the pharmacy to certain floors," Olivia explained. "And though you and I couldn't hide inside, a child could. Or a dwarf. The cabinet was kept locked, but I don't think that would have stopped Lowell from getting in."

"I'll see if New Bern will bring in their K-9 unit," Rawlings said.

After Olivia locked the cottage, she and Rawlings ran to her car. The rain pelted them as they moved. Rawlings held the passenger door open for Olivia and then raced around to the driver's side. Wiping a strand of wet hair from his forehead, he made a succession of rapid calls. While he gave succinct commands, Olivia stared at the water-speckled windshield, lost in thought.

"Back to the station," Rawlings said and put his seat belt on.

Putting a hand on his arm, Olivia said, "We need to get Haviland and then I want to come to the station with you. I'd like to see Violetta's trunk."

Rawlings knit his brows together. "Why?"

"Because Lowell's a thief. He may have wanted to change his ways, but once he heard about the diamonds, I don't think he could resist their allure. I believe he cared about Violetta and that she trusted him, but only to a certain extent. After Hicks died, I think Lowell finally discovered where she hid the diamonds but didn't have an opportunity to grab them until the night Violetta was murdered."

Rawlings was gazing into the middle distance. "That's why he was assaulted."

"Sometime after they'd murdered Violetta, Greg and Amabel must have also figured out where the diamonds were kept and went after Lowell to see if he had them. It's one of the reasons Lowell took off right after Violetta was killed. He was afraid, yes, but he'd committed a crime too."

"If he didn't have the diamonds on him when he was attacked, then he's stashed them somewhere," Rawlings said. "In his car or at the Weavers' house."

"If so, then he won't truly disappear until he stops in Oyster Bay one more time to collect his prize."

Nodding, Rawlings handed her his cell phone. "Call Grumpy. If he isn't at the hospital with Dixie, tell him to go home and keep an eye out for Lowell."

As Rawlings backed down the driveway, Olivia cast a long look at the lighthouse. "Good-bye, Flynn," she whispered in a low, heartsick voice.

Haviland trotted into the police station in high spirits. His brown eyes darted around the lobby, and Olivia suspected he was hoping to catch a glimpse of Greta, Oyster Bay's canine officer. Greta was an attractive German shepherd who enjoyed Haviland's attention, but the female officer manning the front desk informed the expectant poodle that Greta wasn't on duty.

"Every cop on the force is here *but* her," she added sotto voce, but Rawlings heard her nonetheless.

"I know you haven't had much time with your family lately, Officer Brooks, but I also know that you're devoted to this town and its people." There wasn't a trace of rebuke in Rawlings' tone. "We're almost there, Brooks."

The young woman stood a fraction taller. "Yes, sir. We have your back, Chief. We'll see this to the end."

"Let's hope the end happens soon," he said and led Olivia and Haviland down the hall. After depositing Haviland in his office, he took Olivia to the evidence room.

Violetta's massive trunk was pushed against the back wall. It looked forlorn and diminished beneath the weak light of the fluorescent bulbs overhead. "Do you have a flashlight?" she asked Rawlings. He handed her the one from his duty belt. Directing the narrow beam on the trunk's center latch, she said, "Can you see how the leather is a deeper color brown around this area? That's because a padlock hung here. When Lowell dragged the trunk onstage to kick off the performance, he unlocked it. I remember seeing a flash of metal." She gently opened the lid. "Does your inventory list include a lock and key?"

While Rawlings examined the list, Olivia looked over his shoulder. Violetta's belongings were typed into neat columns—her life reduced to a group of words like "pair of black cotton gloves" or "wooden hand mirror." Rawlings set the papers aside. "No padlock. Why is it important?"

"Let me run my theory by Fred Yoder first. I don't want to waste time chasing a false lead." She took out her phone. "Just give me one minute."

"That's about all I have to spare," Rawlings said and began to reexamine the bagged contents from Violetta's trunk.

When Fred answered his phone, Olivia hastily explained that she was at the police station and needed help. As was his way, Fred instantly offered his assistance and then listened as she questioned him about antique padlocks.

"Fred's seen a variety of heart-shaped padlocks made from the late 1800s to the 1920s," she said after ending the call. "There were a few models big enough to have hollows inside the center. A person could hide something very small within the padlock and then solder the two halves together. Of course, to get the treasure out, someone would have to remove the rivets. I imagine you'd need a blowtorch to get to the diamonds."

"I wonder if Grumpy owns one." Rawlings ran his fingers through his salt-and-pepper hair, causing strands to stick up in all directions. "The heart of the old trunk was never a tree. It was always *this* trunk. It was probably Quentin Devereaux's trunk."

Olivia nodded. "Alfred Hicks was misled by Violetta's landmark clues, but Lowell solved her riddle. She added just enough truth in her stories for him to do that." Olivia touched the soft velvet lining the lid's interior. "That's the advice she gave me after her performance. She told me the best stories were an equal blend of truth and lies." Her fingers made little waves in the velvet. "Violetta also said that Oyster Bay was a good Gethsemane—that she liked how the stars reflected on the water. How they shone like fiery diamonds." Olivia shook her head. "Why didn't I remember her saying that until now?"

Rawlings put a hand on her shoulder and squeezed. "You spoke with her once, Olivia. And yet, you've fought for her as if you two were close friends."

"It'll all be for nothing if we can't find Lowell and that padlock." Olivia carefully shut the lid. She stared down at the trunk, unwilling to walk away. Turning to Rawlings, she said, "Could I see Elijah's photo?"

He took a cardboard box from a nearby shelf and placed it on a table. Gesturing at the folding chair, he opened the box and removed an item encased in an evidence bag. "Just put it back when you're done. I'll call you when I can." Kissing her on the forehead, he left the room.

Olivia waited until she could no longer hear his footsteps before she picked up the bag containing the old photograph. The image of Elijah Devereaux was grainy. The black and white had faded to black and grey with spots of brown along the edges of the square paper.

Elijah was quite young. Olivia guessed that he was five or six when the picture was taken. He wasn't looking at the camera but seemed to be laughing at someone standing to the right of the photographer. He was a cute boy with a mop of unruly black hair, a wide smile, and luminous eyes. Olivia had no idea if they were the same sapphire hue as Violetta's, but they were certainly as captivating. His face, neck, and bare arms looked darker than hers, and Olivia assumed that the family's genetic condition had tinted him a deeper shade of blue.

"You're so thin," Olivia told the boy in the photograph. His limbs were twiglike. His face was gaunt. His oft-mended clothes hung from his slim frame, but his smile spoke of innocent delight, and Olivia hoped Violetta was the cause of his happiness. Because in the moment he'd been captured on film, Olivia believed he'd been happy. She also realized that while Violetta had become a renowned storyteller, she'd never allowed herself to love another person. Elijah had captured her heart, and her heart had broken when he died.

Maybe Flynn was wrong, she thought. *Maybe Violetta wasn't simply looking for a dramatic ending to her story. Perhaps she was tired of grieving. Of being angry and unable to forgive. Of the suffocating loneliness. Maybe she was weary of pretending. Or wanted the kind of peace she didn't think she could find in this life.*

Olivia put Elijah's photograph back into the cardboard box and paused.

Shouldn't someone hold on to him? Someone who loved him? Olivia knew she didn't dare do anything that could compromise the case, so she reluctantly put the box away. She wondered if, when all was said and done, Amabel would want to see Elijah's picture. Perhaps she might find comfort in remembering how her little brother looked before he got sick. Before he died and her family fell apart. Before Violetta left and Amabel's hatred for her sister began to bloom inside her like a thorny black rose.

The photo belongs to a girl named Mabel, Olivia thought. *Or whatever remains of that girl inside the woman called Amabel. A woman who plotted the murder of her own sister.*

Olivia called Dixie from Rawlings' office.

"Any sign of Lowell?" she asked.

"Not even a glimpse," Dixie said. "And it's not like the Carolina coast is teemin' with dwarves in hospital gowns." She raised her voice to be heard over the wailing of the storm. "When I heard he was out of that coma, I sang all the way to New Bern, but now I'm back to that doom-and-gloom feelin'. The weather's not helpin'. Grumpy and I are drivin' around lookin' for Lowell, but I can barely see the road with all this rain."

Olivia glanced out the window. The thinner branches of the crepe myrtles separating the building from the parking lot were being whipped about by the wind. The rain pummeled the leaves and deep puddles were forming in the depressions near the roots. "Are you in Oyster Bay?"

"We are. I figured Lowell had to come back here. He needs his car. Two cops are waitin' at my house, and my kids think this is the most wonderful thing since peanut butter, but I could do without the drama. It's fine when I hear about things happenin' to someone else, but I don't like it this up close and personal."

"What did the doctors say about Lowell's condition?"

Grumpy shouted at another driver, and Dixie told him to calm down. "They said he seemed normal. A little weak and in need of a few days' rest, but normal. The cops were lookin' inside that robot when we left. Looks like that's how he snuck away. But he can't hot-wire a car and drive off into the sunset. He can't reach the pedals." She released a heavy sigh. "What's he thinkin'? Why is he actin' so damned crazy?"

Olivia shared her theory about the diamonds being hidden in the heart-shaped padlock. "The police don't have it, and I don't think Greg or Amabel do either. I believe Lowell stashed the lock somewhere in town and will come back for it before disappearing for good."

Dixie was silent for a moment. "He swore he'd changed. I wouldn't have let him stay with us, be near our kids, if I didn't think he . . ." she trailed off. "Couldn't Flynn have the lock? From what you told me, he—"

"No," Olivia said gently but firmly. She knew Dixie was hoping that the thief was anyone but her cousin, but Olivia thought Lowell was the most likely suspect. And she wasn't ready to talk about Flynn's suicide. She couldn't speak of it. Not now. Not for a long time. She was trying not to think about it. To become so involved in Lowell's disappearance that her mind would stop replaying the sound of the gunshot. "Have you checked every inch of your house?" she asked Dixie. "Maybe the padlock is hidden in plain sight. In the tackle box or mixed in with Grumpy's tools or in one of the kids' rooms. Could Lowell have talked any of them into keeping a secret?"

After exchanging a few words with Grumpy, Dixie replied, "Don't think so. Grumpy threatened to take a hammer to their video games if they kept info about Lowell from us."

"I suppose he could have hidden the padlock anywhere in the woods. Is there a back way to your house?"

Dixie snorted. "None that Lowell could find, and it's a long hike. The cops are waitin' at that end and in our closest neighbors' yards too. He can't sneak his way in."

Olivia, who'd been pacing around the office, kicked the desk chair in frustration. It spun lazily around, and Haviland sat up and started barking. "Where else would he go?" she mumbled aloud.

"We've asked the same question a million times," Dixie said. "This feels so wrong, 'Livia, to be out huntin' him like he's a rabbit and we're the foxes. We thought he ran off because he was scared, but that wasn't the reason, was it? It's those damned diamonds."

"I'm sure fear is playing its part," Olivia said. "The murderers are in custody, but no one can rest easy until they've been formally charged and locked in a cell. And that's only a cause for relief if the police have enough evidence to win over a jury. It won't be easy to get Amabel to confess. She'll fight like a cornered cat or shift the blame on Greg or Flynn. Lowell has to come forward and name her and Greg as his assailants or—"

"Wait a second!" Dixie cried. "There's another place he could've stashed the lock. The diner! He's been in most every day, and he could slip in through the kitchen door without bein' seen."

Olivia thought of all the cabinets and niches in the diner. It would be a simple thing to stick a padlock inside a sugar bowl in the far corner of a high shelf. "You might be on to something, Dixie. You two head over there and I'll drive through the alleys. Since Lowell can't operate a car, he must have found another way to town."

"None of the taxi drivers picked up a dwarf. I asked the cops at the hospital, and they'd checked with the taxi companies first," Dixie said after telling Grumpy to head to the diner. "But he could have been hidin' in someone's trunk or backseat. He can make himself real small when he's got to."

For a moment, Olivia's mind formed an absurd picture of Lowell jimmying the trunk of an Oyster Bay police cruiser. "He must be feeling desperate. Be careful, Dixie."

Olivia paused to ask the female officer manning the front desk to get a message to Rawlings. After scribbling a note saying that Dixie thought Lowell might head for the diner, Olivia and Haviland ran through the rain and hopped into the Range Rover. Putting her windshield wipers on high, Olivia joined the search for the only person who could restore a sense of normalcy to Oyster Bay.

"No one's walking around in this storm," she pointed out to Haviland. "Let's check the alleyways."

Maneuvering through the narrow, pothole-ridden lanes behind the shops, Olivia drove slowly, keeping her eye out for movement. After thirty minutes of fruitless scanning, she ended up at Grumpy's.

Haviland raised his nose and sniffed. "I know you're thinking about bacon, but this isn't the time to beg for snacks," Olivia scolded.

She knocked on the back door to avoid startling the Weavers and then stepped inside the kitchen, Haviland close on her heels. "Dixie?"

"In here!" came the reply. Though she'd spoken only two words, Olivia sensed an unusual gravity in Dixie's tone. When she entered the dining room, Olivia saw why.

Lowell was seated at *The Phantom of the Opera* booth. He wore a white lab coat over his hospital gown and was drenched. Water had run off his clothes and bare feet, and puddled on the floor.

"Am I glad to see you." Olivia couldn't help but smile. "Are you all right?"

"I'd be better with a hot cup of coffee, but Dixie won't give me so much as a napkin unless I tell her where Violetta's diamonds are. And I don't have them."

Dixie stood near the counter, arms crossed over her chest. Her mouth was set in a stern frown. "All you're gonna get from me is a swift kick in the ass if you don't start fessin' up."

Olivia approached Dixie and took her hand. "Why don't you let me talk to Lowell? I'd trade both of my restaurants for a pot of your famous coffee."

Dixie hesitated, but when Grumpy nodded, she relented. "I'll fix you some, but if the dwarf tries to leave, sic Haviland on him." She turned to the poodle. "I hear he tastes just like pork chop."

Haviland's ears perked up, and he gave Dixie his most winsome smile. Unfortunately for him, she was too hurt, angry, and worried to notice.

"It's all over, Lowell," Olivia said, taking a seat across

from the sodden dwarf. "Amabel and Greg are in custody. And Flynn . . . he's come clean." She swallowed the lump forming in her throat. "Forget about the diamonds. Tell me who assaulted you."

Lowell was silent for a full minute. He wouldn't look Olivia in the eye but seemed intent on studying the Phantom of the Opera's mask. "Another freak," he whispered. "His story didn't end any better than Violetta's did. The other guy got his girl, and folks went after the masked man with torches. I never saw the play, but Dixie's talked about it so much that I feel like I have."

"She cares about you, Lowell." Olivia spoke gently. "Please don't let her down. Dixie Weaver is one of the finest people I know."

"I'm glad she has a friend." He waved his hand to incorporate the whole of the diner. "Folks respect her in this town. I like to come in and watch her work. Only the tourists stare at her like she belongs in a circus. The rest of you accept her. She's lucky."

"You could stay in Oyster Bay too. You don't have to run anymore. Start over. That's what I did when I came back here."

Lowell gave a humorless laugh. "Dixie will never want me around her kids after this. I've blown it."

"Then make it right," Olivia insisted. "Who attacked you? Amabel and Greg?"

"Yes." Lowell seemed to deflate after the admission. He sagged against the booth cushion and wiped a drop of water from the point of his chin. "They showed up at Dixie's place and said they were going to frame me for the murder unless I gave them the diamonds. All I could think of was getting those two out of there before the boys came home. I had the dogs, sure, but I wasn't close enough to grab the rifle from behind the door, and I didn't know if that pair of psychopaths were armed, so I went with them."

Olivia couldn't begin to imagine how frightening that moment must have been. "You made a very noble decision."

"Not really," he said dismissively. "It was me or the kids. Real simple. I didn't protect Violetta, but I'd be damned if I let something happen to Dixie or her family."

"Then make sure it doesn't," Olivia pleaded. "Press charges against Greg and Amabel. See that they're locked away. If you don't get involved, they could walk, and Dixie will never rest easy again."

Lowell wiped his face with his hands and sighed. His gaze returned to the Phantom mask. And then he looked at Olivia and nodded. "I'll do it, but I'd like to have a cup of coffee first."

Smiling, Olivia said, "Have two. I'm buying."

Lowell drank his coffee, and when he was done, Grumpy agreed to drive him home so that he could change clothes before heading to the police station. Dixie rode along with Olivia. The two women stood like sentinels by the station's front door until Lowell arrived. After Lowell followed Rawlings into the conference room, the two friends sat in the chief's office and listened to the rain.

Dixie was the first to break the silence. "Lowell says he doesn't have the padlock, but I don't believe him for a second. I hope your man worms the truth out of him."

"Me too," Olivia said. "And I still can't figure out how Lowell got to Oyster Bay from the hospital."

Dixie grimaced. "All he said was that he got to know which of the nurses lived out our way. I'm sure he stowed away in her car. And you were right about him hidin' inside the robot, though Lowell's always hated tight, dark spaces. After what he's put us through, I hope he was absolutely miserable inside that thing."

Olivia took Dixie's hand. "Don't be too hard on him. In the end, he chose to come forward, and he nearly died making sure the killers didn't get near your kids."

"I suppose that's somethin', but we won't be gettin' out the good towels and askin' him to stay in the guest room anytime soon."

Olivia laughed and Dixie joined in, and for a moment, the sound of their mirth was stronger than the storm.

A week later, after the media grew tired of reporting on the murder of Violetta Devereaux and vanished to cover a shark attack off the coast of South Carolina, the Bayside Book Writers met at their usual time in the lighthouse keeper's cottage.

Laurel made it through the first fifteen minutes before bursting into tears. "I'm sorry," she sobbed. "But I can't handle your leaving, Harris. Not after what happened to Violetta. Not after Flynn. And now there's a "for sale" sign taped to the front door of Through the Wardrobe." She sniffed. "I don't want to lose anything else. Any*one* else."

Harris put his arm around Laurel. "I bought a round-trip ticket," he whispered into her ear, but Olivia caught the words and her spirits rose just a little.

"Okay," Laurel said and dried her tears with a napkin. "I guess I can live with that."

"What about you, Chief?" Millay asked, obviously trying to change the subject. "You must be totally wiped."

Rawlings studied the splinters of light being cast on the counter by his green beer bottle before answering. "I am tired. But this"—he waved his hand to incorporate all of them—"gives me strength. This fellowship, for lack of a less cheesy word, renews me."

Millay rolled her eyes. "Look out, he's going all Gandalf on us. Rawlings the Grey. Or Sawyer the Salt-and-Pepper."

Everyone laughed and Olivia felt some of her own weariness melt away. They would all recover. The tragedy would change them and possibly scar them, but it wouldn't cripple them. They would work and write and talk and laugh. They would try to make each day memorable.

"I keep thinking about Violetta's performance," Millay said. "The way she seemed to know she was going to die here. And now, she's become as big a story as the ones she told. I bet she would have liked that. Maybe she even wanted that. To be part of a story no one would ever forget."

Olivia considered that for a long moment. "She seemed to care more about stories than people. I think losing Elijah did that to her."

"During an interview session, Amabel told me that stories were a big part of Violetta's relationship with Elijah," Rawlings said. "Every evening, she'd snuggle with him under a pile of quilts and spin tale after tale. She created entire worlds for her brother. She gave him a place of delight and wonder and escape. She gave him things to dream about. And Amabel never forgave them for excluding her from their nightly ritual."

Laurel pointed at Millay. "Just think of all the people who'll read your book someday. Do you wonder how it might change them? Inspire them?"

Millay shrugged. "Assuming it gets published, all I want it to do is make them feel something. I don't care what the emotion is as long as they have a reaction."

"There's no way anyone could read your novel and not be moved," Harris said sincerely, and Millay shot him a shy, grateful smile. He nudged Olivia with his elbow. "And who's going to be next to go agent shopping and have a shot at immortality? You?"

"Definitely not," Olivia said. "Violetta gave me some amazing advice, but I've yet to put it to use."

"I've got another six months before I'm done," Rawlings said and turned to Laurel. "I guess it'll have to be you."

She laughed. "Not a chance! I'm way behind the rest of

you. I trashed my first novel and started over again, remember?" Grabbing a throw pillow, she tossed it at Harris. "It's all you, Harris. Polish that manuscript and send it out."

"I'm going to be really busy at work, but I'll try," he said.

"You'd better do what she says or the four of us will show up at your Texas office and force you to e-mail a dozen literary agents," Millay threatened.

Harris's mouth curved into a wide smile. "That would be awesome."

No one was in the mood to proceed with a critique session, so the five friends ate and drank and talked instead. Knowing this was the last time they'd be together for half a year made the occasion especially bittersweet, but Olivia wouldn't have traded a second of it.

Eventually, Millay announced that she had to get to work. She scooted over on the sofa and gave Harris an awkward hug. He didn't let her go right away, and the words he didn't speak hovered in the air between them as heavy and thick as thunderclouds.

Laurel came next. She promised not to cry, but when she embraced Harris, her cheeks were shiny with tears. "You'd better Skype us *and* e-mail us *and* call us," she said in the stern voice she used to reprimand the twins.

Rawlings shook Harris's hand and then pulled him in for a one-armed man-hug, and when it was Olivia's turn to say good-bye, she kissed him and whispered, "I upgraded your seat on the flight to Dallas. After all, you're a VIP now."

"Thanks." He paused on the threshold and then said, "You'll take care of her, won't you?"

"I'll be a friend to her. And I'll always be yours too." Olivia gave him another squeeze. "Now get out of here before we all start blubbering."

Harris got in his car, and Olivia and Rawlings stood

outside the front door and waved good-bye. Even Haviland seemed to know that something major had just happened. Long after Harris had driven away, he stood in the driveway and stared off into the night.

Olivia slept unusually late the next morning. The recent nights of broken sleep had finally caught up with her, and the sun had risen high in a clear blue sky by the time she slipped on a pair of flip-flops and went down to the beach in search of Rawlings and Haviland.

Cresting the last row of dunes, Olivia paused in surprise. Someone had set up a red-and-white-striped beach umbrella and a folding lounge chair on the sand, well out of reach of the waves.

Olivia glanced around, but the beach was deserted. She didn't even see foot or paw prints around the umbrella, so she had no idea if Rawlings or a trespassing stranger had placed the items in the sand.

Squatting by the chair, Olivia noticed a plain white envelope weighted down by a large rock. Her name was written on the front in Rawlings' hand.

Olivia felt a pang of anxiety as she opened the envelope and withdrew a small piece of paper from within. She read it softly to herself:

When I saw this I thought of you. The woman with the moonlit hair and eyes like the sea. Try it on, Olivia. You don't have to answer me right now. All I ask is that you try it on and see what forever feels like.
   I love you.

Always, Sawyer

She reread the note three times before turning her attention to the lump at the bottom of the envelope. Reaching inside, her fingers closed around a cool piece of metal. She drew forth a ring—a simple band of platinum embedded with a row of dark blue sapphires. It was understated yet sophisticated and exquisitely beautiful.

"Oh, Rawlings. What have you done?"

She pivoted the ring this way and that, admiring how the gemstones soaked in the morning light. It reminded her of moonlight on the ocean, of the path she'd seen as a girl from the lighthouse balcony. The ring felt old and carefully crafted and, to her surprise, absolutely perfect for her. As if it had been made just for her.

Sighing, she looked at the ocean as if an obvious answer might form in the waves, but the water did nothing but whisper on the shore. Glancing at the lighthouse, Olivia thought of how Flynn had never stopped loving Violetta and how his life lost its meaning once she was gone. Unlike Flynn, Olivia knew she could go on without Rawlings. She'd survive as she always had, but she didn't want to merely survive. She wanted the rest of her days to be filled with his presence. The sound of his voice, the warmth of his body next to hers, the scent of his cologne, the sight of his paint-speckled fingers, the splinter of gold in his pond-green eyes, his tacky Hawaiian shirts—all of it. She needed all of him.

Olivia wanted Sawyer Rawlings to be a part of her story.

"All right." She breathed. "All right. Let me just give it a try."

Slipping the ring on the third finger of her left hand, she looked at it and smiled.

Afterword

~~~~~~

A week later, Olivia was on the floor of her nephew's nursery, watching him kick and swat at the plush toys dangling from a padded arch over his belly.

"It's called an infant gym," Kim explained when she came into the room with a folded stack of Anders' clothes.

"He seems to like the lion best," Olivia said and laughed as Anders grabbed the lion's brown mane in his pudgy hand and gave it a violent shake. "Either that or he really hates it."

"The boy is a hair grabber," Kim said. She arranged the clothes in a drawer and lowered herself into the rocking chair with a grateful sigh. "Why do you think I wear mine in a ponytail all the time? That poor lion will be bald by Labor Day."

Olivia laughed again. It was a balm to be with her nephew. She'd stopped by to play with him more than usual this week, and Kim had welcomed her without peppering her with questions. Often, Kim would brew coffee and sit with Olivia while she fawned over the baby. Olivia spent time with Caitlyn after school too, but she preferred to drop by right after Anders had gotten up from his morning nap. Just seeing him helped renew her spirit. She loved the little noises he made and the way he seemed to stare right through her with his dolphin-grey eyes. She knew she was biased, but Olivia firmly believed that he was the most beautiful baby in the world.

"Are you sure you don't want one of your own?" Kim asked as she rocked gently in the chair, a patchwork teddy bear on her lap.

"I'm positive. Why would I mess with this setup? I get to swoop in, bestow gifts and kisses, and then make a swift departure when he spits up or has a full diaper," Olivia said with a wry grin.

Kim sniffed the air. "You're probably safe for another thirty minutes." She smiled indulgently at her son. "What about you and the chief? Everything going okay?"

After a moment's hesitation, Olivia took off the long silver chain she had tucked under her shirt and held it out to Kim. At the bottom of the chain, the ring Rawlings had given her spun around and around. The gems embedded in the band of platinum caught the stray sunbeams coming through the window and glinted like tiny stars.

"Oh, wow." Kim's voice was a breathy whisper. "Is this what I think it is?"

"Yes, but I haven't given him an answer yet," Olivia said. "He told me to take the time I needed to think the whole thing over. To try it on for a few days."

Kim snorted. "Honey, if you don't accept him, then you are clean out of your mind. First of all, this is the most gorgeous ring I've ever seen, and second, you two are good together. Actually, you're better than good. You're perfect for each other."

"I agree, but this is *big*. I've never been married. Never

even came close. My longest relationship lasted six months, and that was over a decade ago." Olivia put her palm on the baby's warm belly. He squealed and kicked his legs in delight, and she gently tickled the bottom of his feet until he squealed again.

"I can help you decide," Kim declared. "I'll ask you a simple question, and if the answer is yes, then you should marry the chief. Are you ready?"

Olivia stared at the ring in her sister-in-law's hand and said, "Really? You can make it that easy? Fine, fire away."

"When you wake up in the morning, are you happier to have your man in bed beside you or are you happier to be alone?"

"To have him there," Olivia replied instantly. "Absolutely. Even when I know he's not going to be there, I reach for him. I reach for him while I'm still dreaming."

Kim threw her hands in the air. "There you go. Marry him."

"That's it?" Olivia laughed. "That *was* easy."

Handing back the ring, Kim said, "Seriously. Try to imagine morning after morning without him." When Olivia frowned, Kim gave a triumphant clap. "See? You don't like the thought. You want to be with him. You two are way past the overnight-bag stage. There's no going back now. It's scary, I know. It's a huge change, I know. But isn't it worth the risk? To never be lonely again? To have the person who makes you laugh and pushes your buttons and holds you when you cry and leaves the toilet seat up—it's all worth it when you open your eyes first thing each morning and he's there. He'll always be there. That's true love. Not the stuff we see on TV or in the movies. But that familiar lump in the bed. That's the real thing."

Olivia was astonished by the emotion behind Kim's speech. She had no idea her sister-in-law was so insightful. "You should write that down."

Kim waved off the notion. "Go on, let me see how it looks."

Taking the ring off the chain, Olivia slid it on to her finger.

"It looks right at home on your hand." Kim's eyes grew moist. "Oh, Olivia. Don't take it off again. Not ever."

Saying nothing, Olivia scooped Anders into her arms and blew raspberries on his neck and cheeks. He smelled like sunshine and promises of days to come. His wordless coos and iron grip on her fingers made her believe that anything was possible. Even the kind of love that she'd always longed for. The forever kind.

The next day, Olivia met Laurel and Millay for lunch at Grumpy's where Dixie was hosting a farewell lunch for Lowell. Her cousin's testimony had been instrumental in convincing Amabel and Greg to admit to their crimes. Subsequently, he'd become something of a local hero.

Considering how Lowell had spoken of gaining respect with such longing the last time she'd seen him, sitting in *The Phantom of the Opera* booth in his stolen lab coat, Olivia found it strange that he was leaving Oyster Bay. He didn't have a job lined up, and Olivia suspected that his police record would make it difficult to obtain one. However, Lowell told Dixie that he was leaving because he felt compelled to bring Violetta's ashes home to the mountains.

"I'm going to bury her with her brother," he'd told Olivia several mornings ago as they shared a pot of Dixie's fabulous coffee.

"Isn't that illegal?" she'd asked.

Lowell had raised an eyebrow. "What if it is? She belongs with him."

Olivia couldn't agree more. "And you? Don't you belong with Dixie and her family? What will you do once you've laid Violetta to rest?"

"I've got a few notions," had been his cryptic reply.

Seeing that Dixie was busy chatting with the customers in the *Evita* booth, Olivia had leaned forward and said, "I don't care what you do with the diamonds, Lowell. Just don't let Dixie find out. Not ever. She's really proud of you. Don't break her heart by sending her a wad of cash or stopping by to visit in a modified Ferrari." When Lowell opened his mouth to protest, Olivia silenced him with a withering stare. "If you must lead that kind of life, then go ahead and lead it, but don't let her know about it. Deceive her if need be. Let her believe that you've truly turned a corner. She needs to hold on to that hope."

When Lowell said nothing, Olivia slid a piece of paper across the table and tapped on it. "There's a price for my silence. It's a small one compared to how much you'll make selling those stones, but it'll change a young man's life. I also believe that you'll derive some satisfaction from investing in him. To be an anonymous benefactor is very rewarding."

Lowell read the name and frowned. "I met Captain Fergusson the other day. I liked him. Didn't know he had a kid." He kept reading the instructions Olivia had written. "The kid wants to go to college I take it."

"That's right. Toby's a bright boy, and his parents have struggled all of their lives just to get by. They've done honest work, Lowell. Hard work. But they could never swing his tuition. They're also too proud to accept charity, but they'd take a scholarship or grant in a second. It has to sound bona fide, so I've written down how to word the letter to Toby's parents and how to send annual payments to the school. Toby Fergusson should be in college studying to be a meteorologist instead of pulling shrimp nets out of the ocean."

"Assuming I have what you think I have," Lowell had said cagily. "This is all you want? You're not asking for anything for yourself?"

Olivia had touched the back of her neck where a silver chain rested against her skin. "I'm pretty sure I have everything I need."

Now, as she watched Lowell shake hands with Dixie's regulars, Olivia wondered for the twentieth time where he'd stashed the heart-shaped padlock. She knew that Dixie had chosen to believe Lowell when he swore that he didn't have the lock, but neither Grumpy nor Olivia were convinced. At the moment, however, Olivia realized that what she thought didn't matter. Dixie's raucous laugh and vibrant smile were all that mattered.

Despite Harris's absence, Laurel and Millay were in high spirits, and Olivia did her best to enjoy the party. Haviland was having a fine time. He maneuvered around the guests, accepting bites of food and affectionate pets, his tail wagging feverishly. He received a big hug from Leona Fairchild, and Olivia was overjoyed to see how healthy the head librarian looked.

"Did you read Harris's text?" Laurel asked. She rubbed her hands together with glee. "Doesn't sound like he's loving Texas, does it?"

"He misses the water," Millay said.

Laurel waved a forkful of salad at her. "And us."

"I just hope he finds time to polish his book. I'd love to see what happens with it." Olivia dipped a French fry into a puddle of ranch dressing and popped it in her mouth. She'd decided to indulge in a bacon double cheeseburger with a side of fries for lunch. After all, they were celebrating. "Any word from your agent?" she asked Millay.

"Actually, yeah. I was going to tell you before we left." She paused to spread mayo on her club sandwich. "There's been some interest."

Laurel gaped. "From a publishing house?"

Millay tried to stifle her grin but was unsuccessful.

"Yeah. The editor loves it. She's got to check with her boss before making an offer, but we should hear something within the next couple of days."

"I can't believe it!" Laurel shrieked. "This is so exciting! What are we going to do to celebrate?"

"Please don't say Snickertinis at Decadence," Olivia begged.

"I won't," Millay assured her. "How about dirty martinis at The Bayside Crab House?"

Olivia gave her a thumbs-up. "You're on." She dipped another fry into the dressing, swirling it around and around. "Are you going to take the first offer you get or see if you can use it to get other editors to offer on your book?"

Millay shrugged. "I don't know. My agent thinks we should do what you just suggested. She's pretty sure more than one publishing house will want my book."

"Did you ever imagine you'd be sitting here talking about this scenario?" Laurel asked. "Okay, my soon-to-be-famous friend, you need to promise me one thing here and now."

"Depends what it is." Millay's tone was leery.

"I get to be the first reporter to interview you. The *Gazette* will follow your career as you become the next J. K. Rowling."

Millay pulled a face. "Seriously? Does Tessa remind you of Harry Potter in any way?"

Laurel tried again. "Suzanne Collins? Stephanie Meier?"

While Laurel rattled off the names of every YA author she could think of, Olivia finished her burger and then rested against the vinyl booth back. She was too full to eat another bite. Looking around the room, she sipped her iced tea and realized that the town was already healing. Like her, people were remembering what it felt like to be relaxed and content again. Hearing Captain Fergusson's gravelly laugh, she saw that he was being entertained by Lowell. When the dwarf caught Olivia's eye, he winked and then turned his attention back to Fergusson.

Olivia wondered if the wink had something to do with the favor she'd asked of him the last time they'd met. Though she suspected it did, she'd have no proof until Toby packed his bags to return to college in August.

If he ends up going back to school, Dixie will eventually tell me. Olivia was reassured by the thought that very little went on in Oyster Bay without her friend catching wind of it. When Dixie skated over to check on the food, Olivia congratulated her on hosting the best party of the summer.

Blushing with pleasure, Dixie performed a little curtsy and then twirled on the toe of her skates, causing her rainbow tutu to flutter. The Dixie Olivia knew and loved was back. Her eyelids were covered with a sparkling gold shadow, her hair was in pigtails, and she wore neon-pink tights with matching arm warmers. Straightening her My Little Pony T-shirt, she listened to Millay's news with delight and insisted on bringing the three women a banana split to share.

"No ice cream for me. I'm stuffed," Olivia said.

"We'll eat yours," Laurel promised. "After that, we'll have to tie a rope around Haviland so he can pull us out of the booth."

Laughing, Olivia excused herself and mingled with the other guests for a little while. She then wished Lowell good luck, told her contented poodle to heel, and left the diner.

Back at her house, she tossed her keys on the kitchen counter and noticed the blinking light on her answering machine. After examining the caller ID, she pressed the button to play her new voicemail.

"Ms. Limoges, this is Millicent Banks." Olivia felt a thrill of expectation at the sound of the Realtor's voice. "I'm sorry to inform you that there's been a complication regarding the building Flynn McNulty owned. Mr. McNulty took out a loan against his house to make improvements on the bookstore, but he also took out a second loan from a third-party lender to cover additional operating expenses. The bank will put his house up for short sale, and the third-party lender, a company called West Park Management, has paid off the remainder of his mortgage on the bookstore property. They now own the building. When I called and asked if it was available for purchase, I was told quite firmly that it was not for sale. Please call me if you have further questions. Perhaps we can find another property to suit your needs."

Olivia was disappointed by the news. She immediately conducted an Internet search on West Park Management and found it to be a small but reputable firm based in Manhattan. Suddenly, she felt a twinge of alarm. She examined on the company's website until she found a link leading to the profiles of the management team. The moment the page loaded, a familiar face appeared under the Partner heading.

"Oh, no. Not you," she whispered angrily. "What the hell do you think you're doing?"

The man with the smug smile was not only a top executive at one of the nation's most successful television networks and a partner at this lending firm, he was also her biological father. She stared at the familiar and completely foreign face belonging to Charles Wade, twin brother of Willie Wade, the man who'd raised Olivia until the day he abandoned her in a fog-shrouded dinghy and sailed away to lead a different life.

"I told you to never come back to Oyster Bay," she growled at her biological father's photo. "What are you going to do with a bookstore?"

Olivia hadn't planned on contacting Charles Wade ever again, but now she knew that she'd have to break her own vow. She wanted to see that Through the Wardrobe not only remained open, but also became a successful independent bookshop, no matter the cost. She needed to do this for Flynn.

"I'll deal with you later," she promised her father's grinning image and then closed the website so she wouldn't have to look at him anymore. "I have something much more important to do."

Checking her watch, Olivia swore and slid the deck door open. "Come on, Haviland. Rawlings will be here any second. His shift was over ten minutes ago!"

Together, she and Haviland hurried down to the beach. Despite her discovery that her father was the new owner of Flynn's building, Olivia's mood was still buoyant. Nothing could put a damper on this day.

Humming, she set up the umbrella and folding chair Rawlings had placed in the same spot a week ago. She then unfolded a second chair and positioned it next to the first.

While she worked, Haviland raced through the surf. He swam a little and then bounded out of the water, barking at the gulls flying overhead. Olivia knelt in the damp sand close to the edge of the waves and carefully arranged shells until they formed letters.

When she heard the sound of Rawlings' car engine, she stood up, dusted sand from her legs, and took a seat under the umbrella.

"Go get him, Haviland."

Issuing a final bark to the gulls, the poodle charged over the dunes and disappeared from view. Several minutes later, Olivia could hear Rawlings' voice as he spoke to Haviland.

And then he was there, smiling down at her, his pond-green eyes glinting with gold. "Ah, you've found a mermaid." He directed his words to Haviland. "Well done, boy. I couldn't have asked for a more wonderful surprise."

"You left a pretty big surprise for me under this umbrella," she said softly, smiling up at him. "You also asked me a question. And I'm ready to give you an answer."

Rawlings seemed to steel himself for her reply. "Should I have a seat?"

Shaking her head, Olivia pointed at the water. "It's down there."

Rawlings hesitated for a moment and then walked toward the ocean. When he reached the collection of shells, he stopped. He stood motionless for a heartbeat and then swung back around to face her.

He didn't say anything. He merely opened his arms in invitation.

Laughing joyfully, Olivia ran into them. Rawlings embraced her, spinning her round and round until they ended up dancing through the seashells, which Olivia had used to spell out a single word.

The clams, scallops, lightning whelks, sand dollars, and moon snail shells had spoken Olivia's answer on her behalf.

And the answer was "Yes."

Dear Reader,

Thank you for spending time with Olivia Limoges, the Bayside Book Writers, and the other colorful characters of Oyster Bay, North Carolina.

Now I'd like to invite you to visit another unusual and intriguing small town. Havenwood, the fictional hamlet featured in my Charmed Pie Shoppe mysteries, is located in an isolated region of northwest Georgia. Home to heroine Ella Mae LeFaye, a pastry chef with an uncanny ability to enchant her food, Havenwood is filled with quaint shops, delightful eateries, and a host of magical residents.

To whet your appetite, please enjoy a chapter from the forthcoming Charmed Pie Shoppe mystery, Pecan Pies and Homicides.

Happy reading,
Ellery Adams

"Do I have icicles hanging from my beard?" asked a small elderly man as Ella Mae LeFaye ushered him into her pie shop. She tried to shut the door quickly against the cold, but a breath of winter stole inside. The other customers hunched their shoulders and shivered as the brisk air snaked under the collars of their heaviest sweaters. Cradling their coffee cups, they launched into a fresh round of complaints about the record lows northwest Georgia had been experiencing for the past three weeks.

"Don't get your scarves in a knot, folks. I'm comin' around with coffee as fast as I can!" announced a middle-aged woman with nut-brown hair and the sharp chin and high cheekbones of a pixie. She filled half a dozen mugs and then intercepted Ella Mae on her way to the kitchen. "You've gotta warm these people up. And you know I'm not referrin' to the thermostat. What's in the oven? Somethin' real special, I hope."

Ella Mae gestured at the chalkboard menu mounted

behind the counter. "Lots of health-conscious dishes. It's the beginning of January, Reba. The whole town is on a diet. Except for you. You're in perfect shape, as always."

"Don't try to butter me up. And I know what the specials are. I'm a waitress, for cryin' out loud. You've got a fine list of hot dishes written on that blackboard. Cheesy quiches and meat and potato pies. Warm berry cobblers and molten chocolate tarts. But where's the *heat*?" Reba put her hands on her hips. "I know you've been feelin' wrung out lately, but these folks need somethin' *more*." She shot a quick glance around the room and then lowered her voice to a conspiratorial whisper. "It'll do you good to give them a dose of magic. You haven't used any in weeks."

Ella Mae pivoted to look at her customers. As a whole, their faces were pale and wan. The Charmed Pie Shoppe was normally an animated place, full of conversation and laughter, but today it felt lifeless and dull. Ella Mae's gaze swept over the room and she couldn't help but notice the empty tables. A few months ago, there wouldn't have been a vacant seat in the place. Frowning, Ella Mae was about to turn away when her eyes fell on the elderly gentleman she'd let into the pie shop. He was clutching the lapels of his wool coat with the thin fingers of one hand and reaching for his coffee cup with the other. His lips had a bluish cast and his scraggly beard did nothing to hide the gauntness of his cheeks. At that moment, he looked up and caught Ella Mae staring. In his pale blue eyes she imagined too many long and lonely winter nights and wondered if he spent most of his evenings sitting in front of a fire, dreaming of springtime and warm memories. Though she couldn't recall his name, Ella Mae knew that the old man lived a solitary life in a crude cabin off the mountain road. The fact that he'd driven to town in this weather made Ella Mae realize that he must be desperate for a homemade meal and a little companionship.

The old man lowered his face so that it hovered above his mug. He closed his eyes as the steam flooded over his wrinkled skin and Ella Mae could see the slightest loosening of his shoulders. She turned back to Reba. "Okay, I'll do it. I'll bring him a summer day. I'll give him heat and the drone of insects and the sound of fish splashing in the lake. I'll remind him that he belongs to this community—that he matters. I'll make him smile from the inside out," she promised, and pushed through the swing doors into the kitchen.

Ella Mae had just begun to comb the shelves of dry goods in search of a particular ingredient when Reba entered the room. She perched on a stool and pulled a red licorice stick from her apron pocket. "What do you have up your sleeve? A little cayenne pepper? Some dried jalapeños? Curry?"

"Red Hots," Ella Mae said, dragging a step stool in front of the shelves. She climbed to the top step and reached for a plastic tub of bright red candy. "There you are."

"That old man's dentures don't stand a chance," Reba muttered.

"Don't worry about his or anyone else's dental work. I'm going to bake them into a pie. An apple pie," Ella Mae said, jumping off the stepladder. "Trust me."

Reba put a hand over her heart. "With my life. Always." She popped the rest of her licorice stick into her mouth, plated two orders of spinach and mushroom quiche with a side of field greens, and left the kitchen, humming as she walked.

Ella Mae peeled, cored, and sliced apples. While she worked, her mind began to wander.

"Hot," she murmured as her knife flashed side to side and up and down, chopping the apples into bite-sized pieces. The word automatically called forth an image of Hugh Dylan, the man she'd been in love with since high school. She could practically feel his muscular arms sliding around her back, pulling her in for a deep kiss. "No. That is not the kind of heat I need to generate. I need something with a PG rating."

Adding the cinnamon Red Hots and a tablespoon of lemon juice to a saucepan, Ella Mae cooked the mixture on low heat. As the candies melted, her thoughts drifted back to her childhood, to a steamy July afternoon on the banks of Lake Havenwood. She remembered how her mother and her three aunts, Verena, Sissy, and Dee, were stretched out on picnic blankets. The four beautiful sisters sipped Tab soda and gossiped while they sunbathed. Ella Mae's mother, who wore a polka dot bikini and a wide-brimmed straw sunhat, looked every inch the movie star to her gangly, freckled daughter.

"Mom," Ella Mae whispered, jerking the wooden spoon out of the saucepan. "I can't think about her. If I do, all of my customers will be sad. I need to find a memory that can't be tainted by my present problems. Something innocent and sweet."

Removing the pan from the heat, Ella Mae poured honey and a pinch of cinnamon into the mixture and began to stir it with slow, deliberate strokes. The aroma of the honey made her think of the bees that gathered around the raspberry bushes along Skipper Drive during the peak of summer. Suddenly, she was a teenager again. It was another humid day. This one was in August, and Ella Mae was older than she'd been in the memory involving her mother and aunts, though she was still gangly and freckled.

In this memory, she was fifteen. School would be starting soon. Determined to savor every last moment of freedom, Ella Mae had ridden to the swimming hole with a towel and a transistor radio in her bike basket. She wore a cherry-red swimsuit under a Bee Gees T-shirt and her favorite pair of cutoffs and felt completely carefree.

Because a street fair was being held downtown, the other

kids of Havenwood were unlikely to be at the swimming hole that day. And when Ella Mae dumped her bike at the top of the dirt path and raced down through the dense trees to the water, she saw that she had the popular hangout spot all to herself. Shucking her shirt and shorts, she climbed to an outcrop of rock and dove off, a blur of long limbs and a tangle of whiskey-colored hair rocketing toward the cool water.

Once the dust and sweat had been washed away and she'd grown tired of floating on her back and gazing up at the circle of trees, Ella Mae climbed out of the swimming hole and found a flat boulder to sit on. Dragonflies flitted through the air and she could feel the heat from the warm stone soaking into her skin. She lay back against its smooth surface, feeling every muscle in her body relax. She rested like this until the sun had dried the last drops of water from her skin and she felt the stirrings of hunger.

Ella Mae got up to gather wild raspberries from the nearby bushes. When her hands were brimming with berries, she brought them back to the flat stone and ate them one by one, relishing each sweet and slightly tart bite. When she couldn't eat anymore, she leaned back on the stone again and sang *How Deep is Your Love* at the top of her lungs. She didn't care that she was off-key or that the echoes of her song startled a pair of whip-poor-wills from their nest in a pile of leaves. She shouted an apology to them as they rose into the clear sky, flying higher and higher until they were tiny pencil dots on a canvas of endless blue.

Years later, Ella Mae now stood in her pie shop's kitchen and remembered every moment of that perfect summer afternoon. Holding on to that feeling of warmth and utter contentment, she scooped up a handful of apple pieces and loosely arranged them in a pan lined with her homemade piecrust.

Smiling, she poured the melted candy mixture on top of

the apples and then dropped tiny squares of butter over the fruit filling. After weaving a lattice top crust, Ella Mae brushed the dough with a beaten egg yolk and then sprinkled it with finishing sugar and put it in the oven.

She was cutting a ham, wild rice, and caramelized onion tart into generous wedges when Reba reappeared. "Perfect. I've got six folks waitin' on that tart." She raised her nose and gave the air a sniff. "You did it! I don't even have to taste the pie to know that it'll light a fire inside your customers— like they've gone and swallowed a pack of sparklers. The magic is thick as a cloud around you. You're gettin' real strong, Ella Mae."

"What good has magic ever brought me?" Ella Mae demanded with a surprising flash of anger. "Being enchanted has robbed me of my mother, forced me to keep secrets from the man I love, and has made me terrified to hire another waitress to help out around here."

Reba made a strangled sound in the back of her throat. "We learned somethin' about checkin' references more carefully, didn't we! But we still need an extra pair of hands. The two of us can't run this place from dawn to dusk. I could ask around. See if any of our kind are lookin' for a part-time job."

Ella Mae shook her head. "Hiring someone to take the position as a way of paying homage to my family won't work. It was my mother who sacrificed herself to keep all of us safe, not me. I don't want people doing me favors because she was brave and selfless." She finished adding garnishes to the tart orders. "No, I need to hire a waitress from outside Havenwood, though finding someone interested in moving to an isolated mountain town in the middle of winter to serve pie isn't going to be easy. If I'd held interviews when this place was packed, when it was hip and fun, then it would have been more of a draw. But now? I hear people whispering that The Charmed Pie Shoppe won't see its first anniversary. Maybe they're right. We have smaller and smaller crowds every week."

"My tips have been mighty lousy too," Reba complained. "I keep tellin' you that it's time to snap out of it. I know Christmas was awful rough without your mama, but you're not alone. You've got me and your aunts and your best friend, Suzy. And you've got sweet Chewy and that beautiful fireman. Your louse of a husband is now officially an ex-husband, so you and Hugh are free to do all sorts of things together." She fanned herself with her order pad. "Lord help me, but I'd better think about somethin' else or I may just spontaneously combust."

Grinning, Ella Mae grabbed a handful of flour and tossed it at Reba. "Don't you have customers to serve? What about that old man?"

"His name's Mr. Crump," Reba said. "And he's takin' his sweet time over lunch. I don't think he has much to go home to."

Glancing at her watch, Ella Mae inhaled a breath of cinnamon, baking apples, and buttery dough. "Whatever you do, don't let him leave. I made this pie specifically for him. Just keep topping off his coffee."

"The poor guy's gonna float away," Reba mumbled. After placing the ham and onion tarts on a tray, she made room for a slice of cranberry and almond pie and a pear crumble drizzled in warm cardamom vanilla custard and left the kitchen.

Ella Mae stared at the empty cooling racks next to the oven and thought that not so long ago they'd been loaded with pies and tarts. Last autumn, Ella Mae had barely been able to keep up with the in-house and take-out orders. She'd had to turn down catering requests because she was too busy baking and serving half the town on a daily basis. She drove around Havenwood in her retired U.S. Mail Jeep, waving at friends and neighbors like a homecoming queen. Everyone recognized her raspberry-pink truck. One of Aunt Dee's artist friends had transformed the white Jeep, painting a luscious cherry pie on the driver's side door and a peach pie with a lattice crust on the passenger side. Silver stars shot across the hood and the name, location, and phone number of the pie shop had been painted in a butter-yellow font across both side panels.

"This is the most beautiful car I've ever seen!" Ella Mae had exclaimed when Dee revealed the transformed mail truck. But now the Jeep was encrusted with dirt and needed an oil change. Like everything else in Ella Mae's life, the lovely truck was showing signs of neglect.

Until I can find a way to free my mother, nothing else matters, Ella Mae thought. For the thousandth time, her mind returned to the moment in which her mother had sacrificed herself to renew the magic of Havenwood's sacred grove. Adelaide LeFaye had spread her arms and leaned against the rough bark of the shriveled and dying ash tree. In the space of a few horrible and spellbinding seconds, the tree and Ella Mae's mother had merged. Instantly, the grove's power had been restored and everyone had celebrated. Everyone but those close to Adelaide. In the beginning, Ella Mae had been able to communicate with her mother, but with each passing day, she became less and less human. Eventually, she would forget that she had a daughter.

The oven timer beeped, jarring Ella Mae from her maudlin reverie. The Red Hot apple pie was done baking. Grabbing a pair of pot holders, Ella Mae opened the oven door and a blast of cinnamon-spiced air rushed out to greet her. Unlike the sharp, wintry wind that had snuck inside the shop with Mr. Crump, this was a warm and gentle caress.

Without waiting for the pie to cool, Ella Mae cut a large wedge and plated it. Pushing through the kitchen's swing door, she carried the dessert to Mr. Crump and set it before him. "This is on the house," she said, smiling. "When you mentioned having icicles hanging from your beard I felt inspired to bake you something special. I promise that it'll only take one bite to transport you to a place of sunshine and birdsong." With that, Ella Mae moved behind the counter and began to assemble take-out boxes that she didn't need. From the corner of her eye, she watched Mr. Crump study the pie warily. Eventually, he lifted a forkful to his mouth.

Ella Mae held her breath.

Reba came around the counter to refill the coffee carafe. "Don't worry, hon. You were born to inject food with magic. To influence how folks feel. That, and so much more. Watch Mr. Crump there. Watch how he changes for the better. If you'd just believe in the good your gifts can do, then you'll realize that you're capable of anythin'. You can rescue your mama, unite your kind, and bake a helluva pie. Watch and believe."

Reluctantly, Ella Mae complied. She saw Mr. Crump chew, swallow, and hesitate. He stared down at the food on his plate as if he couldn't comprehend what he'd just tasted. Clearly surprised, he took another bite. A glint of light surfaced in his eyes and as he continued to devour the pie, his entire face started to glow. His sallow cheeks turned pink and his mouth curved into a wide, boyish smile. After one more bite, he was shrugging off his coat and unwinding the threadbare scarf wrapped like a noose around his thin neck.

"What's in this pie?" he shouted. His voice was no longer weak and reedy. It resonated with strength and virility.

The other patrons stopped talking and turned to see what Mr. Crump was eating.

"It's a Red Hot apple pie," Ella Mae said, stepping out from behind the counter. "I was hoping it would warm you up."

"It's done more than that, my girl!" Mr. Crump sat back in his chair and grinned at her. The joyful expression transformed him, erasing years from his skin and making his eyes shine like sunlight on the lake. He stood up, tossing back the dregs of his coffee as if it were a shot of whiskey, and turned to face the other customers. After clearing his throat, he began to sing.

Ella Mae didn't recognize the melody or the lyrics about woods and fertile meadows, but the song painted a picture of the mountains surrounding Havenwood. She could visualize the blue hills as they looked in springtime, dressed in green leaves and sunshine.

At first, the pie shop's customers gaped at Mr. Crump, but by the time he'd reached the third stanza, their gazes had turned wistful and several of them swayed in their chairs.

And then, a woman who'd been sitting alone near the rotating display case slowly rose to her feet and added her soft, sweet soprano to Mr. Crump's rich baritone. Together, they sang. The words soared through the pie shop like graceful birds, casting a spell over everyone in the room.

> *"Hail to the blue-green grassy hills;*
> *Hail to the great peaked hummocky mountains;*
> *Hail to the forests, hail to all there,*
> *Content I would live there forever."*

When the song was finished, Ella Mae and her patrons clapped heartily and someone cried, "I'd like what he had for dessert!"

The request was taken up by all of her customers.

"You'd best get back in the kitchen, girl," Reba said with a sly wink. "Keep on singin' folks," she announced gaily. "A slice of Red Hot apple pie in exchange for a song."

As Ella Mae hurried through the swing doors, she heard

the organist from the Methodist church sing the opening line of the hymn, "Another Year Is Dawning."

Surrounded by music and warmth, Ella Mae began rolling out dough.

Two hours later, she peeked into the dining room and was stunned to find that none of her customers had left. Some had changed seats to chat with other diners and the organist and the town florist were playing cards with Mr. Crump, but every person was still there. The room had grown loud. Gone was the subdued lunchtime murmur. Story swapping and raucous laughter existed in its stead.

"Has a nice ring to it, don't you think?" Reba asked, looking smug.

Nodding, Ella Mae reached for the tray of dirty dishes Reba had set on the counter. "Okay, you're right. I've been moping far too long. My mother wouldn't want that. She'd want to see what I'm seeing: the people of her community coming together to share a meal, a song, and a laugh."

"Like I said before, anythin' is possible," Reba said gently as the two women returned to the kitchen. "Break your mama's spell. Yes. But don't forget to weave a few of your own. Speakin' of that subject, Suzy Bacchus just came in. She looks like a kid waitin' to ride the Ferris wheel. She's so antsy that I couldn't even get her to sit down. Want me to send her back?"

Ella Mae, who'd been busy loading cutlery into the dishwasher, froze. "Please. And can you ask her to bring me a cup of coffee? The day feels like it's lasting forever. Not that I mind. I'm thrilled with what's happening in that dining room. I just need a jolt of caffeine before I clean the kitchen."

"Sure, I'll let Suzy play waitress. But I'm not sharin' my tips," Reba teased and then vanished through the swing doors.

Suzy Bacchus owned Havenwood's book and gift store, an eclectic shop called the Cubbyhole. Like Ella Mae, she had special abilities. Suzy had a photographic memory. Despite the fact that her mind was a storehouse of knowledge, she was humble, bubbly, and fun. Whenever she entered a room, she immediately filled it with positive energy. When she breezed into The Charmed Pie Shoppe's kitchen, Ella Mae felt as if the lights shone a little brighter.

"I have big news!" Suzy said, setting a coffee mug on the wooden worktable. She yanked off her fuchsia hat and a pair of hand-knitted mittens and tossed the accessories on top of a crate of potatoes.

"I'm all ears."

After pushing back a strand of honey blond hair from her cheek, Suzy took a deep breath and said, "I know we've spent the past few months poring over any and all references to the Flower of Life in hopes that it would free your mom. We started at the beginning by researching the Gilgamesh legend. That story described the original Flower of Life."

"Suzy, we've read everything under the sun about Gilgamesh. I'm sick to death of the guy. He got his flower. We need to find another one. Preferably, within driving distance."

Suzy grabbed Ella Mae's hands. "That's what I'm here to tell you! According to the Gaelic scroll I found in your family's library, these magical blooms can be found near our sacred groves. In other words, if a sacred grove is located near a body of water, then there's a flower of life growing in the deepest part of that water."

"Like a lake? As in Lake Havenwood?

Suzy's eyes glimmered with triumph. "I think so, yes." Her exultant expression dimmed a little. "There's just one teeny tiny complication."

"Naturally," Ella Mae grumbled, then quickly squeezed her friend's hand. "I'm sorry. You've been such an amazing friend. I have no right to take my frustration out on you."

"Now that you mention it, I should be angry. Do you realize that I've gained ten pounds since we started hanging out?" She gave Ella Mae a wolfish grin. "Speaking of which, what's got your customers feeling so merry? It's like Christmas in that dining room."

Ella Mae cut a wedge of Red Hot apple pie for Suzy. "You can have the whole pie if you'll finish telling me what you learned."

"You've got yourself a deal!" Suzy popped a bite into her mouth and nodded enthusiastically. "Hmmm. This is *good*." Licking her lips, she said, "To make a long and complicated story short and complicated, I'll begin by saying that over two hundred years ago, a local man wrote a book called *Lake Lore of the Americas*. I can only find references to this book in other authors' bibliographies. But apparently, this nifty little tome was all about lake magic. Native American shamanism. Elemental spirits. Sea foam women appearing to the colonists. That sort of thing. There's also a whole chapter devoted to the rare and powerful objects *within* certain lakes. And while I can't track down an actual copy of *Lake Lore of the Americas*, I believe I know someone who can. Are you ready to hear the awesome part?"

"I am." Suzy's optimism was contagious. Ella Mae could feel it singing through her blood, more beautiful and sweet than any of the tunes she'd heard today.

"Because the author was from Havenwood, his family might have a copy of his book. I bet the print run was quite small and since the subject matter was obscure, the title's virtually disappeared off the face of the earth. Still, I like to think that at least one copy would have been kept by his descendants."

"Let's hope so." Ella Mae touched the burn scar on her palm. It was shaped like a four-leaf clover and she often rubbed the smooth, puckered skin when she was anxious.

She'd gotten the burn several months ago when a piping-hot glass pie dish had slipped from a pot holder and made contact with her skin. According to legend, the mark indicated that she might be the Clover Queen, a woman born of two magical parents who would one day unite the descendants of Morgan le Fay and Guinevere and forever break the curse placed upon their kind by the warlock, Myrddin.

Suzy shot a quick, fascinated glance at the burn before meeting Ella Mae's gaze. "The only drawback is that you don't exactly get along with his people."

"Let me guess," Ella Mae said miserably. "He's a Gaynor."

Suzy nodded. "And I know exactly when to broach the subject of the book with your old pal, Loralyn."

Saying nothing, Ella Mae only raised her brows.

"I've been invited to a party at their place tonight," Suzy continued airily. "Guess who's going to be my plus one?"

Ella Mae groaned.

"That's the spirit! Now why don't you go home, take a long, hot bath, and put on your nicest dress? We can have a cocktail before we head over to . . . what's the name of their estate?"

"Rolling View," Ella Mae said. "Listen, Suzy. I know that you're on good terms with the Gaynors and really, I'm happy about that. The feud between our families is just that. A feud between our families. But they won't be pleased when I show up tonight. I haven't been to their house since Loralyn's seventh birthday party."

"What happened at that party?"

Smiling, Ella Mae said, "I hit Loralyn with a Wiffle ball bat."

Suzy's jaw dropped. "You went Babe Ruth on the birthday girl?"

"I was aiming for the piñata, I swear, but I was blind-folded and Loralyn's friends had spun me around so many times that I didn't know which way was up, so I just stumbled forward and swung away." Ella Mae smiled wickedly. "You should have heard the *smack* the bat made when it connected with Loralyn's cheek. I hightailed it out of there without even bothering to pick up my loot bag."

Suzy started laughing. She threw back her head and let the laughter bubble out of her. She couldn't seem to stop. Before long, Ella Mae was laughing too.

Reba entered the kitchen a moment later and glanced at the two friends. "I don't know why the two of you are hootin' and hollerin' like hyenas on crack, but I came back to say that I've started kickin' folks out. It's time to close and I've made enough cash to enjoy myself at the bowling alley tonight." She gave her apron pocket a satisfied pat. "All thanks to your special pie, Ella Mae."

"And Mr. Crump?" Ella Mae asked. "Is he still feeling good?"

Reba snorted. "I haven't seen a happier man in ages. Well, other than the ones who wake up next to me, of course. Mr. Crump's been invited to play Bingo tonight and Bunco next Monday. And if he wasn't a churchgoer before, he's gonna become one real fast. That organist is sweet on him. Cal Evans wants to go ice fishin' with him. That man's calendar is fillin' up." Reba studied Ella Mae. "What about yours? You have any special plans for tonight?"

"Yes," Ella Mae said. "I'm going to fortify myself with a few shots of whiskey, pack my Colt in an evening bag, and crash the Gaynors' party."

"That's my girl," Reba said, beaming.

DON'T MISS THE FIRST NOVEL IN
THE BOOKS BY THE BAY MYSTERIES FROM

ELLERY ADAMS

A Killer Plot

In the small coastal town of Oyster Bay, North Carolina, you'll find plenty of characters, ne'er-do-wells,
and even a few celebs trying to duck the paparazzi.
But when murder joins this curious community,
writer Olivia Limoges and the Bayside Book Writers are determined to get the story before they meet
their own surprise ending.

penguin.com